W9-BJU-643

He's gorgeous.

Bobbie could have thoughts like this with the comfortable distance of a woman who didn't really care. Now that much of the mess was cleaned up and she felt calmer, she could observe Nate with detached interest. Tall, lean, hazel eyes with stubby lashes, nice nose, Saturday-morning stubble around a straight mouth that was a little tight. He didn't smile much. She was willing to bet he had a dynamite smile when he used it.

She wondered what had happened that his nephews were living with him. He seemed to be good with them, although she sensed an undercurrent of antagonism from the older boy.

She could list Nate's qualities without a stirring of feminine interest because she had a life plan that didn't involve a husband and children. She was going to Florence, Italy, to study art. It had been a dream since she was sixteen, and the past year had turned it into an obsession. She was in remission, but she didn't have forever. She had to go now. The need to make art lived inside her, trying to break out, and she had to follow the masters to study and learn. To find the depths of her talent.

Bobbie watched the three walk across the yard to the big yellow house next door, the man and one of the boys hand in hand, the dog lumbering along beside them. She smiled at the sight.

Nice, but not for her.

Return to
**GREENFORD
COMMUNITY
LIBRARY**

Dear Reader,

Hello, again! I'm thrilled to be back at Harlequin. Life took me away for some time, but I'm delighted to return with a book to offer you.

My younger sister, Diane, is a cancer survivor. I thought her very heroic in her battle and when I was asked to come up with an idea for a Harlequin Heartwarming book, her struggle came to mind. Combining her experience with my husband, Ron's, career as an artist was an easy leap. My hero's work as a CPA comes from my last seven years as a receptionist in an accounting firm.

So, my heroine wants to travel to Florence to learn about the artist inside her, and my hero has custody of his two little nephews and a business and must stay home. What to do?

Love, of course, will find a solution.

Best wishes to you!

Muriel Jensen

HARLEQUIN HEARTWARMING

Muriel Jensen

Always Florence

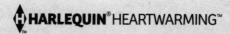

If you purchased this book without a cover you should be aware that this book is stolen property. It was reported as "unsold and destroyed" to the publisher, and neither the author nor the publisher has received any payment for this "stripped book."

Recycling programs
for this product may
not exist in your area.

ISBN-13: 978-0-373-36635-4

ALWAYS FLORENCE

Copyright © 2013 by Muriel Jensen

All rights reserved. Except for use in any review, the reproduction or utilization of this work in whole or in part in any form by any electronic, mechanical or other means, now known or hereafter invented, including xerography, photocopying and recording, or in any information storage or retrieval system, is forbidden without the written permission of the publisher, Harlequin Enterprises Limited, 225 Duncan Mill Road, Don Mills, Ontario, Canada M3B 3K9.

This is a work of fiction. Names, characters, places and incidents are either the product of the author's imagination or are used fictitiously, and any resemblance to actual persons, living or dead, business establishments, events or locales is entirely coincidental.

This edition published by arrangement with Harlequin Books S.A.

For questions and comments about the quality of this book, please contact us at CustomerService@Harlequin.com.

® and TM are trademarks of Harlequin Enterprises Limited or its corporate affiliates. Trademarks indicated with ® are registered in the United States Patent and Trademark Office, the Canadian Trade Marks Office and in other countries.

Printed in U.S.A.

www.Harlequin.com

MURIEL JENSEN

Muriel Jensen and her husband, Ron, live in an old foursquare Victorian looking down on the Columbia River in Astoria, Oregon. They share their home with Cheyenne, a neurotic husky mix, a tabby hoard (there are only two, but they seem like more) and Rosie, a stray cat who's been coming and going for years and still doesn't trust them. Muriel says she helps keep alive those complicated inner workings of a mind dealing with a troubled past that is the source of all good plotting!

They have three children, eight grandchildren, four great-grandchildren and a collection of the most interesting and generous friends and neighbors. They feel truly blessed!

To Mike and Suzanne, and the staff at WWC Business Solutions, who kept me employed (and fed!) and Jim Defeo and Tony Danton and the staff at the Astoria Coffee House who provided a port in the storm while my leg was broken.

CHAPTER ONE

"WHAT'S SHE *DOING?*" Sheamus Raleigh, seven years old, hid with his brother behind a balding rhododendron and watched the woman at work in the garage next to theirs on the shared double driveway.

Dylan, ten, was a little mystified by the very large pot at her feet and the big stick she used to stir whatever was inside. He'd wondered about her since she'd moved in last month, but Uncle Nate said she seemed to want to keep to herself. Sometimes she smiled at them if they were getting into their cars at the same time, but she never spoke or waited to see if they wanted to. His uncle said they'd skip her house when they went trick-or-treating next week. That she had a right to be private if she wanted to.

So they didn't know why she always wore baggy black clothes and a woolly hat. Or why she always worked in the garage with the door open and kept the car in the driveway. There were strange noises when she worked, and she chanted. Whatever she was doing was probably just weird and not bad, but the chance to mess with Sheamus was too good to pass up.

"That's a cauldron," Dylan said, in the knowledgeable tone he used to let his little brother know he was still in charge. He didn't really feel that way anymore. Nothing was the way it used to be. Their parents were gone. Their uncle, who used to be so cool, now made their lives miserable. And worst of all, Dylan didn't seem to know things anymore. Before the accident, he'd started to feel he was beginning to understand how being with people worked. Then his parents had died, and now his life was like a big black hole. Unless he was working on one of his experiments, or making Sheamus cry.

His brother deserved to cry. He was afraid of everything. And it wasn't a world for sissies.

"What's a cauldron?" Sheamus whispered. He put an arm around Arnold, their uncle's apricot mastiff mix, who went everywhere with them. They weren't supposed to be in the neighbor's yard, but Dylan didn't care about that. His uncle was always mad at him. Well, not mad exactly, but he acted as if he didn't understand him. And that was dumb. Adults were supposed to understand kids.

Dylan made a big circle with his arms.

"One of those pots witches use to make potions and things."

Sheamus's blue eyes were huge. "You mean like on the card Stella gave us? With the bugs and bat wings going into the witch's pot?"

"Yeah. Just like that. Only this lady's probably got kid parts in there, too."

Sheamus's eyes got wider. "What kids?"

"I don't know. Kids she kidnapped and locked in her house."

Sheamus stood up, getting panicky. Arnold got up with him. Dylan's plan was starting to work. He felt a twinge of guilt, but it was easy to get past that. Sheamus had blond hair like their mom and his eyes were the same color hers had been. It was easy to hate him.

He yanked his brother back down again. Arnold stood poised for action. "It's all right. She won't want *you*. Only brave kids go into the pot, because the potions are to make big things happen. Like explosions and lightning. It doesn't work with fraidy kids."

Sheamus's eyes brimmed with tears and his lip quivered. Dylan knew his brother was curious to know what the woman was doing, but too afraid to find out. He pointed to the big bush at the edge of the driveway, very near the garage. "Let's go get a closer look."

"No!" Sheamus tried to grab his arm, but

Dylan shook him off. He waited until the woman leaned the stirring stick against the pot and turned to get a glass of something red from a shelf behind her. Then he covered the distance in a military crouch.

Unfortunately, at the same moment a big orange cat leaped onto the shelf near the woman's drink. Uncle Nate said mastiffs were usually lazy, but Arnold was half Labrador retriever, and Labs never missed an opportunity to cause trouble.

Arnold leaped for the cat with an excited bark. The woman fell back against the shelf and screamed. The red drink flew, the cat screeched and the sound of tumbling lumber filled the air as woman and shelf crumpled together. Dylan heard Sheamus run for the house, yelling for their uncle.

He should have run, too, but he was stunned by how much destruction that one leap had caused. Before he could plot his escape, he was hauled to his feet by a hand that wasn't much bigger than his, but very strong. The hat had come off the woman's head and the red stuff was running down her face. She had brown eyes that looked mad.

Great. He was probably facing another night without his Game Boy when his uncle heard about this.

NATE RALEIGH PACKED the dishwasher and thought back to what Saturday mornings *used* to be like, back in the Portland Pearl District. Actually, he'd slept through them, because Friday nights had been all about dating and the Brody Theater, dinner at the Park Kitchen and friends going back with him to his condo looking over the river.

Saturdays hadn't begun for him until lunch at the Dovetail Bakery with a client who had some payroll or accounting issue that couldn't wait until Monday. He'd prided himself on being able to resolve them, or if not, he'd mull over possible solutions with his brother. Ben always had an answer.

God, Nate missed him. And not just as a partner at Raleigh and Raleigh Accounting Services. Mostly he wished his brother was here to tell him how to deal with his boys....

Ben had been two years older than Nate and the kind of kid, and then man, who seemed to know instinctively what to do about everything. Of course, it had been more than instinct. In school, he'd studied all the time and done extra work because he found everything about accounting and finance exciting.

As an adult, his gift in the field had taken their small tax-return business in a strip mall to the fourth floor of an elegant downtown

Portland office complex, where they offered a multitude of accounting and estate planning services. They eventually opened an Astoria office on the Columbia River and two more down the coast.

Pain stabbed at Nate. As an anniversary gift, he'd given Ben and Sherrie the charter fishing excursion that had ultimately taken their lives. Guilt, combined with a terrible loneliness and a dark anger he couldn't shake, were braided into a sort of barbed-wire band around his chest.

He had to fight his way through every day. He usually managed to put the pain and loneliness aside, but the anger was always there. That was the hardest to deal with. He'd been the cheerful Raleigh, the charmer, the one who saw the upside of life.

Now he was mad all the time. He understood the source of his anger, but seemed powerless to overcome it. He was mad at Ben for dying, mad at himself for having given him a gift that placed him in harm's way and not knowing how to cope with that, and mad at the boys because they reminded him of Ben and him all those years ago.

He was able to live day to day without yelling at everyone, but suppressing the inclination was exhausting. He didn't know what to do about it, so he just kept going—sad, mad and, much as he hated to admit it, a little lost.

Nate added soap to the dishwasher, let the door close with a slam, and set the dial. "Suck it up, buttercup," he told himself.

Saturday nights, he recalled, continuing to torture himself, had pretty much been the same as Fridays, but Sundays had been about football at Fernhill Park, then pizza and beer at Mississippi Pizza.

Now, Stella Bristol prepared most of their meals. She was Hunter Bristol's mother. Hunter had helped run the Astoria office of Raleigh and Raleigh with Ben before Nate had given Ben and Sherrie the charter boat trip to celebrate their thirteenth wedding anniversary. They'd met aboard a similar boat fifteen years previously. Nate had volunteered to stay with the boys so that his brother and sister-in-law could enjoy a romantic dinner and watch the sunrise as they'd done the night they met.

Instead, a sudden squall and the captain's belated decision to return to port had resulted in the loss of the boat and everyone aboard. One of the witnesses to the sinking had said that Ben dived under the boat over and over, presumably in search of Sherrie, and finally just didn't come up again.

Nate stayed with the boys in their home and took his brother's place in the Astoria office. And the life he'd known was gone forever.

That was all right. He knew his nephews had lost far more than he had, but the life he'd led had not prepared him for the life he'd inherited.

The accident happened to coincide with Stella's recovery from hip replacement surgery, and a desire to find useful work. She had no nanny experience, but she'd kept house and raised children. Nate figured that qualified her.

He just wished he felt more comfortable in his position as stand-in father. He'd gotten along so well with the boys when he'd simply been their uncle. Now that he had to make rules, they didn't like him. Stella reminded him over and over that parenthood wasn't a popularity contest, but he could see grief in their young eyes and hated the knowledge that he seemed to exaggerate it rather than relieve it. He strove to keep the anger he struggled with himself out of his voice and his touch, but in the end the boys had their own anger issues to deal with.

He awoke every morning determined to do better that day. Usually, he was shot down by 10:00 a.m. Either he got in the way of one of

Dylan's *MythBusters*-wannabe experiments that was eventually going to kill them all, or Sheamus burst into tears because Nate sent him back upstairs to get his jacket before letting him out to play. Sheamus was convinced there was a monster in his bedroom closet.

They'd at least reached a temporary solution for the monster issue by putting Sheamus's jacket in the downstairs closet.

Nate picked up toy cars and trucks off the living room floor and was about to put them in a big wooden box next to the fireplace when he heard Sheamus's shrill shout: "Uncle Na-a-ate!"

It had taken Nate a month in his role as guardian to realize that the boys' bloodcurdling shouts didn't necessarily mean death or dismemberment. They might just want a banana or a pudding pop. So he dropped the toy vehicles carefully into the box and was heading for the kitchen when the door burst open and Sheamus appeared. His blond hair stood up in spikes. His blue eyes were filled with terror.

He pointed a grimy finger in the direction of the backyard. "The witch's got them!" he said breathlessly, his bony chest heaving under his Seattle Mariners sweatshirt. To add emphasis, he grabbed Nate's arm and pulled him toward the door. "Hurry!"

"What witch?" Nate drew Sheamus back to him, then got down on one knee. "And got who?"

"The witch next door! Dylan and Arnold! She's not just a lady, she's a witch! And she's stirring a pot with bat wings and spiders and feet from little kids!"

Nate felt a familiar exasperation at his younger nephew's never-ending terrors. A four-letter word sprang to his lips, but his one success since moving in with the boys was that he'd cleaned up his language.

He caught the weeping seven-year-old by the hand, slapped the back door open and headed across the yard, ready to put an end to this latest fear.

"See!" Sheamus pointed to the little tableau near their neighbor's garage. The woman, who never spoke to anyone, had Dylan by the arm and was leaning over him, her expression angry.

Nate stopped Sheamus at the edge of their property, dropped his hand and told him not to move, then covered the distance to Dylan and their neighbor in three long strides. He circled the woman's wrist with his thumb and forefinger, pulled her hand from Dylan and moved the boy behind him.

"Is there a problem?" He tried to sound reasonable, but Dylan looked worried and Nate's protective instincts flared.

The woman looked up at him in surprise and opened her mouth to speak. No sound came out for a moment, giving him time to study her. She'd been an enigma for the four weeks she'd been here.

She was usually dressed in a baggy black sweatshirt over skinny black pants, and he hadn't realized until now how slight she was, how pale. It was the first time he'd seen her without a hat pulled down to her eyebrows. Her hair was very short, very dark and all tight little curls. Something red and sticky covered her face, but the overall impression she made was one of fragility.

This was the first time he'd been close enough to look into her eyes. They were wide and brown, with a whole range of emotions he no longer felt qualified to analyze. He'd once prided himself on a respectable knowledge of women, but he hadn't spent much time with any since he'd moved in with the boys. And he was angry about everything, anyway. As he recalled, women preferred good-natured men.

He did think he saw fear in her velvety gaze, and realizing he still held her wrist in a firm grip, he let it drop. Whatever had happened, he'd be willing to bet his season tickets to the Timbers that it was Dylan's fault. He handed her a tissue from the wad he'd started keeping in his pocket. "I'm sorry," he said. "What's the problem here?"

BOBBIE MOLLOY ACCEPTED the tissue with a grudging "thank you" and a scolding glance at the dark-haired boy. "It's not a problem, exactly." As she wiped her face, her fingertips brushed the fine hair on her head. She looked around for her hat and found it on the ground, covered in grass and raspberry-hibiscus tea. She tossed it at a small table—the only thing nearby that hadn't been overturned.

"Your son was spying on me," she explained, "and your *pony* destroyed several days' work and tried to kill my cat." She indicated the collapsed shelf behind her, most of the tools and supplies it had held now floating in her pot of paper pulp. Monet, her orange tabby, looked down on them from the top of the oil tank against the wall, tail swishing. Below him, the giant dog with its black muzzle and wide mouth, black tongue lolling, studied the cat.

Bobbie looked over the destruction. Stress was her enemy, so she drew several steadying breaths. To be fair, the man Sandy had told her was new to the neighborhood—almost as new as her—appeared to be as frustrated as she felt.

And he was looking at her hair. It had grown back to at least cover her scalp in a cap of tight curls, and her eyebrows were back. She looked better than she had a couple months ago, but the glossy, shoulder-length hair in her art school graduation photo was a thing of the past. Worse, she knew her face showed the wear and tear of chemotherapy and radiation.

She hated that she cared. Cancer survival, and life in general, were all about what you had inside, not what adorned you outside. But she'd never get over her love of clothes and makeup and all things girlie. Though she was an artist and wore grubbies when she worked, she loved to dress up. In the past, that had earned her admiring looks, but these days it was easy for others to see what she was dealing with. Most men took an unconscious step back. Cancer was scary stuff. No one wanted to be near it if they could help it.

This man, though, stood his ground. It was entirely possible he hadn't figured it out yet. Sandy had told her she had a handsome, single neighbor and Bobbie had told her she didn't want to hear anymore. Sandy had tried to add interesting details but Bobbie had refused to listen. He called the dog to him, told him "sit!" and patted his head.

"I'm sorry. Arnie is very big and can't help making a mess. But he wouldn't hurt a flea." Her neighbor turned slightly to catch the arm of the boy he'd placed protectively behind him and pulled him forward. "This is Dylan. He's fascinated by everything. I'm sure he didn't mean any harm." He gave the boy a firm look. "But it isn't polite to spy on people. Please apologize."

Dylan folded his arms. "She was chanting while she was stirring," he said. "People who aren't witches don't usually do that, do they?"

Chanting. Bobbie had to think about that a minute. Then she realized what he must have heard, and had to laugh. "Okay, I don't have a great voice. But I was singing to ABBA."

"Who?"

"ABBA," the man repeated for her. "Remember when Stella made us watch *Mamma Mia* for her birthday? The movie about the wedding in Greece and all the singing?" When the boy winced and nodded, he explained, "That was music by a group called ABBA. They're from Sweden."

"Weird name."

"Yeah. There are four members and I think it's their first initials. About the apology…"

Dylan complied. "I'm sorry." Then he added to Bobbie, as though it was important, "I'm not his son. I'm his nephew."

"Oh." She'd been watching them come and go for the past month and assumed they were father and sons. She hadn't noticed a woman, except for the older housekeeper. "I just assumed…"

The man extended his hand. "I'm Nate Raleigh," he said.

"Bobbie Molloy," she replied.

Seeing the handshake, the younger boy apparently felt it was safe to come closer. He hid behind his uncle's arm and pointed to the garage. "What's in there?"

"This is Sheamus," Nate said. "I'm sure he wants to apologize, too."

She smiled at the boy and made a conscious effort to be understanding. "Hi, Sheamus. That's my studio. I'm an artist."

"You paint pictures?" Dylan asked.

"Sometimes. Other times I use clay and sculpt things. Right now I'm making paper." She pointed ruefully at the mess behind her.

"I'd show you, but I think I'm going to have to start over."

Sheamus looked confused. "You're supposed to buy paper in the store."

He had a pinched little face and the most beautiful light blue eyes. His brother was darker featured, like his uncle. And there was nothing pinched about him. He gave an impression of energy and attitude.

She gestured to the boys to follow her to the pot, where she pulled out pieces of shelving that had fallen into her soaking pulp. They dripped with the mucky grayish mixture, and she put them aside on newspaper she'd spread earlier to protect the garage floor.

She took the old oar she used for stirring and swept it through the contents. "This is paper pulp, and I stir it and sort of beat it with this to break it down. It's made of linter and…" She saw that she was losing them and backed up. "It's stuff we get from a cotton plant, and when I mix it with water and do a few things to it, it makes beautiful paper. That's how they used to make it in the old days. When it's ready, I dry it on a rack." She moved over to show them a sheet that was already drying. Fortunately, the flying debris had missed it and the precious, specially made frame it was drying on.

"But this isn't the old days," Dylan said. "Why do you do it this way?"

"Because I have a commission," she replied, her spirits buoyed a little as she talked about it. "I make this special paper and paint a saying on it, then put it in a frame."

Sheamus looked up at his uncle. "What's a commission?"

"When somebody hires an artist to make a special picture, that's called a commission. And when the work is done, the artist is paid."

Dylan asked, "Artists don't always get paid?"

"Sometimes artists make things they think people will like and put them in a gallery— that's a place where they sell artwork. The artist only gets paid if somebody buys it. And then he or she shares the money with the gallery."

"Who hired you?" Dylan asked Bobbie.

"A law office in Astoria. A friend of mine from college works there. She showed them something I made for her birthday, and they hired me to do four pieces for their conference room."

Dylan looked around at the mess. "So, you won't get paid until this is finished?"

"Right." She appreciated the distress on his face and felt herself begin to relax a little. "But I know this was an accident. I have one big piece in the house that's already dry, and I've got one piece drying here that seems okay. I'll do the calligraphy on those while I'm getting more pulp ready. It'll work out all right."

"Calligraphy?"

"It's like painting words, only you do it with a pen with special tips instead of a brush."

"Well, we're going to help you clean this up." Nate pushed up the sleeves of his plain gray sweatshirt. "Come on, guys." He pointed the dog to a spot on the lawn. "Stay, Arnold." He turned to Bobbie, all business. "Where's your garbage can?"

"You don't have to clean up. I…"

He wasn't listening. He went to the side of the garage, then peered inside and saw the can at the back. He stepped carefully over the rubble and carried the can out to the grass. "You separate what has to go from what can be fixed. We can replace that shelving for you."

She got down on her knees and began to sort through the broken earthenware pots and saucers, the rusty tools, the old army blankets she used for her paper press. "Thanks, but I can put up new shelves. Most artists worth the name are carpenters, too. Otherwise we spend a fortune on stretchers and frames."

"But you didn't break it, so you shouldn't have to fix it. And Dylan's pretty good."

As his uncle began tossing into the can the things she put aside, Dylan looked surprised, then pleased by the compliment. But his pleasure showed for only a moment. He bent over the broken shelf. "We have boards left from a bookshelf we made for Uncle Nate's room." He turned to him. "Can we use those?"

"Go ahead," Nate said. He looked Dylan in the eye. "Nothing fancy, okay? No power tools. Those boards should be just the right size, but measure them against the old one. If anything needs cutting, call me."

Dylan picked up two pieces of a broken shelf and headed off to the basement entrance at the side of their house.

Bobbie wondered if trusting the boy to do as he was told might be a stretch after what she'd experienced, but she was sure his uncle knew the risk. He watched Dylan head off, mild concern pleating the spot between his eyebrows.

"You can go with him," she suggested as she dropped a rag into the can. "Sheamus and I can take care of this."

Nate shook his head. "No. Dylan would

hate that. I put the power saw away after he cut my workbench in two on his last unapproved project, so he'll be okay." He turned his attention to Sheamus and nudged him with his elbow. "I'm not finding any kid feet, are you?"

Bobbie reached for the broom and turned, certain she'd misheard them. "What? *Kid* feet?"

Sheamus looked into the pot of now brown, mucky pulp, then smiled up at her. "Dylan told me you were a witch and that you were making a... I forgot the word. It's the stuff that a witch has in her big pot and it makes explosions and lightning and loud noises."

"A potion?" Bobbie guessed.

"Yeah. And he said you put bats and bugs and parts of little kids in it."

Bobbie was aghast. She hadn't spent that much time with children, except for the few she'd met when she had her treatments, and they were, sadly, very adult. She was startled by what went on in the minds of little boys.

"I promise I'm not a witch," she told Sheamus seriously. "That was probably pretty scary for you to think that."

He shrugged a small shoulder. "Dylan said you wouldn't take me, because only brave kids would work."

She saw his uncle straighten up from the trash can and frown. "You ran to get help when you thought your brother was in trouble," he said, patting the little boy's head. "That was brave. Come on and help me clean off this table. Grab that brush and dustpan." He pointed to the ancient set propped in a corner that had been in the garage when she moved in.

After salvaging what she could, Bobbie went inside and put half the brownies she'd made that morning into a freezer bag, and took it out to Nate and Sheamus. They were placing the lid on the trash can. The garage floor was remarkably clean. Nate carried the can back to where he'd found it.

"What do you want to do with the ruined pulp?" he asked, peering into the pot. All kinds of dust, shavings and debris were now mixed in its murky contents.

"I've got an old plastic bucket with a lid." She pointed to a shelf above the oil tank. Nate reached up to bring it down. "If you can pour it into that and put the lid on, I'll keep it for later. It might still be useful for something."

Sheamus helped him replace the lid, then he put it in a corner, out of the way.

"Thank you for cleaning up," she said, handing Sheamus the bag.

The boy looked thrilled. "Brownies!" Arnold sniffed interestedly.

Nate dusted his hands on his jeans and thanked her. "Brownies are something all of us agree on. But I'm not sure you should be giving gifts to the kids who caused the damage."

He's gorgeous, she thought with the comfortable distance of a woman who didn't really care. Now that much of the mess was cleaned up and she felt calmer, she could observe him with detached interest. Tall, lean, hazel eyes with stubby lashes, nice nose, Saturday morning stubble around a straight mouth that was a little tight. He didn't smile much. She was willing to bet he had a dynamite smile when he used it.

She wondered what had happened that his nephews were living with him. He seemed to be good with them, though she sensed an undercurrent of antagonism with the older boy.

She could list Nate Raleigh's qualities without a stirring of feminine interest because she had a life plan that didn't involve a husband and children. She was going to Florence, Italy, to study art. It had been a dream since she was sixteen, and the last year had made it an obsession. She was in remission, but she didn't have forever. Follicular non-Hodgkin's

lymphoma was less aggressive than the B-cell form, but it was a lifelong disease. She had to go now. The need to make art lived inside her like the creature in *Alien,* and was always trying to break out. She had to go to the birthplace of classical European art. She wanted to study and learn, to find the depths of her talent.

She offered her hand again. "I'm happy to share. It was nice to meet all of you."

"Again, we apologize for destroying your work." He shook her hand. "We'll bring the shelves over soon. Is there anything else we can do before we go?"

"No, I'm good."

"I'm glad you didn't have kid feet in there," Sheamus said.

She pinched his chin. "Me, too. They would have looked awful sticking out of my paper."

Sheamus laughed infectiously.

Bobbie watched them walk across the yard to the big yellow Craftsman-style house next door, the man and the boy hand in hand, the dog lumbering along beside them. She smiled at the sight.

Nice, but not for her.

CHAPTER TWO

NATE LOOKED THROUGH the rack of Halloween costumes, spotted the bright red and blue, and triumphantly pulled out Spider-Man. They'd been to four stores, found Dylan's Iron Man right away, but had been searching all afternoon for Sheamus's choice. Everyone was now tired and grumpy.

Certain this find would change the mood, Nate was surprised when he held up the costume and turned around, only to discover Sheamus close to tears—again. Nate drew a breath for patience.

"I thought you wanted to be Spider-Man."

"I want the one with the muscles." Nate looked to Dylan for help. Dylan, holding the bag with his own costume in a death grip, reached up to a shelf of masks for a skull with a rubber snake crawling out of the mouth. "Would you lend me a hand here, please? What is Sheamus talking about?"

Dylan rolled his eyes, clearly disdainful of his uncle's ignorance. "Some of the superhero costumes have built-in muscles. They're more expensive."

"Built-in muscles," Nate repeated under his breath. What he needed was built-in patience and endurance.

A smiling older clerk gave him a sympathetic look. "Musclemen are over there." She pointed to a long rack across the floor. A half dozen parents and children were rummaging through it.

Sheamus ran in that direction. Dylan shook his head. "He's not going to be able to reach it. Then he'll start crying again."

"Why don't you go help him," Nate suggested, nerves frayed after the grueling afternoon, "instead of making fun of him?"

"Because he's such a baby!"

Nate directed him toward Sheamus, who was already being pushed aside by older kids. "You find things hard sometimes, and he's a lot younger than you are. You should try giving him a hand rather than telling him the neighbor is a witch who collects body parts of little kids."

"Who'd believe that, anyway?"

"He's seven, Dylan. And he's scared."

"So? Isn't everybody scared?"

The profound question stopped Nate in his tracks, but the frantic shoving going on at the rack precluded a discussion. And Dylan had already wandered away, looking as though he regretted that admission.

Nate spotted all the red-and-blue costumes hung together, and reached for a small one at the same moment that a beautiful, pregnant young woman did. Prepared to fight her for it no matter how bad it made him look, he was relieved when she grasped another size instead. He yanked the small outfit off the rack and got down on one knee to hold it up against Sheamus. Stitched to create the appearance of muscles across the torso and along the arms, the costume brought a smile to the boy's face. Sheamus wrapped his arms around Nate's neck. "Thanks, Uncle Nate! We got it!"

"Great. Now we have to get candy for the trick-or-treaters."

"How can we give out candy?" Dylan asked. "Aren't we going to be at the Monster Bash?"

"Stella's going to stay until we get back," he said.

Nate cringed inwardly at the thought of the event. The city-sponsored Halloween celebration held in a Parks and Recreation building was intended to keep children safe while letting them enjoy a ghoulish experience. He heard it was an ordeal for parents, who often commiserated with each other about having to go.

There was a brief discussion over the merits of mini chocolate bars, small boxes of licorice and sour candy. Nate bought several bags of each.

"Can we get something to drink?" Dylan asked at the checkout. "I'm thirsty."

"Sure." Nate pictured a tall gin and tonic, but led the boys to the Starbucks on the other side of the store. "We shoulda brought the brownies with us," Sheamus said on the drive home. "They would taste good with this."

Nate found the boy's reflection in the rearview mirror. Sheamus drew on the straw of his smoothie so hard that his thin cheeks sucked in. "We can have them for dessert tonight. Stella left us mac and cheese for dinner."

Dylan grumbled. "She's a really good cook, but I like the mac and cheese in the box better." Then he asked seriously and without warning, "Do you think Bobbie had cancer?"

His older nephew's out-of-the-blue observations never failed to surprise Nate. Mostly because they were usually on target.

"Her hair looks like a man's. And she looks

kind of like she has a bad cold. You know what I mean?"

Nate knew exactly what Dylan meant. Their neighbor had beautiful eyes, but they were a little soupy, as though she wasn't quite well. And he, too, had wondered about her hair.

"Yes, I do. But we shouldn't mention it unless she does."

"She's kind of skinny," Sheamus contributed. "But I like her. We should have her over for dinner sometime. When Stella makes that Mexican stuff with the chicken and the corn chips."

"Mexican chicken casserole." Nate nodded. "I like that, too. But Bobbie has a lot of work to do. Especially after what happened today." He let that hang in the air a moment for guilt effect. It was probably bad parenting, but he was just an ignorant bachelor pressed into service.

"She could come on game night," Dylan suggested. Nate studied the boy, wondering why his nephew suddenly seemed keen on the woman. Could it have been the brownies? "When Hunter comes over to watch our big TV."

Hunter had lost his own accounting business when his office manager embezzled

from him, then disappeared. Hunter had liq-
uidated all his assets to pay creditors and
his employees, then moved into the Grand
Apartments with a few pieces of furniture
he'd saved, and an old television he'd bought
at Goodwill. He loved coming over to watch
big games and play-offs on Nate's plasma TV.

"We'll see how it goes." Their neighbor had
kindly given them brownies, but he couldn't
imagine she'd want any more to do with them.

"I don't think she has a husband." That was
from Sheamus, who thought Nate needed a
wife. Nate had explained over and over that
he had more than he could handle with the
two of them and the business, but the boys'
mother had been a wonderful, warm, funny
woman, and Sheamus was trying hard to put
those qualities back into his life. He didn't
realize that not all women were like Sherrie.

"I didn't see a ring." That was from Dylan,
who enjoyed stirring things up.

"She could have a boyfriend." Nate paused
to sip at his coffee and thought longingly of
that gin and tonic. "There's no way of knowing that."

"If she isn't married to him," Dylan said,
"it doesn't matter. She's still available."

"That's a big word."

"I'm a smart kid."

"I don't know. A smart kid would stop annoying me by trying to get me married off."

Dylan met his eyes in the mirror, smiled grudgingly and the subject was dropped.

Nate pulled into their driveway, congratulating himself on a day that had turned out better than it had begun. He'd made peace with their neighbor, found the right costume for Sheamus and had a conversation with the boys that hadn't ended in tears or with Dylan stomping away.

And they had brownies. All in all, a successful afternoon.

BOBBIE DUNKED AN English Breakfast tea bag into the hot water in her favorite pink mug and picked up her ringing phone. The caller ID read Molloy, D. J. She prepared herself to lie through her teeth.

"Hi, Dad!" she said cheerfully, carrying her tea to the kitchen table and sitting down. Monet leaped onto the table and rubbed against her face. He smelled of fabric softener. He'd been sleeping on top of the dryer again. She pulled him onto her lap. "How are you doing? How's the arthritis?"

"Under control." His voice was deep and gentle. It had soothed many a patient in his long career as a general practitioner. He was

retired now, and Bobbie's health had become his focus. "I'm taking my glucosamine chondroitin and getting my exercise. How are you? Still thinking the move to Astoria was a good idea?"

When she'd left Los Angeles to come here, she'd had a hard time convincing him she'd be fine on her own. He'd watched over her treatment, moved in with her to manage her recovery, and hovered over her with suggestions about diet and exercise until she knew she had to get away. Not just for herself, but for the single women in Whittier, California, who were interested in him but had taken a backseat to his daughter's illness and recovery. Bobbie wanted him to reconnect with his own life so that she could go to Florence with a clear conscience.

The commission from Sandy Evans's office had come at the perfect moment. Bobbie could have completed it in Whittier, but the lease was up on her apartment and she didn't want to sign another one, or move in with her father. When she'd explained her predicament to Sandy, her friend had offered her the monthly rental of this tiny two-bedroom in Astoria that she'd inherited from her aunt. The selling point had been the two-car garage that Bobbie used as a studio for messy papermaking.

"I love it here," she said. That was true. The hilly old neighborhoods with their turn-of-the-twentieth-century homes were wonderful for walking, collecting leaves and flower petals, and enjoying beautiful vistas. Even in tightly built areas there was the occasional empty lot where she could see the broad Columbia River and the Washington hills on the other side. "I walk all the time and the air smells of wood smoke and pine."

"Mmm. That sounds heavenly."

Encouraged by his approval, she went on, stroking the cat as she talked. "Sometimes, on the river walk, which is this wonderful paved strip that runs a couple of miles right along the water, you get a whiff of fish and diesel because of the fishing boats, but I've come to love that, too. It's a very lively, working waterfront."

"Are you getting acquainted with anyone? You're not just spending all your time working in your studio and walking alone, are you?"

"I am meeting people," she fibbed. "Of course, I have to spend a lot of time on the commission, but Sandy has introduced me to her friends." Bobbie hesitated a moment.

That was a big lie. Sandy was a single mother with two little girls and a full-time job. She was always working for one worthy project or another, and barely had time to go to the bathroom, much less party with friends. But Bobbie's father must have lost the lie-detector skills he'd had when she was in high school, so she forged on. "And just today, I met my neighbors. Well, I've seen them come and go, but there hasn't really been time to talk until this morning, when Nate and the boys came over."

"And his wife?"

"Nate's a single dad. Well, an uncle, actually, and I'm not sure what happened, but his two nephews live with him."

"Really."

She heard it in her dad's voice. Speculation on the possibilities.

"I'm not getting married, Dad," she stated quickly, firmly. "I explained it all to you. A couple of times, as I recall. I'm going to Florence in January."

"Did I say anything?" He sounded innocent and a little injured.

"You didn't have to. I can read it in your voice."

"Hmm. New skills acquired through chemotherapy, no doubt. Because in the past, you've always *heard* my voice, but I've never noticed that you *listened* to it."

"Ha, ha. Very cute. I'll be thirty in February. It's time I did what I was born to do."

"We're born to love and be loved," he said gently.

She agreed. "We are, but I love Michelangelo, Tintoretto, Monet, Renoir, Giacometti.... And when I see their work, it's as though they love me back."

She heard her dad draw a breath, and knew he wanted to take issue with that, but he changed the subject instead.

"I'm coming to see you," he announced abruptly.

Oh, God, no. It had been hard enough to pull away from him once—for him and for her. It would be awful to have to do it again.

"I thought you were going to come and visit when I get to Florence." Her voice sounded high and a little strained. At least that way she'd have made it to Italy.

"Well, I want to visit you there, too. But I thought we should spend Thanksgiving together. I know it'd be too hard for you to come here, so I'll come up there. I got a new van, did I tell you that? Actually, it's new to me but a couple of years old. I can throw all my stuff in the back, a sleeping bag, and be gone at a moment's notice."

"No, you didn't tell me. And...wow." Her attempt at excitement fell a little short.

"You don't mind, do you?"

"Of course not." She answered quickly, decisively. She couldn't hurt his feelings. The cat looked up at her, as though sensing her ambivalence. "It'll be fun. When will you be here?"

"How about the Monday or Tuesday before Thanksgiving?"

"Perfect." She just had to make sure her commission was completed so she could show him around. She could do this.

"Great." She could hear the smile in his voice and was glad she'd made him happy. Then he added with a sudden burst of speed, "I'll stay through Christmas, then we can say goodbye."

She closed her eyes and pressed her lips together to prevent anything he wouldn't want to hear from coming out. Through Christmas? He'd done that deliberately. He'd been a very astute father and he'd always read her like a book. He knew she wanted to be on her own to prepare herself for Florence. Leaving family and friends behind was difficult, but she was desperate to do this, so she'd started with the move to Astoria. And now he was doing his best to foil her plans.

He didn't want her to go. He'd been clear about that more than once. He considered her still too delicate to be on her own in a foreign country with what some considered less sophisticated medical options. Or—she had to face this—he was afraid she'd die there and he'd never see her again.

But she felt sure she had time. She didn't have forever, but she wanted to spend all the time she did have stretching the artist in her to the furthest reaches of her talent. And she couldn't do that with her father's arms around her. Or a husband's.

She ramped up the cheer in her voice. "That'll be fun, Dad. I'll love showing you around. This is the most beautiful place, everywhere you look."

He expelled a breath. Relief, she guessed. "Good. Good, Bobbie. I'll see you in about a month."

"Okay, Dad."

"Okay. I love you, baby."

"Love you, too, Dad. See you soon."

"Bye."

She turned off the phone and growled and stamped her foot. Monet jumped down and meowed in protest. Bobbie stroked him with the sole of her shoe. She wanted to cry, but she didn't let herself do that anymore. It was a waste of energy and she had too much to do.

She could *do* this. She could walk into her father's embrace one more time and be able to let him go at the end of it. She just hoped he could do the same.

She sipped at her tea and carried the cup to the second bedroom, where she had a drafting table and her paints and inks. She put her cup safely out of the way and leaned over the piece she was working on. A quote from Oliver Wendell Holmes about dying with one's music unsung was partially complete. It was going well. She wouldn't say that aloud, of course, because it had a way of jinxing a project, but she could admit to being happy with her progress.

She had just pulled her stool into position when there was a rhythmic knock on the front door. Sandy. "Come in!" Bobbie shouted.

Tall and red-haired and just a little plump, Sandy Evans breezed into the room in jeans and a short, pumpkin-colored jacket. Her two little girls, Adalyn—Addie—and Zoey, were with her. Three and four respectively, they were fair-haired like the father, who'd walked away after Addie was born, claiming to be overwhelmed.

Sandy didn't know what the word meant. She worked full-time as an office manager, was completely devoted to her daughters and still found time for community involvement. She made Bobbie feel like a slug.

She dropped a white paper bag on Bobbie's table, then came around to look over her shoulder at the artwork. She was distracted for an instant when Zoey reached out to touch a jar of paintbrushes. "Hands in your pockets, girls," she said. "No touching. This is all important stuff to Aunt Bobbie, and we don't want to break anything."

Leaning over Bobbie's shoulder, she breathed an "Oh!" of approval. "That's going to be gorgeous!" She pointed a pumpkin-painted fingernail at a pale blue flower petal in the paper. "What is that?"

"I dried hydrangea, and took one of the petals." She indicated another spot. "That's a hawthorn leaf. And that longer yellow petal is from a forsythia I saved from the spring."

Sandy gave her shoulders a squeeze. "You are so clever. And that's what I came to talk to you about."

Bobbie opened the white bag. Sandy had brought a berry scone from the Astoria Coffee House downtown, one of Bobbie's favorite indulgences.

She looked up at her friend suspiciously. "Thank you, but what do you want from me that requires a bribe?" The girls came closer at the possibility of treats. "Can I give them a bite?"

"Just a little one."

Bobbie broke off two chunks and offered them to the girls, who accepted greedily. Then she tore one off for herself.

"Astor School needs someone to help with a couple of art classes for the lower grades. The budget for that kind of thing is gone this year. Would you do it?" Sandy waited expectantly.

"How do you know they need someone? Your kids aren't even in school yet."

"My boss is on the school board, and our office is donating supplies if we can find a teacher."

"But I'm here only until January."

"Holidays are when the kids get restless, and art gives them something fun to focus on. What do you think?"

"Sure. I guess." She wanted to help, but wasn't certain she was qualified. "I don't know a lot about teaching children. I suppose I can find projects on the internet."

Sandy opened the big tote she carried as a purse. A sock monkey wearing a tutu and ballet shoes tumbled out as she withdrew a large paperback. She held it up. The title was *Holiday Art Projects for Elementary Grades*. She handed it to Bobbie, while Zoey rushed to rescue her ballerina monkey.

"Thank you." Bobbie flipped through the book. The projects were simple and she'd seen them before, but that was probably good for children. Maybe she could handle this.

"So, you'll do it?"

"What's the schedule?"

"Once a week, Friday mornings, ten to eleven-thirty—until the kids get out for Christmas break."

"I'm still working on the pieces for your office, remember."

A wave of Sandy's hand dismissed that as a problem. "I know you to be brilliant. You'll get it all done. And what's an hour and a half a week?"

Bobbie hadn't intended to get this involved in her temporary residence, but she remembered how exciting her art periods had been in grade school. She liked the thought of providing that sense of fun and discovery to kids. And her father would love knowing she was spending time away from her studio.

"Okay, I'll do it. Should I call the teacher?"

"I put her name, number and email on the bookmark." Sandy indicated where it protruded from the book. "She'll be thrilled. Great! Okay, girls." Bobbie's friend shepherded her daughters toward the door. "Can we come by and trick-or-treat?"

She got up to walk them out. "I'd be disappointed if you didn't. In fact, I made you something to put on your front porch."

The three followed her into the kitchen, where she retrieved a medium-size pumpkin sporting a cat face. She'd cut off the top and cleaned out the seeds, then carved part of the eyes and nose. With a special tool, she'd removed only the orange skin and thinned out the pumpkin flesh in a few places, defining the cat's features so that a candle would shine through. The cat had a whimsical expression, wide eyes, whiskers, and a tongue protruding from his scalloped mouth. She'd placed a flameless candle inside and turned it on to demonstrate.

The girls giggled and squealed. Bobbie felt as fulfilled as if she'd sold a 24" x 36" oil on canvas.

She pointed to two smaller pumpkins she'd made with less interesting faces, but that she'd drilled to hold a wire loop. She held one up in each hand. "Or do you like these better? You can hang them in the tree in the front yard."

The girls both voted on the cat pumpkin.

"Okay. I'll carry it out to the car for you."

Sandy strapped the girls into their car seats, but there was great protest when she tried to put the pumpkin in the trunk.

"If I set it on the seat between you," Sandy explained, "it might fall over when we go down the hill."

Logic didn't sway them. Bobbie ran into the open garage, found a box the right size and placed the pumpkin in it, then set the box between the girls. Each rested a hand on the pumpkin, delighted.

"There!" Bobbie exclaimed, hugging Sandy. "Peace reestablished."

"You're really very good at this, Bobbie. You sure you want to devote your life to art rather than children?"

There was no question. "I'm sure. Now, get out of here so I can get back to work."

"Incidentally…" Sandy opened the driver's door, then stopped. "What do you hear from Laura?"

Laura Kirby had been having chemotherapy at the same time that Bobbie had her first infusion. Sandy managed time away from work and her mother was able to babysit so that she could provide moral support. Bobbie and Laura had become fast friends, bonding over their mutual need to accomplish pressing goals. Laura's was to have a baby—something she and her husband, a law student, had put off until his graduation. Fortunately for Laura, she'd been given none of the drugs that played havoc with a woman's fertility.

Laura and Bobbie had lunch occasionally, and since Bobbie had moved to Astoria, kept in touch through email. Sandy had seen Laura just that one time, but had liked her and was happy that she and Bobbie had forged such a strong friendship.

"*Is* she pregnant yet?"

"Latest report, not yet," Bobbie replied. "But they're having fun trying."

"Great! Next time you email, tell her I said hi."

"I will.

Bobbie waved off Sandy and her girls and went back inside. Monet wandered out from behind the sofa—his usual hiding place when children visited—and followed her into the kitchen to a favorite spot on a sunny windowsill.

Before going back to work, Bobbie went out to the garage to get the hat and jacket she'd left there. They'd been soaked with tea and should be thrown into the laundry.

She stopped in surprise at the sight of three pristine shelves leaning up against the inside wall. She slipped one onto a surviving bracket and found it a perfect fit.

Feeling guilty that the boys had probably gotten into trouble for the morning's escapade, she picked up the two small pumpkins Addie and Zoey had rejected in favor of the cat-faced one, and headed next door.

The Raleighs had left earlier, but she'd noticed the car was back. She walked around to the front. The tall mountain ash on the deep lawn was covered in red berries. Birds chirped and fluttered, so that the tree seemed alive. Bobbie stopped to take in the pleasure of the moment. There was such richness in nature for her now. She'd always been aware of it, but since she'd been ill, she felt more a part of it—as though everything in the universe was connected, herself included.

She stepped over a toy truck and climbed the steps to the wide front porch of the yellow house. A seasonal figure made of straw and wearing overalls and a baseball hat sat on a wooden bench. Two pumpkins, obviously carved by children, sat beside him.

She knocked on the front door with its classic Craftsman leaded window, and heard Arnold's deep bark, followed by the sound of running feet.

The door was yanked open and she was

greeted by…well, she wasn't sure who. She'd apparently walked into a comic book.

"Hi, Spidey!" she said, recognizing the blue-and-red costume worn by the smaller boy. But she wasn't sure which character the red-gold-and-black costume represented. "Who's your friend?"

"I'm Iron Man," Dylan replied, striking a pose.

"Ah. I'm sorry I didn't recognize you."

Arnold, standing between the boys, wagged his tail and reached up to lick her hand when she patted his giant head.

Dylan did a turn. "Iron Man is really Tony Stark. He made armor to escape terrorists in Afghanistan."

"Iron Man can fly," Sheamus said, "but I can shoot spiderwebs."

"Iron Man can fly without having to hold on to spiderwebs or anything else."

Sheamus shrugged off the implied criticism of his powers and pointed to the pumpkins in Bobbie's hands. "What are those?"

"Miss Molloy." Nate appeared behind his nephews and opened the door wider. He now wore a dark blue sweater and had shaved. She couldn't help staring a little. He looked fresh and crisp, but he still wasn't smiling. The "what are you doing here?" look in his eyes seemed to mirror his polite but cool greeting.

Still, he *was* handsome. She felt the smallest flutter behind her breastbone. Of course, she'd had radiation there, and a burn remained as a result. There *was* a little bit of a laserlike quality to his expression.

"The shelves fit okay?" he asked.

"They're perfect. Thank you." She remained on the porch, but held out the pumpkins. "I have only a minute. I made a few pumpkins for myself and a friend's children, and had these left over. I thought the boys might like them. But I see they already have some really cool ones on the front porch."

The boys pulled off their headpieces and each reached excitedly for one of her pumpkins before she could withdraw them.

"Whoa!" Sheamus held his up, then turned to study Dylan's. "I like mine better. It has a smiley face."

Dylan's had a saw-toothed mouth to indicate distress or fear. He seemed to like that. "Who wants to smile on Halloween? It's supposed to be scary. This one's the best!"

"You can hang them on the plant hooks on the porch," Bobbie said, "or in the tree in the yard." She reached into Dylan's to show Nate the flameless candle. "No fire, so you don't have to worry about where they put them."

"Good idea." Nate duly admired each one. "We do have our share of disasters around here. I'm happy not to have to deal with fire. Thank you. That was very thoughtful." He said it in the same tone one might use to say, "And don't let the door hit you on your way out!"

She ignored him and smiled at the boys. "I have to get back to my work. Be sure to come by trick-or-treating. I'm making something special."

Sheamus jumped up and down. "We'll come to your house first!"

"Thanks, Bobbie." Dylan's smile was wide. "I'm going to put my pumpkin in my room."

"Me, too!" Sheamus ran off toward the stairs. Dylan followed more slowly, holding his up to study it as he walked, Arnold at his heels.

"You made them very happy." Nate stepped out onto the porch, the statement sounding a little like an accusation. She frowned up at him, wondering what his problem was. "Thank you," he added grudgingly. "I sometimes have trouble doing that."

Ah. She'd overstepped somehow. But

she'd be darned if she'd apologize for having pleased his nephews.

"Gotta go," she said with a pretense of a smile. "Thank you for the shelves."

She was halfway down the stairs when he ordered, "Wait!"

She stopped in her tracks, holding on to the railing to get her balance. She turned to ask what he wanted, and found him right beside her. He caught her arm. "Sheamus left one of his trucks at the bottom of the steps." He tightened his grip and led her around it. "I've told him a million times about leaving his toys out, but he never remembers."

Nate's eyes were turbulent suddenly, that remote, unsettling quality gone. It made it somehow easier to talk to him.

"How did you become a parenting uncle?" she asked. She thought the answer to the question might help her understand him. Not that she had to make a connection here. By all indications, he didn't want one, either. "On second thought," she said quickly, turning to start across the lawn, "it's none of my business. I apologize for invading your space."

"No." Again he stopped her with a single word. "You did no such thing. And there's nothing secret about it. Their father was my brother. He and my sister-in-law died in a boating accident six months ago."

"Oh." The small sound expressed her horror at that information. She felt sudden sympathy for him. "I'm so sorry. How awful for all of you."

He made a one-handed gesture of helplessness. "It is what it is—at least that's what everyone says about things they can't explain or do anything about." He stopped on the lawn, his expression grim. "I guess the suggestion is that since you can't change it, you have to accept it. I'm having a little trouble with that."

She nodded in understanding, his admission forcing her to reassess her opinion of him. "I get that. I tore my curtains off my bedroom window when my mother died. I was in my teens. Then I had to replace a window in my kitchen door after my teacup went through it when I got my cancer diagnosis." She smiled in self-deprecation. "Sometimes it's just too hard to pretend that we're adult and in control."

He frowned as his eyes went to her hair. "I wondered if that was the case. Not that it's any of *my* business."

"It's all right. Nothing secret with me, either. Millions of people deal with cancer every day, and my prognosis is better than many." She ran a hand self-consciously over her head. "And my hair's back. Well, mostly. So, all in all, things aren't too bad."

His eyes roved her hair, then slowly and with an interest that pinned her in place, moved over her face, feature by feature. He lingered for the barest moment on her mouth, then went back to her eyes.

"So, the cancer is gone?" he asked.

"Ah…" She had to pull her thoughts away from his close scrutiny. She swore she could feel fingertips everywhere his gaze had touched. "No. But I can live with it for a long time. It doesn't go away, but it's not as aggressive as other types."

"You seem to have adjusted," he said. "Or maybe the better word is *accepted*. How did you reach that point?"

She didn't have to think. It was the decision to move to Florence that had finally put her on her feet. "You're right. It is what it is. Nothing says it quite so well. I couldn't change it, and I was tired of pouting and being scared, so I started to make plans."

She began to walk across the yard. She was surprised when he kept pace with her.

"What kind of plans?"

"I'm moving to Italy after the holidays to pursue an art career."

"I thought you had an art career."

"What I do now is commercial. I want to go where the masters worked, to study their genius and try to learn and absorb. I want to see if there's fine art in me. You know, art that changes the world."

"That's a big dream."

"Well, when you flirt with death, you tend to think big. I mean—I think I have time, but I don't have forever. So, if I'm going to get to it, it's now or never."

He took her hand as they reached the row of chrysanthemums that bordered his side of their adjoining driveways. She talked to cover a little nervousness. His grip was strong, the skin on his hands smooth. "And I feel really good. My father is a doctor and moved in with me during my treatments. He cooked all the right things for me, and when I came here, made up a diet that I try to follow. If he hears I'm eating badly he'll come and take over my kitchen again."

"Ah. The hovering parent." Nate freed her hand and they walked side by side around his car, then her truck. "I know something about that. My mother died of cancer when Ben and I were in high school, but my friend's mother is my housekeeper and she's a dragon where the boys' and my health are concerned. When she thought I wasn't getting enough sleep, she bought me bed pillows made of Hungarian goose down mingled with herbs that are supposed to help with stress relief."

"I'm sorry about your mother," Bobbie said gravely. Then she smiled. "Buying you goose down pillows is just caring and concern. My father cooked every meal for me with fresh organic produce and grains, and hid all my chocolate."

Nate questioned her with a look. "Isn't *that* just love and concern?"

"I guess it is," she conceded, stopping to study her dormant rhododendron. "He taught me to fend for myself, and now wishes he hadn't. And separating me from my chocolate is a suicidal move." She plucked at a dead flower in the middle of the bush.

"Stella—that's my housekeeper—says it's as important to accept help as it is to give it. Maybe you should give your dad a break. He sounds like a great father. And I'm just learning how hard it is to be a good parent."

"He's wonderful. But healing the body is simpler than healing the soul and the emotions." She frowned sympathetically. "And you're in pain, too. If you don't feel like the perfect stand-in father, I think you should give *yourself* a break."

She reached farther in for another dead flower. "My dad's coming for Thanksgiving. He called me today to make sure I was getting out and meeting people and not spending every waking moment in my studio. I guess you have to be an artist to understand another artist."

"Have you met people?"

"I've been here just a month. And I'm working on the commission, so there hasn't been a lot of free time. But the friend who got me the commission just talked me into teaching art classes at the school once a week." She laughed softly. "At least I'll be able to tell Dad I know a lot of children."

"Astor School?" he asked. When she nodded, he said, "The boys go to Astor. What grades?"

"It sounds like they'll be combining a few of the lower grades for my class."

"Sheamus is in second grade. Dylan, though, is a fifth grader, so he probably won't have access to the class. And he's the one who shows definite artistic abilities. He's really smart all around. He's crazy about the *MythBusters*. Do you ever watch that?"

"No. Not much time for TV. Except *Dancing with the Stars*."

Her neighbor closed his eyes. "Saints preserve me. Anyway, when I was just his uncle, we used to watch it together, and I used to think his love of exploring and experimenting was fun. The two hosts take accepted myths and action scenes from movies to see whether they could really happen. Even the president and his daughters watch it, and asked the show to prove an old myth about Archimedes's death ray."

"Archimedes…" Bobbie repeated the name, trying desperately to remember who he was.

"Among other things, he was a physicist and an astronomer. He's supposed to have set fire to an invading Roman fleet by positioning his army to direct mirrors that reflected the rays of the sun. The hosts of the show used five hundred students with mirrors, but it didn't work. Anyway—now that it's my job to keep Dylan from killing himself, I don't enjoy the show as much anymore."

"You mentioned the power saw this morning. What was he doing when that happened?"

"Trying to build a bike ramp. We got off lucky. I hate to think what he could have done to himself with the saw or the ramp if he'd finished it. I locked up my power tools and asked Stella to be extra vigilant. Meanwhile, I've got to get him busy with something."

"I have a thought." Suddenly inspired with

a positive solution for Dylan, Bobbie withdrew her hand from the bush and started off
toward the house.

At the sight of a large spider on the back of
her hand, she stopped in her tracks and shook
her arm frantically. The spider held on. She
screamed.

Nate caught her wrist in one hand and
swatted the spider away with the other. "You
confront a major disease with heroic resolve
and freak out over a spider?" He almost
smiled, but not quite. "It is Halloween, after
all. They're supposed to be here."

She did a sort of all-body shudder and
brushed both arms. "Okay," she allowed. "But
not on *me*."

"I guess Nature doesn't know that." The
remark was teasing, but he still didn't smile.
"You said you had a thought," he prompted.

"Right." She gave up trying to figure him
out and ran lightly up the back porch steps.
"If Dylan's interested in art, I can give you a
sketchbook and some pencils."

Nate hesitated, then nodded. "Sure. If you
can spare them."

"Come with me." She pushed open the back
door. "I've got pastels I never use, too. But
that can get messy."

He followed her inside. "I don't care about

the mess, if he'll be occupied with something that carries low injury potential."

"Great. Wait here for a minute. I'll find some things for him."

NATE WALKED INTO her small living room while she disappeared into the back of the house. He was curiously uncomfortable in her presence, though he wasn't sure why. Possibly because there was such brightness about her and it seemed intrusive in his dark, angry world. But if she had something that would interest Dylan, Nate would be happy to have it.

The walls in her living room were a go-with-everything off-white that would have seemed dull but for the berry-colored sofa and chair, the coffee table painted with stylized flowers and vines trailing down the legs, and all the unrelated but individually striking paintings on the walls. There was a seascape, a still life, a wild pattern of some sort, a languorous nude in the grass and a large canvas covered with what looked like a conveyor belt with rabbits on wheels careening off it. A bright sun shone, smiling birds flew around the rabbits and in the background ducks on a pond bathed happily. He stepped forward for a closer look.

The painting defied explanation. He'd always thought he preferred representational art—a pot of flowers, a portrait, a familiar scene—but this brought a smile and seemed to inspire in him a sense of good cheer. It was ridiculous, but somehow enjoyable. The signature on the bottom right read "RLM."

He heard light laughter behind him. "That's called *Hare Raising*." It was Bobbie's voice.

He continued to study the canvas. "Really. It's wild. I'm surprised that I like it, but I do. Who's RLM?"

"I am."

He turned to her in surprise. She had an armload of books, papers and boxes, and a canvas tote she was trying to put it all in. He took the bag from her and held it open. "So, Bobbie is for, what? Roberta rather than Barbara?"

"Right." She dropped everything inside, then took the bag from him and gave it an adjusting shake. She handed it back. "Roberta Louise Molloy. That was my one foray into surrealism."

"I think of myself as a traditionalist, but I really like it."

"I did, too, when I did it. It was toward the end of my first round of chemo and I had to dig deep for energy and enthusiasm, so I tried something new. I had a dream one night about a similar scene. I added the birds and the ducks just because I like them. But I haven't been able to find that feeling again."

He looked at the painting once more, then at her. "The feeling of a frightened rabbit on a wild ride?"

She blinked and stared. He was obviously on target, but he felt sure she didn't appreciate it. Something shifted in her eyes as she lowered them and closed him out. He could almost hear the sound of a slamming door.

She gave him an artificial smile. "Yes. That was perceptive. I think you probably understand the boys better than you think you do." She walked ahead of him to the door and opened it for him.

He paused in the entry before she physically pushed him out. Instinct told him that was coming next. "Thank you." He held up the bag. "Dylan will be very happy."

"You're welcome. See you on Halloween."

He stepped onto the porch as the door began to close.

It was clear that, for whatever reason, she didn't like being understood. Which was probably best. He didn't want her to become a chummy neighbor and understand that he was a deeply angry man who wasn't dealing very well with his life, and had no idea how to raise two lost and frightened little boys.

God, he missed Ben.

CHAPTER THREE

"COOL!" Dylan studied the art supplies spread out on the kitchen table. He picked up a sketch pad and flipped through the blank pages. "Really?" he asked Nate for the third time. "Bobbie gave you all this for me?"

"Yeah." Nate turned off the burner under the whistling teakettle. "She was telling me she's teaching art at your school until the holidays, but just for the lower grades. I told her that was too bad, because you like to sketch. She thought you might like to have some stuff to work with."

"Wow." Sheamus hung over Dylan as he zipped open a green fabric envelope that contained pencils, some new, some stubs. There was a large-format paperback on basic sketching and a box of pastels. Dylan held up a two-inch-square gray object wrapped in plastic.

"What's that?" Nate asked.

"The wrapper says it's an eraser."

"I've never seen one like that."

"It's probably for real artists. Wow."

Nate turned back to the stove before Dylan could think he was too interested. That would certainly ruin his own fascination with Bobbie's gift. After pouring boiling water over the cocoa powder in the mugs, Nate added two ice cubes to each, then topped them with miniature marshmallows. He poured himself a cup of coffee.

He put the cups on the end of the table, away from the supplies. Sheamus, wearing a pout, sat down in front of his cup. His hair was disheveled and a smear of dirt ran across his cheek like a scar. Stella would be horrified that Nate had seated the boys at the table without making them wash first, but there should be some advantages to an all-male weekend.

"She doesn't like me, does she?" Sheamus asked, his voice a little strained. "'Cause I thought she was a witch."

Nate gave him a gentle shove. "Of course she likes you. But this is for Dylan because he's interested in the same thing she's interested in. And she gave you a carved pumpkin to hang in your room."

That didn't help. "But Dylan got one of those, too."

"Remember when we bought you a new

winter jacket, but we didn't get one for Dylan because he didn't need one?"

Sheamus was horrified by the comparison. "That's clothes! Who cares about clothes?"

Nate bit back laughter, having to give him that one. "I'm sorry. You can't have everything he has, and he can't have everything you have. It's the way the world works."

"It sucks!"

"I know."

Sheamus blew out air and sipped carefully from his cup. He gave Nate a pleading, put-upon look over the rim. "Can we buy me a new game for my Nintendo?"

"No."

He sighed noisily. "Then can I have a cookie?"

"Sure. Help yourself."

Dylan put everything in his bag and picked up his cup. "I'm going to look at this in my room."

"Bobbie said the pastels are messy," Nate warned. "So be careful, okay?"

"Okay." Dylan walked away, the bag slung over his shoulder, the cocoa held carefully ahead of him. Arnold, curled up under the table, stood—unsure whether to follow Dylan or stay with Sheamus. Then he heard the cookie jar lid and the decision was made.

Sheamus came back to the table with three

cookies. He handed one to Nate, held one out to Arnold, who snatched it greedily without touching the small hand with even a tooth, then sat down again.

"Thank you," Nate said. Sheamus sloshed his cocoa and Nate handed him a napkin.

"Maybe I could be an artist, too." Sheamus twisted his sandwich cookie apart and scraped cream off the bottom half with his teeth.

"Maybe you could. I have paper in my office. We'll get you some."

"Artists use *special* paper."

"Right. Maybe Dylan will give you a sheet."

Sheamus gave Nate a look that told him he knew better than that.

"My mom would buy me something to make me feel better," he said, trying another tack. "Maybe some different kind of art stuff."

Nate pushed his cup aside, crossed his arms on the table and leaned closer. "No, she wouldn't. She never let you whine, remember? And she didn't like it when one of you had to have something just because the other one did."

Sheamus's eyes filled with tears suddenly. Nate could see this was no artful manipulation, but real emotion. "I don't like to remember," he said, a quiver in his lips.

Nate reached for his arm and drew him onto his lap. "I know. Sometimes I don't, either. But if you don't ever think about them, then you can't remember the really nice things."

Arnold whined in concern and came to sit beside them.

Sheamus leaned into Nate and kicked out with a grubby tennis shoe. "When I think, all I think is that they're not here."

"Yeah." He couldn't deny the truth of that. "I really miss them, too. When your dad and I were little, we were a lot like you and Dylan. We did a lot of things together and we fought a lot, but when we got older, I realized how smart he was. We stopped fighting so much and started helping each other. Someday, you and Dylan will be like that."

"I don't think so."

"I do. And when your dad met your mom, I would have been jealous because she was so pretty and so special. But she and your dad were so happy, and when you guys were born, it was hard not to be happy with them."

There was a moment's silence, then Sheamus asked worriedly, "Do you think they're still happy?"

"I do. They're together, so they're happy."

The boy thought about that, then sat up in Nate's lap and rested an elbow on his shoulder. His blue eyes were troubled. "Okay, but you're not going anywhere for a long time, are you?"

"No, I'm not." He prayed that fate would support his conviction.

NATE DROPPED THE boys off at school Monday morning, then detoured a block and a half to the Astoria Coffee House to pick up a triple Americano. By the time he parked in the transit center lot just steps from his office, his cup was almost empty.

It had been an awful morning. Mondays were tense for the boys anyway after two days of not having to conform to a schedule. But today was Halloween and Sheamus was so excited he was practically airborne—without benefit of a spiderweb. Nate hated to think what the added sugar after trick-or-treating would do to him.

Dylan pretended to be taking the day in stride, but Sheamus was driving him into a foul mood more easily than usual. The ride to school had been loud and contentious. Trying to focus on the road, Nate had heard Sheamus accuse, "You're on my side of the seat!"

Dylan rebutted with typical hostility. "How can I be on your side? You're in a stupid little-kid seat!"

Nate looked in the rearview mirror just in time to see Sheamus fling a hand at Dylan. His brother caught it and squeezed. Sheamus's screech felt as though it drove a spike through Nate's ears.

He'd pulled up to the school and turned to frown at both of them. Sheamus was crying and rubbing his hand, and Dylan's expression could have drawn blood.

"I'd love to make this trip once," he said, suppressing the bellow in his throat through sheer force of will, "without the two of you screaming at each other before we even get here."

"He broke my hand!" Sheamus wept.

"You hit him first." Nate came around the car to help Sheamus out of his seat. "When you react by hitting, you have to expect the other person to hit back." He leaned over the little boy and gently manipulated his hand. It felt intact, though there was a slight bruising on the back. "Can you close it tight?"

Sheamus made a fist and didn't even wince.

"I think it's fine. Now, don't hit anybody else, okay?"

Sheamus looked abused and misunderstood. "I don't ever hit anybody. I just hit *him* 'cause I hate him!"

"I hate *you* more!" Dylan replied venomously.

"You don't hate each other," Nate insisted, pained over the thought that they really might. "You get angry because life is hard, and you take it out on each other."

They looked at him as though he were a Klingon come to life. It occurred to him to be grateful that at least they agreed on that.

"No," Dylan insisted seriously. "We really hate each other."

Nate gave Sheamus a gentle shove toward the school yard, where kids ran and shouted and waited for the bell to ring. "Remember that tonight you're Spider-Man and everyone's going to give you candy."

"We have to go to Bobbie's," Sheamus said over his shoulder. He'd stopped crying, and excitement now battled the misery in his eyes.

"Right. First thing." Nate caught Dylan by the shoulder and stopped him from following Sheamus.

They boy squirmed, trying to escape. "I'm going to be late!"

"You've got four minutes." Nate held on to him. "Look, Dyl. You have to stop being so mean to Sheamus."

"But he…"

"I know. He swung at you first because he's even more scared than you are, and you're always awful to him. I know he can be exasperating for you, but try to have patience. Try to help him out a little."

"He's a dork."

"He's seven."

"I'm not scared. I'm just…"

When Dylan hesitated, Nate offered carefully, "Lonesome?"

Dylan looked into his eyes and for just an instant the vulnerability he struggled so hard to hide was visible. He opened his mouth to speak. Nate waited, hoping. Then the bell rang and the moment was gone.

"Now I *have* to go," Dylan said.

Nate dropped his hand and straightened. "Right. Try to have a good day. Think candy."

Dylan seemed to consider whether or not to be amused by that blatant example of bad adult advice, but decided against it. He simply turned and ran for the door, his Iron Man pack slapping against his back.

Nate returned to the present as Hunter pulled open the office door for him. His friend took one look at him and the empty coffee cup and made a face. "Rug rats getting to you, huh? I want to sympathize, man, but the Astoria Food Bank Fund-raiser Committee is in the conference room and they've been waiting for you for a good fifteen minutes."

Nate said something he'd never let the boys hear. "Forgot they were meeting here today. We have to get doughnuts." Not only had he taken over Ben's place in the Astoria office of Raleigh and Raleigh, but he'd found himself taking over his brother's place as a community volunteer. He could deal with never having a free moment, but with charity work he faced a learning curve, since most of his previous activities—both professional and social—had been focused on self-interests. Still, the people involved in this particular fund-raiser were hardworking and appreciated the use of the office conference room. And they probably accounted for all he had in the way of a social life these days.

"Jonni went to Danish Maid Bakery, and Karen is making coffee and hot water for tea and cocoa. I told your committee that you had to stop first at a client's." He pointed to the cup Nate still clutched. "The Coffee House is a client. I didn't say you were doing business, just that you had to stop there."

Hunter was several inches shorter than Nate, but had a build more appropriate to a quarterback than an accountant. He had the dark blond hair and blue eyes of his mother's Scandinavian ancestry. Ben had trusted him completely, and now Nate did, too. Hunter had saved his hide more than once in front of clients. He never missed a detail and seemed to have memorized the tax code, complete with current changes.

Nate felt fractional relief. "You should have been a lawyer rather than an accountant."

His colleague laughed lightly. "They don't have a tax season. Who'd want to miss that? Here's Jonni."

An attractive woman in her mid-fifties wearing a dark skirt and matching jacket ran from a silver compact at the curb to the office door. Nate held it open for her. She was the workplace counterpart of Stella, without whom nothing would function smoothly. She had bright blue eyes, silky blond hair and an easy, efficient manner that had saved him more than once.

She handed him the bakery box and a tub of cocoa mix with one hand, and took his briefcase with the other. "Go," she said. "Karen and I'll bring in the coffee and water. Your committee notes are on your chair at the conference table."

"You're a treasure," he told her.

"Yeah, yeah." She disappeared down the hall toward the kitchen as Nate carried the appeasing doughnuts into the conference room.

The previous renter, a law firm, had had a nautical bent, and the walls of the room were decorated with ship's wheels, navigation charts and paintings of ships. The pictures made him think of Bobbie and the bright artwork on her walls. These pieces seemed suddenly pale and staid in comparison.

The five people around the table greeted him with pointed verbal abuse.

"Just because you've recently adopted two children, don't think you can keep us waiting." Sandy Evans, who worked for his attorney and was in charge of developing concepts for the fund-raiser, harassed everyone with equal fervor. "I mean, one of them is ten years old. I have two under five and I was here on time. And I don't have the luxury of meeting in *my* office."

"Go easy on him." Jerry Gold was the shop teacher at the high school. He was very tall and reedy and wore a University of Oregon jersey over jeans. His wife had given birth to their first baby in August. "He probably got to sleep in and had trouble getting moving. I mean, I haven't slept in weeks, so it was easy for me to be on time."

"And I came from across the river." Clarissa Burke had a fashion boutique in Long Beach, Washington, and one in Astoria. She was a white-haired woman who was the epitome of grace and style—even after her husband left her for one of her young sales associates. "And you'll see that I—"

Nate put the doughnuts in the middle of the table. "I know. You probably braved pirates to get here in a leaking kayak you had to drag across the river the last mile with a length of rope in your teeth. Right?"

She cocked an eyebrow. "It was a length of leather," she corrected, "and I was still here on time."

"And remarkably dry." Mike Wallis owned the building and The Cellar, a wine shop in the basement, under Nate's office. He was small in stature but big in ideas.

"I'm just saying," Clarissa added pointedly, "that punctuality is important in small-town service. There are less of us to do more work, so it's a good thing if we don't hold each other up. Your brother understood that."

Even Sandy groaned at the comment. "Clarie, he's a bachelor with two little boys and no parenthood experience. Cut him some slack."

Nate gave Sandy a grateful smile. He wanted to shout at Clarissa that he'd had one hell of a morning, and that while he wished more than anything that Ben were still here, he hated the comparisons to him because he'd always felt that he'd never measured up to his older brother. It was Ben who'd made the skills Nate did have work for the business.

Instead, remembering what he told the boys to do when they'd been misjudged or misunderstood, he fought for patience. He nodded politely to the older woman. "You're absolutely right. I won't be late again."

At that moment, Jonni and Karen carried in thermal pots of coffee and hot water, a stack of white, diner-style plates and cups, and paper napkins.

"Perfect." Nate smiled his thanks.

The two disappeared quickly, closing the door behind them.

After doughnuts were selected and beverages poured, Clarissa, the committee's chairwoman, started the meeting. For all the group's frivolity, the items on the agenda were efficiently worked through one by one. By ten o'clock they'd decided to do several small projects throughout the fall to accommodate all the groups who wanted to help, culminating with one formal event with a Christmas in Old Astoria theme.

"How formal?" Jerry asked worriedly.

Sandy made a broad gesture, apparently seeing the picture in her head. "You know, something really classy. Something upstairs in the Banker's Suite."

"So, dinner and dancing?" Clarissa asked.

The Banker's Suite occupied the second floor of a former bank built in the Greek Revival style. The upstairs had been remodeled in grand fashion for weddings and other special events.

"Yes, but maybe with a raffle—some special items that'll really get attention. What do you think?"

A skeptical look went around the table. Clarissa shook her head. "Those twenty-dollar raffles are a thing of the past these days."

"I know. Bad economy. But what if the tickets were five dollars instead of twenty? People who can afford them will buy several, and people who can't will buy just one."

"What special items do you have in mind?" Jerry asked. "I can probably get tickets to the Mariners." He waggled his eyebrows. "My father-in-law has connections, and he's crazy about his new grandson. Thinks I'm quite brilliant."

Sandy rolled her eyes. "Lydia carried this baby for nine months, gave birth after what was probably a grueling labor if the baby takes after you sizewise, and you're taking credit for him?"

Jerry grinned unabashedly. "I am."

Clarissa joined him. "You do have to admit that season tickets are a brilliant idea. And that is one beautiful baby. I'll contribute several items in a winter wardrobe. And my daughter is a jewelry designer in Palm Springs. I'm sure she'll send us something."

Sandy applauded. "Okay. You guys are on fire! Except for you, Jerry. You're just kind of full of smoke. Nate, what can you get us?"

"A couple of free tax returns? I won't even stipulate that they have to be simple."

"Wonderful. We all know what getting taxes done costs these days." She turned to Mike. "Can we count on you for a couple of gourmet baskets and wine?"

"Of course."

"Great. So what have we left undone?"

Clarissa looked over her notes. "Not much. We're agreed that we'll have a series of small events so that all the groups that want to help us can. The high school kids are having a car wash and bake sale. The grade school kids are selling candy. The Astoria Coffee House and the Urban Café are contributing half the proceeds from a particular weekend to the cause. And the Downtown Association has agreed to devote a Saturday from noon to five where a portion of each business's sales come to us for the food bank. What else? What's Kiwanis doing, Nate?"

"Our plan is to lend support to whatever the committee wants. And we're working on the raffle, too. Hunter is trying to get a really big prize to make everyone buy a ticket. Maybe a European trip, with airfare and hotel accommodations." He went to the door and shouted for Hunter.

His colleague walked into the conference room. "Yes?"

"Can you give us an update on the status of the trip for the raffle?" Nate asked.

Hunter stood near the table, seemingly reluctant to share the news. "It's not good, I'm afraid," he reported. "It's hard for travel agents to comp that kind of thing for us at this point in time. I've got a few local hotels and restaurants, but no one can do anything really big."

Everyone around the table seemed to understand that.

"Does it have to be a trip?" Sandy asked into the quiet.

Nate noticed her eyes roving Hunter's shoulders as she posed the question, then down the sturdy length of him as he replied.

"I guess not. What else would draw interest?"

"I know an artist," Sandy said, with enough excitement to get everyone's attention. "And she's brilliant. In fact, I'll bet we can get a painting out of her for the raffle. Something to support the Christmas in Old Astoria theme."

"Who is it?" Jerry asked.

"Bobbie Molloy. She's living here while she's fulfilling a commission for my office."

Nate looked at Sandy in amazement. "That's who's living in your aunt's old house? She's my new neighbor…. I didn't know you knew her."

"She's kind of a private person. And she moved here to have time alone to work."

"Then are you sure she'd want to help us?"

Sandy smiled sweetly. "I'll talk her into it."

"Didn't you already talk her into teaching an art class at Astor?"

Sandy appeared surprised that he knew that. "Yes, I did. Why?"

Nate wasn't sure why he felt protective of Bobbie Molloy. She insisted that she was doing well, but he remembered vividly how small she seemed, how pale. He wondered if Sandy knew she'd been ill. "Well, she seems a little…fragile."

Sandy met his eyes and he was suddenly sure she knew everything about Bobbie, and maybe resented his interference. "If we don't give her something to do, she's going to spend every waking hour in that studio until she leaves for Italy in January. Her father called me recently to see how she was doing, and I promised him I'd help her get out and meet people." Sandy looked around the table at the expressions on the committee members' faces. Her colleagues obviously thought she presumed too much. "What? She was my roommate at Portland State, before she went to the Pacific Northwest College of Art. I care about her."

"Well, if you ask her for a painting, won't she still be spending every waking hour in her studio?" Nate asked.

Sandy considered that, then said finally, "As a member of the committee, and her neighbor, *you* can help her gather whatever she needs, check on her progress, support the work in whatever way you can. Why? Do you object to my asking her?"

He thought a moment. Bobbie Molloy seemed perfectly capable of taking care of herself. "No," he said finally. "Go ahead."

"I do like the painting idea," Clarissa said as she closed her notebook and stood. "Okay.

Back here next Monday morning same time?" She gave Nate a slightly apologetic smile. "You can be late as long as you arrive with doughnuts again. We'll all try to get whatever donations we can for the raffle at the Christmas dinner dance, right?"

"Right." The reply was unanimous.

The group left in a surge. Nate walked them to the door and waved everyone off. Sandy stopped to talk to Jonni.

"You seem very protective of this Bobbie woman," Hunter said to Nate when he returned. He picked up the last maple bar left on the plate.

Nate scooped the paper trash into a woven basket. "She's just been through a lot."

"How do you know?"

"She told me."

"Hmm."

Nate rolled his eyes. "She's my neighbor. She brought some Halloween things over for the boys."

"You called her fragile. I thought that went out in women along with petticoats and high button shoes." He pointed with his last bite of maple bar to Sandy. "They're now all like her—what's her name?—from your lawyer's office."

Nate put the basket down and elbowed him. "Sandy. And she's got a thing for *you*."

"What?"

"She was giving you the once-over."

He didn't seem to like that. "She's a pit bull. I'm waiting for a…a—"

"A poodle?" Nate asked. Then he added quietly, "You know, she's raising two little girls alone. Can't do that if you're just a pretty face."

"What happened to her husband? Probably drove him away."

"I don't know. But I've seen her at meetings with her kids when she couldn't get a babysitter." He held a hand down, palm parallel to the ground at the level of his thigh to indicate height. "Little things. Younger than Sheamus."

Hunter made a face. "Sounds awful. She probably never gets to watch Sports Center."

Nate laughed and pushed him toward the door.

BOBBIE COULDN'T BELIEVE her ears. She sat across the table from Sandy at the Astoria Coffee House, a funky, converted auto repair shop.

Sandy pointed her fork at the chicken, cranberries and walnuts in Bobbie's salad. "Is that as good as it looks?"

"Yes, and don't change the subject." Bobbie tried to sound severe. It wasn't hard. "You volunteered me to produce a new painting for a fund-raiser? Have you forgotten that you just volunteered me to teach an art class to little children? After helping me get a commission for your office, a project that's falling behind schedule?"

"Come on. You work fast when you're inspired." Sandy took a bite of her Reuben sandwich and remained casual in the face of Bobbie's indignation. "And everything about Astoria is inspiring. It'll be good for you to get out and get material, take photos, whatever you do. And the Kiwanis guys promise their total support. They're gorgeous, you know. Some of them are single and financially comfortable enough to support your art if you decide you like Astoria and want to blow off Italy, after all. And it'll flex your artistic muscles to help us out for charity. It's a win-win."

Bobbie put a hand on her friend's to stop her from taking another bite. "I like Astoria, but I am not staying here. I'm going to Florence, and I do not need to be this involved, when I'm leaving in January. Not to mention that I need *time* to get the commission done!"

"I thought you were down to just needing to do the calligraphy."

"On two pieces, but there are two more."

"You were mixing the mucky stuff."

"Yeah, well, a shelf and a lot of other junk landed in it."

"What?"

She explained about the mishap with Arnold and the Raleigh boys.

Sandy leaned back in her chair with a half smile. "So, *that's* it."

"That's what?"

"Why Nate Raleigh was being protective of you. He felt guilty about the boys putting you behind."

"I don't understand."

"At our committee meeting this morning. I proposed you help us, but he said you seemed fragile."

Bobbie put her fork down, her voice high. "*Fragile?* Me?"

"Calm down." She nibbled on a potato chip dotted with cracked pepper. "Nobody else knows what an Amazon warrior-woman hides in your delicate body. He's going to be your go-to guy for Kiwanis." She frowned. "He seems to think I'm pushy."

"No!" Bobbie said. "How ever could he have come to such a conclusion?"

Sandy dismissed her sarcasm with a wave of her chip. "The truth is, we really need you. The food bank is practically broke, and if this fund-raiser isn't a success, I don't know what the hungry people in this county will do. Now, please. Let's talk about something else. Oh! You'll never believe what Zoey said...."

Bobbie pretended to listen as her friend talked on about the girls. She was privately wondering two things. First, how on earth was she going to fulfill all her obligations by the New Year? Because she had to help with the fund-raiser. She'd been sick and she'd been down, but she'd never been hungry. And the thought of *children* being hungry was an abomination.

Second, why had she ever shared her personal struggle with Nate Raleigh? She'd been holding back, trying not to get too involved in Astoria, since she would be here only through December. But thanks to Sandy, she was in up to her eyebrows in community projects. Of course, if her father was coming to visit, she wanted him to think she was connected to the community so he wouldn't worry.

But if Nate was going to go around calling her fragile, she would have to straighten him out. Even if he meant it kindly, nobody counted her out. She'd fought too hard to get here.

So, she'd add working on the fund-raiser to finishing her commission, teaching the art class and preparing her tiny home and her personal space for her father's visit.

And she'd teach Nate Raleigh a thing or two about underestimating people. Women. Her.

CHAPTER FOUR

By THE TIME Nate left the office at four-thirty, Halloween had taken over Astoria. Traditionally, businesses welcomed trick-or-treaters in the late afternoon before the Monster Bash took place. Hundreds of costumed children, their parents in tow, swooped down upon the merchants in search of treats. Jonni and Karen stood outside the office with plastic pumpkins filled with candy, seemingly having as much fun as the kids.

Nate wound his way home through the chaos, finally pulling into his driveway when the late afternoon sun was low in the sky. He braked so abruptly that the car rocked. There was a witch in his driveway. Narrowing his eyes, he leaned over the steering wheel and took a second look.

She was still there, complete with a conical hat and flowing black dress. The fall breeze caught the irregular hem and fluttered it around slender ankles and small feet in incongruous tennis shoes. She held a star-tipped wand pointed in his direction. It traced a dramatic swath in the air that suggested he would disintegrate, or explode, or something equally dire.

He was surprised to feel a moment's cheer. It was Bobbie. She lowered the wand and came toward him, waggling it between her thumb and forefinger.

He opened his window. "Careful with that thing," he said. "You might turn me into a toad."

She pointed it at him once more, her expression severe. "You already are a toad. I'm here to—"

Sheamus burst through the back door carrying a small orange basket trimmed with black ribbon and fuzzy, phony spiders bobbing on a wire attached to the handle. His arrival halted her explanation of whatever she was "here to do." Ask him something? Tell him? He had no idea.

Sheamus held the basket so close to Nate's face that he went cross-eyed.

"Look, Uncle Nate. Bobbie made peanut butter cookies and some other kind with jam in them and these special ones shaped like pumpkins with orange frosting!"

Nate pushed Sheamus's hand slightly away so that he could focus on the basket with its elegant assortment of treats. The container itself was a work of art.

Stella wandered out with Dylan, who had an identical basket, except that bats bobbed from the handle.

"I think these are going to require a thank-you note," she said, giving Bobbie a quick hug. "I'm happy you moved in next door."

"Yuk!" Dylan made a face. "We did say thank you. And we really meant it."

"When someone cares enough about you to give you something this special…" Stella pointed to his basket. "You have to be sure they know how happy you are to have it. Are you boys ready to go to the Bash?"

"Maybe you should hit the bathroom first," Nate suggested.

The boys ran back inside. Stella followed. "Wouldn't be a bad idea if you took your coats!" she shouted after them before the door closed behind her.

"You know they're not going to want to hide their costumes," Bobbie said.

Her comment seemed obvious and it annoyed him that it hadn't occurred to him first. They were *his* nephews.

"Yes, I do. Thank you for stopping by." He looked to either side, as though searching for something. "No broom?" he asked pointedly. "How did you get here?"

"Aren't you cute?" She touched his shoulder threateningly with the wand. "Remember that I can make you bald and ugly."

"You were going to ask me something," he reminded her. "Or tell me something."

A car stopped behind Nate and a crowd of children leaped out, half of them headed for Nate's house, the other half for Bobbie's.

She pointed her wand at him. "We'll talk again. Goodbye." She ran back across her yard with witchy dignity to intercept the trick-or-treaters.

Monet, sitting on the back porch, ran for cover as the children approached.

Nate pulled the car up into his usual spot, gathered briefcase and computer and went inside as Stella distributed candy into outstretched bags. In the kitchen he dropped his things on a chair and went to pour a cup of coffee, hoping he could down a few sips before the boys reappeared.

"Bobbie's a lovely neighbor," Stella said, coming back inside. She opened a bag of treats and refilled the large orange bowl she'd placed on the table. A bony plastic hand hovered over the candy, descending whenever someone reached for a piece. The boys thought it hilarious.

Nate leaned against the counter and savored the caffeine. He was going to need it. "She's a little bit of a buttinsky," he said absently.

Stella made an impatient sound at that assessment. "I think it was providence that brought her here." She arranged the treats, eliciting a grisly laugh from the bowl as the hand descended on hers. "She's just the kind of woman this household needs.

"You can stop it right now, Stella. You can matchmake for your son, but not for me. And she's a woman with plans, anyway. She's moving to Italy after the first of the year."

Stella nodded. "To study art. She told me. She could do that here for the right man."

"No. She's not some little romantic waiting for her Prince Charming. She wants to study art in Florence. She's determined to dedicate herself to it without the complications of a personal life."

"Well, you certainly would complicate a woman's life."

Nate straightened away from the counter. "I beg your pardon?"

"Come on, Nathan. You're charming and

generous and very appealing, but you're afraid to go the distance."

"Hey!" He only half pretended injury. "I'm going the distance with two little boys and a business. I don't have time for romance."

"I'm talking love, not just romance. You can't be afraid to face it head-on."

"What makes you think I'm afraid?"

"You're thirty-five, handsome, intelligent, successful and you know how to treat a woman. Hunter says your single female clients and a few of the married ones come to the office all the time for your opinion on their finances."

"That's business. And he's not supposed to talk about what goes on at the office."

"He didn't share any details." She gave Nate a knowing smile. "Just that you haven't a clue that they're after you. And you're a smart man. So, you mustn't *want* to know."

The doorbell rang. She picked up the laughing bowl and, with a parting wink, headed for the door. "You boys have fun," she said.

Sheamus raced from the downstairs bathroom as Dylan thundered down the stairs and out the back door. Sheamus caught his uncle's hand and pulled him. "Come on! Hurry!"

Nate let himself be dragged along, thinking indignantly, *Afraid? Me?*

NOTHING SEPARATED THE MEN from the boys quite like Astoria's annual Monster Bash. The excitement generated by hundreds of hyper-charged children, and parents trying to maintain some degree of control, was an all-out sensory assault. Nate felt as though it took over his heartbeat and thrummed through his body like a blood tsunami.

And the candy, cake, punch, contests and prizes only revved the kids higher.

While Dylan and Sheamus posed with dozens of other boys for a superhero photo taken by the *Daily Astorian*'s photographer, Nate tried to stay out of the fray. But two little bite-size fairies collided with his knees. One of the girls spilled punch on his slacks, and the other got frosting on the cuff of his jacket when he leaned down to make sure they were all right. He recognized Sandy's children, Addie and Zoey.

"Hi, girls," he said. He kept smiling despite going mildly nuts with the noise and confusion. But if the other parents could cope, so could he.

"Oh, good grief!" Sandy fought her way

past someone in a Hulk costume who had gotten between her and the girls, and noticed Nate dabbing at his jacket. "What did they get on you? I'm so sorry." She extracted a wet wipe from her purse and grabbed his wrist to work on the frosted cuff.

She wore a wildly colored headscarf, a yellow blouse and long red skirt, and the large hoop earrings of a gypsy. As she worked she smiled up at him in dismay. "I'm really sorry. You always look so elegant and we've messed you up."

Nate pulled away to stop her fussing. "Hi, Sandy. I'm fine, really."

"Girls! Come back!" While she was trying to clean him up, the girls had escaped again. She reached around him just in time to catch Addie's hand and desperately pointed to Zoey, on his other side. "Stop her, Nate!"

Afraid he'd break that small arm if he grabbed it, he caught the little girl around the waist and scooped her into his arms. He was smacked in the face by a sparkly wing as she put her arm around his neck. The little fairy pushed aside her long blond hair and smiled warmly. She smelled of strawberries. "Hi!" she said. "You're Sheamus's daddy."

A little surprised that she remembered him, Nate didn't correct her. He was sure he'd met the girls only once, at a parish picnic at St. Mary's. "And you're Zoey. You have to stay with your mom or you'll get lost."

Addie tugged at his pant leg, clearly competing for attention. "I'm Addie!" she announced in a voice much bigger than seemed appropriate for her size.

He smiled down at her. "Yes, I know. Are you having fun?"

She held up a plastic bag filled with candy. "Yes. You want some?"

"No, thank you. I'm full."

She clearly didn't see how anyone could be too full for candy. "Can you pick me up, too?"

Sandy sighed apologetically. "I'm sorry. They're both man-crazy. I guess because they don't have one in their lives. You really don't have to…"

He reached a hand down for Addie, told her to hang on, and pulled her up against his side. She held on to his neck as he settled her on his arm. She giggled at her sister, then both girls looked around, enjoying their superior view.

He grinned at Sandy. "They seem like a lot of fun." It was strange how vulnerable she seemed as a mother, yet as a community activist, she was a powerhouse.

She glanced at her daughters adoringly. "They are. Exhausting, but fun. They're never still a minute, and I'm trying not to think ahead to when they'll be dating at the same time." She straightened the hem of Zoey's dress and asked casually, "Have you and Bobbie talked about the painting?"

He shook his head and frowned. "You told her I called her fragile, didn't you? Apparently that's a bad word where she comes from, because when I got home tonight, she waved a wand at me and threatened to make me bald and ugly."

Sandy laughed, her hoop earrings dancing. "As though she could make you bald. You have that same wonderful hair Ben had." She smiled reminiscently. "I served on a couple of committees with Sherrie. They were both fun to know. Anyway." She expelled a sigh, pushing the sensitive subject aside. "As for ugly," she added, mischief in her grin, "I'm sure it wouldn't take, no matter how hard she tried."

Nate was left wondering if Sandy Evans had just given him a compliment.

"Hey, guys!" Hunter appeared beside them in a Frankenstein costume. The Kiwanis Club had helped with the decorating. Suddenly recognizing Sandy, he looked a little nervous. "Hi. I'm sorry. I didn't recognize you with your red hair covered."

Nate watched in amazement as Sandy's

gaze softened. She said nothing, but smiled into Hunter's eyes.

It surprised Nate that the girls didn't seem frightened of Hunter, despite his full Frankenstein makeup, complete with a large bolt sticking out of his head.

"Ah…" Hunter dragged his eyes away from Sandy and looked around for another subject. He found it in the little fairies that had alighted on Nate's arms. "How come you have two of those," he asked, "and I don't have any?"

"Clearly, I'm more important. Actually, they're just on loan. I think my purpose here is to provide them with an aerial view. You want one?"

Sheamus walked up to the group, the photo session over, and looked puzzled at the sight of Nate holding Sandy's daughters. "We aren't keeping them, are we?"

"No. Here you go, Hunt. Have both. Girls, how about you let Uncle Frankenstein show you around?"

The amenable pair leaned out of his arms toward Hunter without complaint.

"We were about to join the dancing, Hunter," Sandy told him. "Want to come?"

He looked pleadingly at Nate, who ignored him.

"Do I have to dance?" Hunter asked worriedly.

"No."

"Then, yes. See you tomorrow, Nate." He followed her across the room, his arms filled with her children. It was a good look for him, Nate thought.

"Okay." He put a hand on Sheamus's shoulder and glanced around for Dylan. "Where's your brother?"

"He and a couple of his friends were gonna get some punch."

As Nate looked toward the refreshment table at the other side of the room, he heard a sudden, eerie whooshing noise that was immediately followed by the eruption of a green geyser shooting toward the ceiling. There were cries and screams and a great scattering of children and adults before the geyser collapsed as dramatically as it had risen, drenching everyone nearby.

Nate saw three boys run for the door, one of them a very familiar Iron Man.

He pushed his way through the crowd and reached the table just in time to see the principal of Astor School and the mayor soaked from head to toe in green slime. One of the bad words he'd fought so hard to control in the past few months slipped out. Sheamus, wide-eyed and glued to his side, blinked up at him. "Uncle Nate!"

Nate did the mayor's personal taxes, and he didn't really know the principal, but he'd had a conversation with her about the boys right after the accident. She'd been kind and caring. Right now she maintained the carriage of a royal personage—despite the fact that she was green.

"I'm…so sorry," he said. He looked around frantically for something to help them wipe the slimy stuff off, just as several people ran from the kitchen with a stack of towels.

A woman Nate recognized as the mother of one of Dylan's friends held his nephew by the arm in one hand and a vampire by his cape in the other. A concerned mummy followed them, looking around furtively, as though considering escape. In the end, he chose to stay with his friends.

Nate met Dylan's eyes. Then, in a gesture of deliberate defiance, his nephew pulled off his headpiece and glared at him. Every word that came to Nate's lips should not be used around children, so he remained silent as the principal stepped forward.

She slanted a scolding look at the boys.

"Are you all right, Mrs. Trumble?" the mayor asked as he wiped his face.

"Oh, yes, Mr. Mayor. I can't tell you how many times the Mentos–Diet Coke experiment has crossed my path. Nucleation never seems to get old for children." Then she added a little more severely, "But I think someone's allowances should pay for dry-cleaning the mayor's suit and my dress."

The other parents involved, Steve and Judy Berg, a couple in their forties that Nate had met at an open house, and Kristy Moss, a single mother and the one who'd caught the boys, nodded their approval.

"Good. And now I think the boys should clean this up." Mrs. Trumble smiled at the crowd collected behind them. "Please continue with the party. Everything's fine." To the boys she added more quietly, "What were you thinking? There were already enough Mentos in the lime punch for the bubbling cauldron effect."

"We wanted to see if we could make it hit the ceiling," Dylan said. "But we didn't think you'd be standing here. I'm sorry about your dress. And your suit, Mr. Mayor."

Nate was both proud and angry. Which mystified him, because he hated indecisiveness. Since he was more familiar with the anger than the pride, he decided to go with the pride this time. Dylan was behaving well, despite what he'd done, so maybe there was hope. And he and his friends hadn't intended to hurt anyone. It was simply a kid-friendly experiment for which they'd chosen the wrong time and place.

The principal beckoned to one of the women who'd been working in the kitchen. She was tall and formidable-looking. "Inga, please take the boys and get them each a bucket and a mop, then send them back to me."

Inga nodded, pointed the boys to the kitchen and followed them. Dylan cast a dark look over his shoulder at Nate.

The principal smiled at the parents. "Don't be upset. It's messy but harmless. Blame the sugar and the excitement."

Steve Berg shook his head. "Justin was probably the instigator." He looked apologetically at Nate and Kristy. "He's new to our home, and still trying to shock us."

The Bergs, Nate knew, had a foster home. He shrugged. "Dylan never needs much encouragement to try to make *something* reach the ceiling."

Kristy folded her arms, looking completely demoralized. "Yeah, well, this time it's *me!* I've never been so embarrassed! I can't believe Randy did this!"

Judy sighed philosophically. "It's very humbling to be a parent." She lowered her voice when Mrs. Trumble turned away to speak to the mayor, and there was a wicked gleam in her eye. "But you got to love how straight and high that geyser shot!"

Nate suppressed a laugh. Mercifully, Sheamus was distracted by someone passing in a Chinese warlord costume.

Kristy looked horrified. Judy patted her arm. "We've raised four boys, Kris, and Justin is our eighth foster child. Believe me, it can get a lot worse than an eruption of soda."

When the boys returned with buckets, Mrs. Trumble gave directions for the cleanup to Inga, then left.

"Is Dylan in big trouble?" Sheamus asked as they sat at a table to wait for him.

"That's where he seems to like to be."

Sheamus dug into his sack, came up with a bag of almonds and ripped it open. He grinned at Nate as he poured some into his hand. "It was cool the way it just shot up!" he said excitedly, using his free hand to gesture toward the ceiling. "And it was kind of funny that Mrs. Trumble got slimed!"

"That's the part that wasn't cool, Sheamus," Nate said seriously. "She's a very nice lady, and she works hard to make Astor School special. Dylan and his friends ruined her dress, the mayor's suit, and made them look silly. That isn't nice."

Sheamus appeared repentant, or seemed to think he should. "Yeah," he corrected, striving for sincerity. "Sorry."

The event began to wind down. Nate was chewing on a red licorice vine he'd finally accepted from Sheamus when Hunter appeared beside them.

"How's it going?" he asked Nate, pulling up a chair. He fist-bumped Sheamus. "You guys okay? You got to admit we all want to try the Mentos thing."

"Yeah!" Sheamus agreed heartily. At a disapproving glance from Nate, he went back to examining his candy.

Nate turned the same look on Hunter. "What he did wasn't so bad," he said in a low voice, so that Sheamus wouldn't hear, "but like a lot of things you don't think through before you act on, other people get hurt or embarrassed. And that's not so good."

Hunter nodded gravely and took the last string of licorice in Nate's package. "Right. Sorry." But there was laughter in his eyes.

Nate noticed something was different about him. "Your bolt is missing," he said.

Hunter touched the spot of glue just above his ear. "Zoey didn't like it and pulled it off."

"What happened to Sandy and the girls?"

"Addie was starting to fuss. They had to go home. I offered to take them but Sandy had her car."

"Did she make you dance?"

"Nobody makes me dance. She tried, though. Pushy woman."

"I know."

Dylan came to join them, smelling of pine cleaner and looking belligerent. His headpiece was tucked under his arm. He frowned at Hunter. "Where's your bolt?" he asked. "Your brain's going to fall out."

"That happened years ago." Nate got to his feet and grinned at Hunter. "See you in the morning. Let's go, Sheamus." Noticing Dylan was empty-handed except for his headpiece, he asked, "Where's your candy?"

Dylan shrugged. "I don't know. Lost it after the punch bowl blew up. Somebody probably took it when everybody started running."

Sheamus held up his bag, still filled with treats despite how many he'd eaten. "I got lots. You can have some of mine."

Dylan rolled his eyes and started for the door. Sheamus turned to Nate in confusion, so he put an arm around him. "It was nice of you to offer to share. He's just crabby because he lost his. Good night, Hunter."

"See you guys." Hunter waved them off, but he seemed moody.

Dylan was quiet on the ride home, but Sheamus relived the evening in descriptive detail. At home, Nate stashed the bag of candy in a kitchen cupboard, Arnold watching closely, tail wagging. Nate gave him one of his own treats, explaining why dogs shouldn't eat chocolate.

A short while later Nate tucked Sheamus in, assured him that the closet door was securely closed, turned on his night-light, then crossed the hall to Dylan's room. The door was shut.

That was a metaphor for their relationship, Nate thought. He rapped lightly, and when there was no answer, he pushed the door open. Dylan was in bed with the lights out, facing the window.

Nate turned the light on and sat on the edge of the bed. "We have to talk about tonight," he said, doing his best to sound reasonable. "You didn't do anything awful, but you have to start thinking first, Dyl."

"We didn't mean for that to happen." Dylan spoke without turning.

"I'm sure you didn't." He wasn't really, but

the words expressed some belief in the boy's intentions. "But…you're a kid who likes to experiment with things. Next time, experiment with thinking through the possibilities of what could happen before you do it."

That earned him a puzzled look over Dylan's shoulder. "What?"

"Think first," Nate added more succinctly. "Imagine what could happen if something goes wrong, or just differently than you planned. Then consider whether it's worth taking the chance. Especially if you're doing it in front of a bunch of people who'll probably remember what you did for a long time."

"Yeah." Dylan agreed, but before Nate could feel a sense of relief, the boy added, "And plan enough time to get away."

Nate closed his eyes and bit down on exasperation. He so wished he could channel his brother. "Are you getting my point at all?"

Dylan turned away again. "Yes," he said stiffly. "You were embarrassed in front of some of your clients, weren't you? I know you do some work for the mayor."

Surprised, Nate replied, "I didn't say that."

"Sandy did. She was in the kitchen when Inga was filling our buckets."

"What you did embarrassed you, not me. And most of my clients have their own kids and know that thinking before you act is a lesson that takes time to learn. So buck up. You're not as awful as you want to be. Good night."

CHAPTER FIVE

BOBBIE EXPECTED CHAOS in the large classroom assigned for her art projects, but was pleasantly surprised to find the second and third graders attentive while she explained the plan.

She had initially been reluctant to use the tried-and-true turkey-made-from-paint-on-a-child's-hand project but finally decided it would be a good introduction.

Once the children got their hands in the paint, though, the chaos she'd feared surfaced and quickly took over. They dutifully pressed their hands to the paper. There was giggling and bumping as everyone moved along the table to press their hands into a different color set out in pans on a work table. They pressed their hands into the paper again, but the third pass was too much of a temptation. In their little minds the obvious next step was touching one another. Before Bobbie could react, children were sporting orange noses, yellow foreheads, multicolored blotches on their T-shirts and dresses. The classroom aide had outfitted the students with aprons, but still, paint was everywhere.

The aide, a wonderful volunteer in her midthirties named Fernanda, laughed and patted Bobbie's shoulder when she saw her distress. "It's all right. This always happens. That's why we supply water-based paint. And, of course, water-based children."

Bobbie relaxed, but worried a little about how to keep the children occupied for another forty minutes. Then one of the livelier second graders suggested eagerly, "Let's do monsters! Turkeys are dumb." He waved his unconventional yellow-and-blue print in the air. "Monsters! Can we, please?"

The other children quickly picked up the cry. Bobbie questioned Fernanda with a look.

The woman nodded. "Why not? Whatever keeps them happy for another—" she consulted her watch "—another thirty-seven minutes."

"Okay." Bobbie walked to the middle of the aisle separating the worktables and tried to project order. "Let's talk about what monsters could look like."

Hands flew up and excited suggestions were shouted. "Messy hair! Ripped up shirts! Scabs and blood all over! Mean faces!"

Eddy, the lively second grader, made a

twisted face that sent his classmates into hysterics.

Pleased that the children were so responsive, Bobbie suddenly noticed Sheamus in a back corner, staring worriedly into space, while Fernanda distributed fresh sheets of white paper.

Bobbie wondered what it was he didn't like—art or monsters. He seemed to have enjoyed the turkey project, so it must be the latter. She was certain he wasn't the only child here who worried about imaginary creatures that lurked in the dark.

"All right." She found herself clapping her hands to claim the children's attention. How school-marmish was that? "I want each of you to draw a picture of what you think a monster would look like. If you opened your closet in the middle of the night and found one there, what do you think he'd be wearing? How would he have combed his hair that morning? Would he be wearing shoes, or would he have bare feet?"

One little girl waved her hand.

"Yes?" Bobbie asked.

"Can I have a lady monster?"

"Of course." It was probably an equal-opportunity profession.

Eddy looked up from his work to say profoundly, "There have to be lady monsters or there would never be baby monsters to take the place of old monsters when they die."

Bobbie was amazed. This was turning into an art and philosophy class. Or was it biology?

She wandered up and down the aisle while the children worked, and stopped near Sheamus as he hesitantly made a circle, presumably for a face. She squeezed into the small, empty chair beside him. "That's a good beginning, Sheamus." She saw the concern in his face and spoke cheerfully. "This is just a picture of a pretend monster, so you can look at it and maybe decide it isn't very scary, after all."

He considered a moment before adding a larger circle with stick arms and legs.

"Very good," she praised. "Probably ate too many French fries."

Sheamus looked up at her, his expression grave. "I think he ate some of my Halloween candy. And one of the cookies you gave me."

"Really? Are you sure you didn't eat them when you were hungry, and just forgot?"

"Maybe."

Other children were clamoring for Bobbie's attention. She patted Sheamus's arm, praised him for doing well, and went to the little girl who was creating a "lady" monster.

"She gots lots of hair," the girl said, making yellow crayon curls with great enthusiasm. "And she doesn't let anybody say, 'Shut up!' or, 'That sucks!'"

"That's just a mom," Eddy said from across the room. "We're supposed to make monsters!"

"Sometimes moms are monsters," another boy commented.

Sheamus looked up from his drawing. "My mom was nice. And pretty."

"She died," one child said knowingly.

Bobbie held her breath, wondering how Sheamus would react. But apparently that truth was now a fact of his life.

"Yeah," he said, and went back to his work.

Five minutes before her class was over, Bobbie spread their artwork on two tables at the front to save for next week. Fernanda helped her wash little hands, clean up and pack her supplies away.

Bobbie was delighted that the children seemed enthusiastic about the work they'd done today. She headed home with a new glow in the center of her being. Emailing her friend Laura, she told her about the class, described Eddy and Sheamus, and passed on Sandy's greeting.

The glow remained with her for a long time.

A GOOD DAY'S work behind her, four sheets of paper drying safely inside her closed garage so that no act of nature, boy or dog could set her commission further behind, and dinner dishes finished, Bobbie walked across her backyard toward the Raleighs' house with leftover Halloween candy and cookies.

She had to talk to Nate, and the leftover candy would provide an excuse for the visit.

At the back door, she rapped firmly.

The door opened and Nate stood there in dark jeans and a soft blue sweater that seemed to imbue his hazel eyes with a hint of the same color. He looked surprised to see her. She couldn't tell if he was pleased or not. So she prepared to get right to the point.

She handed him the bag of leftover candy and the cookies, then folded her arms and fixed him with a firm stare. "This is the conversation I wanted to have with you on Halloween, but I didn't want to yell at you in front of all those children. I am *not* fragile, so I'd appreciate it if you didn't go around telling people that I am. I'm perfectly capable of finishing my commission, teaching an art class *and* creating a painting for the food bank fund-raiser."

"I meant…" he began.

She wasn't finished. "All you know about me," she went on evenly, determined to keep her tone calm even though her words were testy, "is that I've had cancer and I'm an artist. That doesn't qualify you to determine anything else about me except that I've had cancer and I'm an artist."

"Sandy…" He tried again.

"I'd appreciate it if you didn't count me out. When you've had a life-threatening disease, everyone wants to sit you down somewhere comfortable, cover you with a blanket and go around you, because they don't know what to do *for* you. Well, I've struggled to get to the point where I can work again, and I will not let you—"

"You will not let me *speak?*" he interrupted, his expression caught somewhere between anger and laughter.

She hesitated, surprised that something about her telling him off amused him. "No, I will not let you—"

"Explain?"

"No!"

"Tell you that I meant to help you, not insult you?" he persisted, "because that was my intention. Maybe you aren't fragile, but you *look* fragile, and pardon me for not wanting Sandy to take advantage of you."

She heaved a sigh and said defensively, "Sandy meant well."

"Okay," he said reasonably. "So did I. She's a hardworking woman, but she's like a runaway tank, and I wasn't sure you could stand up to that."

He certainly understood Sandy. "I can stand up to anything," Bobbie declared.

"Hi!" Sheamus shot around his uncle, hair messy, eyes bright and flatteringly happy to see her. Arnold was beside him, wagging his tail. "Come in!" On second thought, the boy looked up at Nate. "Can she come in? I finished my homework." He took hold of Bobbie's hand while waiting for the decision from his uncle.

"Sheamus, I have things to…" She started to demur at the same moment that Nate stepped aside. She suspected he knew she'd rather not stay, and deliberately took the choice from her.

"Sure," he said. "Please come in, Bobbie."

"Want to see my room?" Sheamus pulled her across the kitchen.

"Is it presentable?" Nate asked in some concern.

"Sort of," Sheamus shouted over his shoulder as he continued to tug on her hand. Arnold tried to follow them, but Nate pointed to his green plaid bed in the corner of the kitchen. Bobbie noticed that it was the size of a single bed.

Sheamus pulled her down the corridor, through the living room to the stairs, talking a mile a minute. She had a quick impression of large pieces of furniture in beige and dark blue, a fireplace, oak tables and kid things all around.

Had Bobbie not picked up her pace, she'd have been dragged up the stairs to the middle room on the west side of the house. Small play figures were lined up on the floor. Green rubber soldiers, pink pigs, black-and-white cows and a variety of dogs stood facing a single stuffed animal with large purple ears, a green-and-yellow-striped nose and fuzzy blue protrusions from his head—antennae, she guessed. Apparently, a diverse community had allied to fight off an alien invasion.

The bed was half-made, with a Spider-Man bedspread that matched Spider-Man curtains. The room was a little chaotic but clearly kid-friendly.

Sheamus opened a wooden trunk at the foot of his bed to show her a jumble of toys and a special box that held electronic ones. "You have to be careful with that stuff," he said, as though quoting an adult, "or it won't stay in good working order."

"That's very true," she agreed seriously, wondering what she was doing. She'd come to give Nate a piece of her mind, and here she was, completely immersed in kid territory.

Sheamus opened dresser drawers so she could see his shirts and pants. He pointed at the top drawer. "That's underwear and socks. And…" His sunny cheer seemed to dim a little as he turned toward the closet. "That's where my cold weather stuff is. And my basketball."

"I like basketball," Bobbie wondered at his change of mood and wandered to the closet. She noticed he took a step back from it. She smiled at him and put a hand to the doorknob, then remembered his expression when they'd begun to draw monsters. "There's a basketball hoop over my garage," she said, "but I don't have a ball."

"It won't be winter for a long time," he said. "We don't have to open the closet until then."

"But what if we want to play basketball?"

"Then…we'll ask Uncle Nate to open it."

His eyes were wide pools of concern. "We keep my jacket downstairs so we don't have to go into the closet."

She dropped her hand from the doorknob and went to sit on the edge of his bed. "Is there something else in there?" she asked casually.

He came to stand beside her, clearly afraid, and embarrassed that he was. He nodded. "It's…a monster."

She put an arm around him and drew him closer. Fear was something she understood. "You know, monsters make good stories and movies, but they're really not real. They're just fiction. Make-believe."

He looked directly into her eyes. "He's in there."

"Have you seen him?"

"No," he admitted, "but I know what he looks like. I can tell. And I hear him all the time."

"What does he say?"

"He doesn't talk, he makes noises."

"What kind of noises?"

"He growls. And sometimes in the middle of the night, he just hums."

Bobbie hugged Sheamus a little closer. "It doesn't seem like we should be afraid of something that hums. That's like a song, but without words. If he's singing in there, that doesn't sound very dangerous."

The boy considered that a moment, then sighed and said, "It's okay if you think it's stupid. Dylan thinks it is, too, but Uncle Nate says sometimes you just can't help how you feel, even if it is stupid."

"I don't think it's stupid at all. Everybody has stuff they're afraid of. But being afraid stops you from doing all kinds of things. Like, what if it gets really cold and you want to go out and play, but you won't go into the closet to get your winter coat?"

"Uncle Nate will get it for me."

"What if Uncle Nate's at work?"

Sheamus smiled disarmingly. "I'll come and get you. You're not afraid of monsters, are you?"

It wasn't good to lie to a child, so she compromised and told a half-truth. "I'm only going to be here until January. And that's when the cold part of winter gets going. Whoever is living in my place then might not want to come over."

"Then I guess I'll stay inside and play with my Game Boy."

Bobbie stood and kissed the top of his head. "It's okay," she said. "One day you'll wake up and feel really brave and you'll open the closet."

"How do you know?"

"I just know."

She heard movement at the bedroom door and looked up to see Dylan standing there, his expression serious. He had one of the pens she'd given him in his hand, and the sketchbook tucked under his arm. He smiled suddenly. "Hi, Bobbie. I thought I heard you. Can you help me? I don't understand some of the things you gave me."

"Which things?"

"My bag's downstairs. Can you stay awhile and show me how to use them?"

"Oh, I don't know. I should…" Again she made an effort to refuse the invitation and go home. But Sheamus already had her hand again and was dragging her back downstairs. "Come on. You can help me with my monster!"

"Is it okay if Bobbie stays for a while?" Dylan asked Nate as the three of them arrived in the kitchen at a run. Bobbie leaned against the doorjamb to catch her breath.

Nate looked her over with sudden sympathy. "Do you want to stay?"

Dylan replied for her. "She's going to show me what to do with some of the stuff she gave me," he said, and went to the table where his art bag hung over the back of a chair.

"And she's going to help me with my picture." Sheamus pulled out a chair at the table, then said gravely to his uncle, "Maybe she should have a cup of coffee, Uncle Nate."

"You're right. Coming up." Nate turned back to the counter as Sheamus pushed Bobbie toward the chair and Dylan sat opposite her.

"I love all the stuff you gave me." Dylan frowned suddenly and handed her the square eraser. "But I don't know how this works."

"Here. I'll show you."

Nate got a mug down from the shelf and watched her and the boys.

"This is no ordinary eraser," she told Dylan, pulling and tugging on it, warming it with her hands until the rubber was malleable. She rolled it between her palms to form a ball, then pulled out a small section almost into a point.

"This is almost like having another color," she went on. "It allows you to take out what you don't want in a sketch and leave white space. And when you manipulate it to make it skinny like this…" She made a mark on a piece of paper with one of his pencils, then removed a small part with the tip of the eraser.

"...you can get the tiniest spot out of a very small space."

She rolled the rubber back into a ball, then used it to remove the entire mark.

Dylan looked on in surprise. "Wow!"

"Isn't that cool? You should work it in your hands when you start. I do it while I'm looking at a sketch and planning what I'm going to do next."

Dylan looked up at Nate in obvious delight. Then, realizing what he'd done, he glanced away again.

"Cool," Nate said simply. He put a cup of steaming coffee in front of Bobbie. "Cream or sugar?" he asked.

"No, I drink it straight," she replied. "Thank you." She took a quick sip and set the cup back down.

Sheamus sat across the table from Dylan and beckoned her over to look at his project. She saw that a sheet of drawing paper was attached to a board with stationery clips. "This is cool," she said.

"Uncle Nate made them for us." Sheamus reclaimed his art. "I haven't gotten very far," he complained, tapping his pencil against the same head and trunk circles he'd drawn in her class.

"We just have to think about this." She

leaned toward his drawing. "So, we know he should have hair. What do you think his hair looks like? What color is it?"

"Your color," he said.

She found the black pencil in the array spread beside him and handed it to him.

"Is it curly?"

"No. It sticks up. Like punk hair."

"Okay. Give him some hair." She peered closer. "Make it just like you see it in your mind."

He made large, irregular spikes atop the head circle. "Like that?"

"What about his nose?"

With the same pencil, Sheamus drew a big circle in the middle of the monster's face. He added dots for nostrils.

"Very good," she declared. "Does he have lumpy ears, too?"

The boy shook his head. "Pointy ears."

"Okay. Let's see what they look like."

Sheamus carefully made bat ears, then leaned back to study his work. "Yeah. That's about right. And he has big shoes with a big buckle on them." He drew the feet, one considerably larger than the other, then added straps and a lopsided but clearly defined buckle on each.

"All right. He's really taking shape."

Sheamus turned to her and said gravely, "He needs a tool belt."

"Really. Why a tool belt?" she asked.

"Because I heard him working in there."

"I thought he was humming."

"That's what I thought at first, but maybe he's using power tools."

"Is he building stuff? Is there anything new in your closet that wasn't there before? Like another shelf, or something?"

He looked at her with a "duh!" expression. "I don't know. I can't go in there, remember?"

Flawless logic. She nodded in apology.

He handed her the pencil. "I don't know how to draw a tool belt. Can you do it?"

"Sure." She took a long pull on her coffee, then moved the board toward her, considering a minute before she began to draw. She created a belt with dangling pockets around his bulky middle, a power drill sticking out of it, and a power hammer dangling from a loop. Bobbie had both tools in her own arsenal in the garage.

Sheamus was delighted. He stood and leaned over her shoulder to watch her work. She could feel his little heart beating against her arm.

Nate came to stand over them. "Handsome dude," he said. "But he doesn't have eyes."

"We're getting to that." Bobbie handed him her half-empty cup. "That's really good stuff. May I have a warm-up?"

"I'm on it. Anyone want cocoa?"

Sheamus shook his head. "I want to finish Shrek first."

Bobbie looked up, completely distracted by Sheamus's reply. Her eyes met Nate's. She could tell they shared the same thought. Shrek was seriously nonthreatening as monsters went. That seemed like a good sign.

"You want to finish your monster instead of having cocoa?" Nate asked with a smile. "Does that mean you're getting to like him?"

"Uncle Nate, Shrek is an ogre," Sheamus corrected.

"What's the difference between the two?" Bobbie asked.

"Um…" Sheamus thought.

Dylan, hard at work on his own sketch, looked up to explain. "Ogres are humanoid. Monsters are really big and usually animal, or parts of animals, or sometimes part people and part animal."

Again, Bobbie's eyes met Nate's in amazement. He patted Dylan's shoulder. "Atta boy," he said. "Dazzle us with your smarts."

Dylan gave the barest of smiles. "Justin has

the Monster Slayer game. You have to have different weapons to get different monsters."

"So, you think my monster should have a different name?" Sheamus tried to reclaim attention.

"How do you know what's in your closet is a monster and not an ogre?" Dylan asked. "Or a troll?"

"'Cause I know," Sheamus insisted.

"'Cause you made him up."

"Dyl," Nate warned.

Dylan went back to work, ignoring the monster construction.

"I think he's *your* monster," Nate said, "and you can name him whatever you want." He angled his head for a better look at the sketch. Bobbie turned it so that he could see. "But maybe he should have a special name. One that just belongs to him."

Sheamus thought. "Like…Bill?"

Bobbie bit back a smile.

"That doesn't sound very scary," Nate said.

Sheamus shrugged, apparently thinking that was all right.

Dylan looked up again. "His name should be something creepy, like Skeletor. I know that's already taken, but something like that."

"No, I like Bill." Sheamus was stubborn.

"Okay." Dylan leaned over his own work again. "But it's dumb."

"What color is Bill?" Bobbie held up a green pencil. "Same color as Shrek?"

Sheamus leaned his elbows on the table. "Brown. Like a bear. He's part people, part bear."

She held up a yellow-brown and a dark brown. Sheamus picked the dark one, so she crosshatched color onto Bill's round face, rotund body and squatty arms and legs.

"Do you think he should have a jacket? You know, since he's in the closet where your winter clothes are."

"Yeah. One of my jackets is green with a hood. I don't like it, so he can have that one."

"Right." A green zippered jacket with a hood took shape. She added a smiley-face button to the collar. "What about a hat?"

Nate took a seat at a right angle to her and watched the drawing progress. When she glanced up, he did, too, and something completely unexpected happened. Electricity. As though the pencil in her hand had become a bare wire. Their eyes connected again. She felt his gaze like a touch.

He looked as startled by the impact as she was.

"I hate to wear a hat," Sheamus said, unaware of anything but his monster. "I bet he does, too."

She refocused on the monster, who was becoming less and less threatening as she built and clothed him. Which was precisely what she'd hoped for.

Sheamus pointed to Bill's throat. "I have a yellow scarf my mom made hanging inside the closet door."

A mild but palpable tension invaded the room.

"Should we put that on him," Bobbie asked gently, "or should we save it for you? When you can open the closet, that might be the first thing you take out."

He considered that, his eyes troubled.

"You have a blue scarf in there, too." Nate spoke softly, leaning closer to study the figure. "It has red and yellow dinosaurs on it, remember? I brought it back for you when I went to New York. Bill would look cool in it."

Sheamus smiled broadly as he remembered. "From the museum. Dylan got a red one with blue and yellow dinosaurs."

"That's right. That was a couple of years ago. You were just little guys."

Dylan didn't look up.

Sheamus turned to Bobbie. "It's kinda little. Can we make it fit Bill?"

"I think we can." She set to work with all the colors Nate had mentioned, and made it fit snugly, its two short ends sticking out of the knot at the side of Bill's throat. The dinosaur pattern was small but visible.

"He should have mean eyes!" Enthusiastic again, Sheamus jabbed a finger at Bill's face.

"At last!" Nate exclaimed, slapping the table. "I was afraid we'd have to teach him to read braille."

Bobbie did as Sheamus asked, but made the eyes comically angry. An inverted eyebrow added tension but in the end he looked more disgruntled than mean. She added color to his cheeks, then drew a snarl that was also more funny than frightening.

Sheamus unclipped the sketch from the board and held it up. He looked unsure at first, but finally smiled. He turned to his uncle. "Can I tape this to the closet door?"

"Sure."

"Will you help me put it up when I go to bed?"

"Yes. Meanwhile, why don't you put him on the refrigerator? We can get used to him before you go to bed."

Sheamus took a yellow power company magnet shaped like a lightbulb and secured the portrait under several postcards and a school lunch menu. Bill was impressive. His dimensions were large, his pose blustery, but his general impression was one of vulnerability.

"Doesn't he need fangs?" Nate asked, a smile in his voice.

"Yeah!" Sheamus agreed.

Bobbie went to the refrigerator with the black pencil and a yellow one. She gave Bill one regular fang, then colored the other yellow. But when she stood back to study it she wasn't happy. "I wish I had a gold pencil," she complained. "That looks more like yellowed decay than a gold tooth."

"Here." Dylan offered a marker she had put in his bag of supplies. Nate took it from him and passed it to Bobbie.

She uncapped it and turned the yellow fang gold, even added a few sparkle lines to depict glitter. She stood back again and laughed aloud. "That's perfect! Thank you, Dylan." She handed the marker to Nate, who passed it back.

"Thanks, Dyl. Just what it needed."

"Sure." He smiled thinly, then added, "Bill's still a stupid name."

Sheamus ignored that. "How come a gold fang?"

"In the old days," Nate explained, with a

hand on the boy's shoulder as they studied the portrait together, "dentists used gold to fill teeth. Pirates usually have at least one gold tooth."

Sheamus studied Bill closely. "I kinda like him," he said. Bobbie silently cheered. Mission accomplished. Almost. He still had to open the closet door.

The living room clock chimed eight. Sheamus poked Dylan on the shoulder. "*Suite Life of Zack and Cody* is on." He turned to his uncle. "Can we go watch TV before bed?"

"Sure."

"And now can we have cocoa?" He smiled winningly.

"Go ahead. I'll bring it in a minute."

Bobbie noticed that Dylan had turned his sketch facedown before getting up. "Can I see what you've done?" she asked, before he could follow his brother.

Dylan stopped in the doorway to consider, bounced a glance off his uncle. "It isn't finished." He nodded reluctantly. "Okay. But don't laugh."

She frowned at him. "Artists never laugh at each other."

He followed Sheamus into the living room.

Bobbie turned his sheet over and studied his sketch with pleased surprise. It was elementary so far, just nicely defined lines indicating beach, ocean and low mountains in the background. There were rocks on the shore, and a bird suggested in the sky.

She went to straighten up and ask Nate what he thought, then felt his face right beside hers, his eyes riveted to the drawing.

"So, he's good, isn't he?" he asked.

"He's good," she confirmed. "Those expressive lines are the sort of thing you can't teach."

"He's been working on that a lot since you gave him the supplies." Nate turned his gaze from the paper to her eyes, and she felt that electricity at work again.

She delved deeply for a full breath. "The more he works, the better he'll become. I'd love to see how this develops."

"Incidentally…" Nate didn't touch her, but his eyes somehow held her immobile. How did he do that? She should look away, just to show him that she could, but contrary to all good sense, she didn't want to. He exuded strength and concern—and crankiness, true, but at the moment he seemed to want to connect with her. "Thank you for helping Sheamus with Bill," he said, his voice rumbling in the quiet room as he emphasized the monster's name. Then he grew serious again. "You were brilliant, drawing all that out of him. I'll bet we're on the road to a closet breakthrough."

She thought so, too, and was almost as happy as he was. "Sheamus was just ready to put a face on the monster. It'll be interesting to see how long it takes him to open that door."

"I'll bet it's just days."

"I hope so. He'll want to get that yellow scarf."

"That was inspired, Bobbie."

She felt her body respond, wanting to reach out to Nate, wondering what that forearm would feel like under her fingers.

But they were two very different people with two very different paths to follow. "I have to go," she said with a forced smile. She tried to come up with a reason, but there wasn't a lucid thought in her head except *Get out. Get out now!*

As she headed for the door, she realized she could feel the heat of his body beside hers. "Let me walk you," he offered.

"No. It's just a few yards." She ran down the back steps.

He stepped out onto the porch. "We have to talk about painting supplies for the artwork you're donating!" he called after her.

The night air was full of wood smoke, pine and the complicated diesel and perfume of the river. And Nate's voice. "I have paints!" Walking backward, she shouted, "I think we're okay!"

"Kiwanis is supporting the event. We'll pay for your supplies!"

"Fine. When I know what Sandy wants, we'll go shop—aahh!" She heard her own small scream carried through the quiet night as she fell back and lost her footing. She crashed against something metal—Nate's car door, she guessed—then slid down so that her upper body was on the concrete driveway and her hips and legs were in the grass.

The chrysanthemums!

Nate was there in an instant with a flashlight. He knelt beside her and turned her, propping her up against his raised knee. He shone the light on her face. "Are you all right?" he asked urgently.

Good grief. Would she ever draw a normal breath again? Now she was aware of his strong leg supporting her back, his arm around her shoulders, his nubby sweater against her face and his powerful heartbeat beneath it.

"Yeah," she said a little breathlessly. She struggled to get up, but he held her down.

"Give yourself a minute," he said.

"Thank you, but we've had this *fragile* discussion, remember." She pushed against him to get to her feet. He rose with her, holding her arm to steady her. "I'm fine. I fell against the car, but I slid down to the concrete, so I'm not hurt." She tried to shake him off. "Good night."

He kept hold of her. "I'll walk you."

"I'm fine!"

Arguing was pointless because they were now almost at her house. He studied her closely once they'd climbed the steps and stood under the porch light. "You might have a little bit of a shiner," he predicted.

She opened her kitchen door, anxious to put some distance between them. "I'll make up a good story to go with it. 'I fell over a row of chrysanthemums' just doesn't do it."

"A bar fight doesn't work, either. It's so not you."

She drew herself up. "You don't think I could hold my own in a bar fight?"

He rolled his eyes. "Well, if you were allowed to *talk,* I'm sure you would." He closed a hand over one of her shoulders. "But you're puny."

She gasped indignantly.

"What?" he questioned. "That's not the

same as fragile. That implies a breakable delicacy. Puny just means you haven't eaten enough. But your father's coming, right? So he can plump you up a little."

She was losing her grip on the conversation. She kept looking at him instead of thinking about what he was saying.

"Thank you for your help," she said coolly, politely. "Good night."

He looked as though he had more to say but thought better of it. "Good night, Bobbie." He walked away, the flashlight guiding his path until he disappeared on the other side of the vehicles.

WHY SHOULD THIS happen now? she asked herself anxiously as she turned on the teakettle and stroked Monet, who leaped up on the counter to nuzzle her. Why, after ten healthy years and no men in them who made her think about a romantic future, should she be attracted to a man with two children? More importantly, why at a time when she was recovering from a bout with a major illness she was destined to fight for the rest of her life? And—please God!—*why* all this when she was preparing to move to another country?

She made a cup of Earl Gray in her favorite mug and checked her email. She snuggled into her chair when she saw a message from laurasean@aol.com. Monet fought with her computer for his favorite spot in her lap as she read it.

Hey, Bobbie, so happy you're having fun with the art class. Tell me more about your neighbor. Sounds hunky even if you say he's kind of serious. There are things in life we should be serious about. Like having a baby. Must don my apricot lace teddy. Sean will be home in fifteen minutes. Love from sunny Southern California. Laura

P.S. Attached is current photo of Sean and me at his mom's birthday party.

Bobbie opened the attachment and Laura's cheerful face smiled back at her. She was bright-eyed and laughing, her straight blond hair gelled into funky spikes. Bobbie laughed in turn, for it reminded her of Sheamus's monster, Bill. She wrote back: You look beautiful. You and Sean will have the prettiest baby. I promise to come home from Florence for the christening, so get busy.

Neighbor is sometimes nice on closer acquaintance, but too complicated. Not much else to tell. Leaving here in January so am focused on the commission. I'm doing my work as you're doing yours. (Mine's probably not quite as much fun.) Dad's coming to spend the holidays. Love, Bobbie.

NATE TIDIED UP the kitchen, not sure whether to be happy or worried that his neighbor was acting oddly. Because he was feeling odd, too. He liked her. He had a feeling she liked him. He should have kept her at a distance the way he'd wanted to when she came over with those Halloween pumpkins for the boys. But she'd been looking at him as though he was a jerk, and he was afraid she'd fall over the dump truck at the bottom of the steps and sue him. So he'd walked her down the steps and across the yard, and learned that she was brave and thoughtful and really, really interesting. He hadn't known a woman like that in a while. And he didn't have time for one right now. He suspected she was experiencing the same feelings about him, and she didn't seem to like it any more than he did, judging by the way she'd raced home.

So, what was he doing? He didn't want a woman in his life. Stella *did* have his number as far as women were concerned. Before the accident, he'd been a happy playboy who didn't want to get serious because it would end the good life he was living.

Now, he couldn't get serious because there simply wasn't time between raising the boys and running a business.

Well. Okay, that wasn't true. Everyone did that—had jobs and raised children, and still managed to have relationships.

What Stella didn't know about him was that his neighbor's illness reminded him of the huge black hole the loss of his mother had made in the middle of his life. It seemed to have gone on forever. Dylan and Sheamus had already experienced the same loss. How could Nate put them in a situation where it could happen again?

Not that he planned to. But his body, his emotions—usually under careful check and lately exhibiting nothing other than *anger*—seemed to have a mind of their own.

Absently, he noticed that, for the first time in months, he didn't feel that ever present darkness dogging him. He felt…good. Maybe not good, but—yeah, it was good. And he knew that Bobbie had made the difference. She'd been able to help Sheamus confront his monster fear, and she'd charmed Dylan into sharing his artwork.

When she'd looked into Nate's eyes and he'd seen her excitement over the boys' progress, he'd felt a shared celebration that had been missing from his life for a long time.

How could acknowledging that be so bad, even if she was going away? He didn't know, but he had a feeling this whole thing had *trouble* written all over it.

Glancing out his kitchen window, he saw the light in hers reaching out through the darkness between their houses. Then it went out, leaving only blackness.

He didn't have to be hit over the head with the metaphor. He closed the door, turned off the kitchen light and went to join the boys.

"Not for you, Raleigh," he told himself. "Not for you."

CHAPTER SIX

DYLAN SAT IN the middle of his bed, his flashlight aimed at the sketch he'd worked on tonight. It was 3:34 a.m. and he was wide-awake. He'd heard the phone ring and the sound of his uncle's voice. A photographer client called all hours of the day or night because he was always in another country.

It must be exciting working as a news photographer, but Dylan wasn't sure he'd like that. He loved experimenting with dangerous things, but there, if you were careful and followed the safety rules, you had a better chance of survival. It was different when someone was shooting at you. Good planning couldn't stop a bullet.

And he didn't want to die anymore. It wasn't that living was so great, but—he hated to admit this—there were more interesting people in his life now than when his uncle had first moved in. Dylan still missed his parents so much it was like a pain in his gut, but when Bobbie came over, he felt better. And when Hunter came on game night, it was like they were just a bunch of guys together, and his uncle seemed to loosen up a little, let him and Sheamus stay up late and drink pop out of a beer glass.

Bill the Monster was kind of stupid, but Sheamus and Uncle Nate had stuck it to the freak's closet door with masking tape, and Sheamus didn't look quite so terrified anymore. He wouldn't open the closet, but winter was coming and he was going to have to sooner or later, or freeze to death. Or maybe Uncle Nate would just buy him another coat. But the scarf their mom had made was in there.

Dylan climbed out of bed, took the flashlight and went to his dresser. He rooted through the bottom drawer until he found the one she'd made him. It was red and plain, and he wrapped it around his neck as he walked back to bed.

He started to cry. He hated that. He was going to be eleven in January. He swiped at the tears with the back of his hand and placed the flashlight so that it lit both the sketch he'd made tonight and the picture of a bunch of boats he'd printed off the internet. He studied them for a minute, then picked one and began to sketch it onto the water slightly to the right of center on the page.

IN DOTS AND DOODLES, an extensive art supply store worthy of a metropolitan city, Bobbie selected a 24" x 36" canvas for the painting as Nate stood by with a basket. He had called her this morning to tell her a client had canceled an appointment and it would be a good time to shop for her supplies.

"I have a lot of the colors I'll need. I unearthed my taboret this morning," she said, stopping at a display of brushes. "But I'll need a couple of flats, and maybe…" Her voice trailed off as she looked through the round brushes for something small enough for facial detail. She turned to him, sure her expression betrayed her hesitation. "I hope I can do this. I usually plan paintings around a palette I'm comfortable with. I don't think I've ever done a seascape, or in this case, a riverscape."

"I'm sure it'll be great," he said supportively. "The work in your living room is very impressive."

She was beginning to relax. Talking about the project was easy. It was almost as if their sparking glances from the other night had not happened.

"Thank you. Then, are you willing to be

my model?" she challenged. "Sandy wants a turn-of-the-twentieth-century ship captain looking out at the Butterfly Fleet. You know, the Finnish fishing fleet with their funny sails. I'd have thought Bat Wing Fleet would have been a more appropriate name, but I'm sure Butterfly Fleet is more palatable to history."

He nodded. "I know about the Butterfly Fleet. But me? Seriously? Do I look salty to you?"

She laughed. "Well, generally, you're a little buttoned-down in your suit, but in the right clothes, you'll be perfect. Sandy's going to get me some photos of the river in the old days, and she says she can borrow an old ship captain's costume from the museum. They're happy to support us."

"Okay, I guess."

"Good. Do you think we could work in your garage? Mine's a little cluttered with papermaking stuff."

"Of course. And I presume I have to supply Thundermuck coffee. You seemed to really like it the night you helped the boys with their artwork. And, of course, I'll have to provide the chocolate."

"If you do that, I promise to make you handsome." She thought about how that sounded. "Not that you aren't already," she added. "You're…" She was talking herself into a hole and he was enjoying her discomfort.

She put several brushes in the cart and started for the counter, ending that line of conversation.

He handed the clerk a credit card. "Are you free for lunch? The Urban has a great Reuben sandwich." When she looked doubtful, he added, "And a half dozen great salads for those of you watching your diets."

"Ah…" She scanned her brain quickly for an excuse. She was more interested in him than she should be, yet circumstances kept forcing them together. At the same time, he seemed to be changing his attitude to her. And while she was happy to be dealing with a more pleasant person, this change in him was increasing his appeal, and that wasn't good.

"Come on," he coaxed. "Neighbors have lunch together all the time. I mean, if you want to pass me off to your father as a friend, you're going to have to know a little about me. Right?"

She was hungry. And she certainly couldn't fault his reasoning about her father.

"Okay," she said finally. She knew she sounded pathetic.

THE URBAN CAFÉ was a chic, uptown restaurant with mirrors, graphics on the wall, half curtains separating spaces and comfortable furniture in a back room where there were also a few pub-style tables. They sat at one in a corner near a giant poster of Marilyn Monroe.

"Now, there's a woman for you," Bobbie teased as they were handed menus. "I loved her in *River of No Return*. She was so good with the hero's little boy."

He nodded. "She must have been something. But I have quite a list of women interested in me, you know." He gave a superior tilt of his eyebrow. "It's an accounting thing. Women love men who are good with numbers."

Bobbie challenged that with a laugh. "Do tell. As opposed to good with baseballs, or race cars, or sophisticated software?"

He grinned at her. "It's true. At this very moment, I'm the object of affection of a very wealthy client of mine in Portland, a supermodel I met while on a cruise two summers ago, and the prettiest little barista at the Astoria Coffee House. Casey is her name."

Bobbie put her menu down and folded her arms over it, enjoying this fanciful side of him. Or *was* it fanciful? Maybe he was telling her the truth and he did have three women on the string.

"And they've actually *told* you how they feel?"

"Not in so many words, but Casey puts a beautiful steamed-milk heart on my mocha every morning."

Bobbie shook her head pityingly. "Nate. Every barista in the world puts a steamed-milk heart on every customer's mocha. It elevates a cup of coffee to an art form. And it helps validate the $4.50 price."

In a theatrical gesture, he put a hand to his heart. "You mean she *doesn't* love me?"

Bobbie patted his hand. "Well, she might, but you can't judge by the heart on your mocha, because she does that for everyone."

His brow wrinkled. "Well, I'm depressed."

She laughed aloud as the waitress arrived to take their order. When she'd left, Bobbie's eyes went to his thick, slightly mussed hair and lingered on it a moment, wondering if it would be silky or wiry to the touch. She met his eyes. "Stop pouting. You are kind of cute. And apparently that opinion is shared by three other women, so stop with this embarrassing need for constant adulation."

He pulled the complimentary basket of chips away when she reached to help herself.

"Hey. I thought we're having lunch to learn how to be friends. You're not getting how this works. Friends are kind and supportive."

She put a hand to her own heart now. "Sorry. As your friend, I thought you should know that your display of neediness was not flattering."

He leaned toward her and said with a hopeful grin, "But you think I'm kind of cute?"

She had to laugh. "Yes, but not when you're being needy. Do you want to hear about my art class?"

He straightened, the silly exchange over. "Sure. How's it going?"

She told him about Eddy, and the little girl who was making a lady monster, and the moment when Sheamus talked about his mother.

Nate dipped a chip in salsa and seemed to lose focus for a moment. "She was something," he said with real feeling. "I was jealous of Ben for finding her. She was everything a man wants in a woman. Kind, caring, supportive, strong, smart." Happy memories seemed to change suddenly to grim ones. He leaned back, obviously still focused on the past. "I put them on that boat, you know."

Bobbie sat up a little straighter, concerned about his mood switch. "What do you mean?" she asked gently.

"I gave them the charter boat tickets for their anniversary."

She leaned closer. "You're not blaming yourself for the fact that they...died?"

"I do. I mean, I know it's not my fault precisely, but I am the reason they were on the boat."

She put her hand on his, and when he didn't look at her, she pinched a knuckle. He glanced up in surprise, the brooding gone from his eyes. "That's self-abuse, Nate, and completely uncalled for."

He almost smiled. "You pinched me."

"I was just trying to get your attention."

"Yeah, well, the fact remains that they'd be here if I hadn't given them the tickets. And the boys miss them so much."

"Here we go." The waitress placed their lunches in the middle of the table, Nate's Reuben smelling heavenly, and Bobbie's pear and strawberry salad colorfully tempting. "Anything else I can get you right now?"

Nate had already bitten into his sandwich. Bobbie shook her head. "We're good, thank you." The waitress left and they continued to talk as they ate

"Fate or the divine plan, whatever you believe, took them from you, not the fact that you gave them the tickets. And you're doing the best you can for the boys." She took a sip of her drink and smiled teasingly. "Don't you think you need a woman in your life? Isn't it time to get serious about the client or the model?"

He made a face. "Right now my life needs certainties."

"What do you mean?"

"Women tend to come and go."

"No, they don't. Well, maybe some do, but many are as committed as you would ever want."

He shrugged and admitted, "I lost the client and the model when I moved here to care for the boys. And, honestly, neither was a till-death-do-us-part relationship, but it goes to show you. And *you're* going," he pointed out.

He made it sound like an accusation, and she was momentarily surprised, because it suggested that he cared more than their relationship would warrant. She was both flattered and upset by that.

"I am," she replied firmly. "But you can't expect to uproot and force maternity onto women who aren't till-death-do-us-part serious. You need to broaden your pool of prospects. I'm sure women would be lining up if you expressed an interest." Bobbie tried to inject a little humor. "You know, clever and cute as you are."

It didn't work. He simply frowned at her.

"I'm just trying to learn this friend thing," she said a little weakly. "I think friends tell you when they feel you're making a mistake."

His mood had turned again. A little edginess crept into his tone. "So, if I think *you're* making a mistake forgoing family for career, you'll take it as an act of friendship if I tell you?"

She considered that and finally replied with candor. "Probably not. I hate being told that I'm wrong. I usually don't take it very well. I once poured a glass of merlot on an art critic who called my work confused and undecided."

Nate barked a laugh. Diners at nearby tables turned to look. Bobbie blushed. The conversation diverted, he seemed to relax again.

"You think my work's confused, too?" she asked.

"Not at all. I think it just means that you're interested in different styles and a lot of subjects, and you're good at all of them so you explore them."

She sat up straighter, relishing his approval. "Why aren't *you* an art critic?"

"Because I know nothing about art. And I'd

have trouble shooting down anyone's dreams if I didn't like their work. But back to you." He leaned closer. "Have you considered that having someone to share your life might enhance your studies and ease the burden of your work a little?"

She'd thought that over so many times she had the answer on the tip of her tongue. "In most professions a helpmate is a wonderful thing. But in art—I'm talking serious, life-changing, world-affecting art—someone who loves you can be a…" she looked up apologetically, because the thought was selfish but still true "…a distraction. It won't work. One of you will end up leaving because you can't get or give what the other needs. And the emotional energy required of a relationship is all time taken from getting at the stuff in your gut." She was silent a moment, then added, "And I don't have the time to waste."

"But you're well," he said. "Your prognosis is good, right?"

"Cancer's a sneaky rat. I could be fine today and gone tomorrow." She hated admitting that to herself, but she'd seen it happen. "I'm not going to live in fear of it, but I'm not going to pretend that I have forever."

"None of us has forever. So shouldn't we be fearless?"

"Every artist is. When I hang a canvas or show a sculpture or a bowl, I'm putting out there all the heart and soul it took to create it, and running the risk that some big-city pseudo-sophisticate who 'knows what he likes' is going to think it's trite or stupid or means something I never intended. But I do it anyway, because it just might really speak to somebody." She paused for a moment, remembering how wonderful that felt. "And that's what it's all about."

"That's what it's about for the artist," he said quietly, "but what's it all about for the woman?"

She replied with another smile. "It's all about the art for me, Nate. I made myself a promise."

He nodded, seeming to accept that. He watched her in silence, then leaned back in his chair with a sigh. "You and your dad want to join us for Thanksgiving? We'll have everything. All you have to do is come. Then you won't have to find time to fix a holiday dinner, and it'll convince your father that you have *good* friends."

"Ah…" It was a lovely idea, but that would make it even harder to keep herself above the cozy pull of this town and its people. And him. Still, she had resolve, and a plan she intended to follow without deviation. And it would be good for her father to see that she wasn't spending every moment in her studio. "That would be nice," she heard herself say. "Do you have pies and rolls?"

"We'll just buy those."

"I'll make them. Pumpkin and apple? Mince?"

He brightened. "You can make mince pie?"

"Yes. It's my father's favorite."

"Mine, too, but I'm usually outvoted. No one likes it but me. The boys and I can help you with the grunt work."

They packed up leftovers and he paid the check. When they arrived home, he helped Bobbie carry everything into his garage. It was filled with bicycles, lawnmower and tools, a shop against one wall, all kinds of implements hanging on another. In the middle was a large table where he put everything they'd bought today.

"When do we start the Old Astoria painting?" he asked.

"Anytime you're free, I'd like about an hour on the waterfront to place you against the background. I know if we make it on a Saturday, you'd have to consider what to do with the boys. But if we do it during the week, there's your work."

"How's Friday morning? That's usually a

short day for me. I'll just catch up in the afternoon."

"Can we make it early? I have the art class at ten."

"I'll come by for you at eight."

"Great. Thanks for lunch. You'd better get back to work."

He loped to his car and she headed off across her yard. She let herself into the house and was greeted with a meow from Monet, who was dozing in the Christmas cactus in the middle of her kitchen table. His orange body was wrapped around the plant and tucked inside the terra-cotta pot.

Except for Monet's one "Hello" the house was quiet. It seemed particularly so after the morning spent wrapped in Nate's deep voice.

Well, she'd better get used to it, she told herself as she changed into her grubs and went to work in the garage. The future would probably be just a little lonely. But she was finally going to see what she was made of.

Canvas and linseed oil, she thought with a laugh. And a lot of coffee and chocolate.

She emailed Laura about the painting project and told her she'd be using Nate as a model.

Talk about finding out what she was made of.

NATE ARRIVED AT the office to find Jonni

in the conference room, her arms wrapped around a sobbing client, while Hunter looked on helplessly. Nate recognized Ellen Bingham, whose husband had MS. They were both in their late seventies and Nate had been helping them with an Offer in Compromise to the Internal Revenue Service.

Jonni held Ellen in one arm and handed Nate a notice from the IRS with her free hand. "They won't even talk to her until she pays the thousand dollar application fee."

He snatched the paper. "But their income is low enough that they don't have to pay it." He glanced over the investigator's figures and saw a tricky but allowable variation in how the income had been calculated. And she'd put a deadline of a week on the fee or "we won't even consider the application."

"Ben dealt with that investigator once," Hunter said. "She believes in the letter of the law and that everyone who owes the IRS money is a deadbeat. He found it easier to do what she wanted in the interest of getting the client the result *we* wanted."

Ellen tried to compose herself. She was plump and gray-haired, and seemed at the end of her rope. Her husband's illness had so debilitated him that they'd had to close the gift shop they'd operated together. Ellen provided around-the-clock care for him herself, so their income was now down to two Social Security checks and little else. A previous debt to the IRS had resulted in a lien on their property, and a reverse mortgage would solve their problems if the IRS was willing to take half what they were owed. The reverse mortgage could not be considered until the lender knew the entire lien would be paid. If the IRS didn't agree, the Binghams' payout wouldn't cover everything.

"Can you borrow the money from one of your kids, Ellen?" Nate asked. "Because I'm sure if we can get this under consideration, you'd win."

She dabbed wearily at her nose. "I'll try. I don't know. A reverse mortgage seemed like such a good idea in the beginning, but it's taken so long that it's involved two appraisals at the tune of five hundred dollars apiece, and the last appraisal was down thirty thousand because of the real estate market. We have nothing left."

He put his hand over hers. "Hang in there with us, Ellen. I think it'll be a slam dunk in the end. The letter you got from your doctor proves that Jim's illness makes it impossible for him to earn money, and because you have to care for him, you can't, either. The debt load from the closing of your business proves you have nothing extra to pay them without the cash coming from the reverse mortgage."

She drew a ragged breath. "If only it was enough to pay the whole lien."

"It's still half the debt," he said bracingly, "and they should be happy to get that, considering your situation. Imagine getting rid of your house payment, and the couple of hundred dollars you pay the IRS every month." He smiled. "Come on. Don't give up. Try to get the thousand dollars. If you can't, we'll see what we can do. There might be other options."

She leaned forward and wrapped her arms around him. "Thanks for trying so hard."

"That's why we're here."

"You're here to make money, not spend so much effort on one client's uphill battle. A client who can't pay you very much."

"Don't worry about that. You and Jim were favorites of my brother."

"He was a good person. And so are you. Are the boys doing well?"

He nodded. "Mostly. We have our difficult times."

"Yes. Who doesn't? Don't think it's you. All children, whether born to you or invited in, can make you crazy. Thank you for doing this for Jim and me when you have so much else to deal with."

Hunter patted her shoulder. "Don't worry about him. He makes *me* do all the hard stuff."

Nate grinned up at him. "That's what you get for being good at everything. Ellen, let me know in a couple of days if you can get the money, and I'll contact the agent."

She hugged him again, then Jonni, then got to her feet and hugged Hunter. "Thanks, kids. I'll be in touch."

Jonni watched her go with a sad smile. "I hope you can make this work for them. I used to love to shop at their store."

"We'll make it work." Nate stood and pushed in his chair. "Hunt, since you're familiar with this agent, you want to call her and tell her the client's working on getting the fee?"

"Sure." Hunter took the notice from him. "I think she secretly has a thing for me, anyway. That's probably why she's so mean and frustrated." He grinned at Nate. "So, how was your lunch with the pretty artist?"

"Good." He walked out of the conference room with Hunter as Jonni ran to her desk to get the phone. "We bought paint, brushes and a big canvas board. Nothing exciting."

"Oh, come on. I was across the room with

Jerry Gold. She was looking into your eyes. I happen to know you're not that interesting. You must have turned on the charm."

"I don't have any charm. But you do, so please put it to work on that agent."

"Right. What'll we do if Ellen can't get the money?"

"I'll think of something."

"What?"

"I don't know. Something. Go."

Hunter walked away and Nate closed himself in his office. He'd been thinking about ordering a new copier for tax season, but he didn't absolutely have to have it. Maybe he could divert that capital to more creative uses. Maybe he'd just send the application fee on the Binghams' behalf, and if they were able to get the money, they could pay him back.

He laughed at himself. Nate Raleigh, superhero.

CHAPTER SEVEN

BOBBIE HAD A little difficulty focusing on the project at hand. Mostly because it involved taking photos and making sketches of Nate in a sea captain's jacket and cap from the late 1800s. He was gazing out over the water as she'd instructed, and she felt lost in time. What difference would it have made, she wondered, if they'd met a hundred years ago and she hadn't been ill, and he hadn't been confined by the need to raise two children?

She shook her head to chase away the thought, and reminded herself that she had a short deadline on this painting. All right. She'd positioned him against the background, using period photos of the waterfront without the bridge to work from.

Today the sky was pewter, and a low bank of fog draped along the Washington shoreline, on the opposite side of the river. Traffic on the water was sparse this morning, just the Coast Guard cutters *Alert* and *Steadfast* moored nearby.

Nate's jacket was a thick, roughly-woven gray wool worn over a blue cotton shirt with a tab collar. The cap was a traditional captain's hat with a bill that Nate had instinctively put at a rakish angle.

She went to him and turned up his collar. "He'd wear it up against the wind," she speculated. "Don't you think?"

Nate dropped the pose to let her adjust the collar. "Sure. And don't I need a handlebar mustache?" He pretended to twirl the edge of one in the tradition of the melodrama villain. "After all, I might have some cargo aboard I wouldn't want to be caught with. Didn't they sometimes smuggle Chinese laborers to work in the canneries?"

She made the smallest adjustment to the hat. It didn't really need it but was a way to stay close to him. "You wouldn't have done that. You'd be picking up salmon to go to Great Britain and Australia. But it might help if you didn't shave for a couple of days."

As she stepped away she had to bite back a gasp. He looked true to the period, despite the lack of facial hair, and the hazel eyes watching her from under the brim of his cap were intriguing—as though he might really have seen the mysteries of the Seven Seas. He was very handsome, not a present-day accountant, but a man of action from another time. A man that any woman might want to accompany her on a trip of self-discovery.

She shook her head again and prepared to take several more shots.

"So, if I was a sea captain in, say, 1898…" Nate looked out to sea again, in character. "I suppose you'd have been a suffragist, and I'd be completely offended by your independence. Or maybe you'd want to sail with me to Florence. You being you, you'd probably still want the same things then that you want today."

"Unless I hadn't had cancer, and didn't feel the urgency I do." As she spoke the words, she felt the first stirring of self-pity since she'd put that destructive emotion behind her right after her diagnosis.

He must have heard it in her voice, and turned to look at her. "It is what it is, remember? You made yourself a promise and nothing's going to change it. Don't be mad at yourself."

She was trying to pull herself out of a sudden, sucking depression when she realized what he'd said. "I'm not mad at myself." She felt argumentative. "I'm happy with my decision."

"Okay. You sounded like you were mad."

"Well, I'm not. I have a right to go."

A sudden gust of cold wind took her back a year ago to the moment she'd made herself the promise. It was as though she were encapsulated in a bubble as she remembered that low moment at the end of her chemotherapy.

She'd been lying on the sofa, too weak and exhausted to move, and her father had been giving her a pep talk. "You have to fight, Bobbie. This is the moment. I know you feel like everything's dead inside you, that the drugs have killed all the good stuff as well as the bad, but you have to believe you can do this. Make your body work. Don't let it give up."

She had rolled her head on the pillow to look at him, the woolly hat she wore to protect her bald head slipping over her eyes. She'd raised a hand to push it back. "I'm tired, Dad."

The lab reports after her previous treatment had shown only minimal improvement and the drugs had hit her like a sledgehammer that day. She'd been vomiting all that morning and was sick of being sick, and sick of the struggle. She'd let herself wonder, for just an instant, what things would be like if she wasn't here. Her father would be devastated, of course, but she wouldn't know because she'd be...she'd be with her mother. That possibility was just a little tempting.

"I'm not saying you don't deserve to rest, just that you aren't allowed to give up. Your labs are going to show considerable improvement this time. I feel it."

"Good." She'd liked that thought but wasn't sure she believed it. "I'd like to see Mom again."

His expression became fierce. "She'd only send you back to me, because you're not through here yet. You have unfinished art. Places to go."

He said something about making lunch and she'd closed her eyes wearily and thought, *Places to go*. In a desperate attempt to rally her bottomed-out spirits, she'd tried to imagine where she would go if she could get up off this sofa.

Then it hit her. Florence! She'd wanted to visit it since she was a teenager. She'd borrowed books from the library and fallen in love with the Renaissance dome of the Duomo, the medieval town hall, Palazzo Vecchio. The works of Botticelli, Giotto, Michelangelo and Raphael in the Uffizi Gallery.

Going to Florence hadn't been possible at seventeen, but with no relationships to worry about and few commitments in her way, it seemed almost doable as she lay on that couch. Or it would be if she didn't have cancer.

If she didn't have cancer.

That had been the moment fear became resolve. She let the images slide across her mind again. She could move to Florence and paint among the masters if she didn't have cancer. So she had to get rid of it. Her body was too weak to sit up, but she felt as though her spirit did. Florence. Florence!

"Bobbie!" She came back to the present at the sound of her name. Nate stood directly in front of her, looking concerned. "Where'd you go?" he asked. "Back to the nineteenth century?"

She squared her shoulders and smiled. "No. Not quite so far." She began to gather up her things.

"Pardon me?"

"Never mind.

"Are we done?" he asked, watching her put her book and camera in her bag.

Curious choice of words, she thought with a touch of fatal resignation. "We're done. Now you have to go back to work, and I do, too."

"No time for coffee?"

"No. I've got to get to my class."

His eyes under the bill of his hat still made him seem a little unfamiliar. "Do you want to come with me to the dinner dance?" he asked without warning, and suddenly he was the man she knew again. The man who challenged everything she wanted. "Come on, it's the holidays. We'll eat great food, do a little dancing, watch them make a fortune on the raffle and your painting, and go home."

She couldn't come up with a good excuse to refuse. "My father's coming," she said lamely.

"Stella can be his date. We'll all go together."

Bobbie looked into the strong planes of his face, saw the wind stir his hair and redden his earlobes. If only it *were* a hundred years ago. "Okay," she said finally. "But just dinner and dancing."

"Right." He grabbed her bag—which was a good thing, because she'd momentarily forgotten she had it—and led her to their vehicles, parked on Commercial Street.

Before getting into her truck, Bobbie stopped to admire the window of Tony's Boutique. In the center of the display was a red jacket with an irregular collar and hem, and a front closure at an angle, running from the right side of the neckline to the left hip.

"Isn't that pretty?" she asked, leaning closer to the window like a child at a candy store.

Nate looked slightly askance at the unusual

design. "Well, I wouldn't wear it," he teased. When she elbowed him in the ribs, he laughed and added, "But I imagine it'd look perfect on you. Very artsy. Too bad you don't have time to try it on."

She turned away resolutely. "No, I have to save my pennies for Florence and a little Christmas shopping. And that shop gives me a terrible case of the 'I-wants.' Anyway..." She smiled. "Thanks for your time today. I'm going to put in as much as I can of the background, then I'll need you to sit for me. The photographs are great, but I'll still need the real you. Maybe a couple of evenings. Can you work that in?"

"Sure. And thank *you*." Rain had begun to fall and he reached down to pull up her hood.

"For what?"

He shrugged a shoulder. "Lots of indefinable things. Call me when you need me. Bye." He slipped into his car and disappeared around the corner.

NATE FELT DRIVEN for the next few days. He'd gone back to the office to find that one of the copiers had died and *had* to be replaced, and at home, Dylan had had a bad day, Sheamus was in tears and even Stella was out of sorts. Apparently her daughter and son-in-law had been invited to Florida for Thanksgiving with *his* parents.

"What about Hunter?"

"He's talking about going on a camping trip with some friends."

Nate was surprised Hunter hadn't said anything.

"You're welcome to join us for Thanksgiving," he told her as he helped her on with her lavender wool jacket. Her white hair was in disarray from breaking up a confrontation between her charges, and her dark eyes were sad.

She smiled a thank-you, but it was unconvincing. "Can I let you know? I may do something radical."

"Radical?" he asked worriedly.

"Yes. You know, like order a pizza."

He made a face at that suggestion. "Bobbie and her father are coming. And I have a complete dinner planned from Safeway."

She nodded. "Then you won't need a housekeeper-nanny, will you? Don't worry. I'll be fine."

"Stella. We'll be expecting you."

She hugged him quickly and left.

He'd been feeling edgy for several days and didn't like it. He hadn't felt secure in his job as his nephews' guardian, or indeed in his life, in so long that he had grown used to it.

And then Bobbie Molloy had moved in next door and changed everything in subtle ways that made it all just a little better and, if he stopped to think about it, a whole lot worse. He'd known her only two weeks, but she'd brought light to his world. And she was taking that light to Italy in January.

Though he knew and even understood that anything other than friendship between them was impossible, he found himself longing for more, anyway. And that was stupid. He hated being stupid. He wanted to remember the cost of caring for someone whose life was short.

Thoughts of her were shredding his resolve to just be her friend.

And he hated the realization that some of the old anger was coming back. He'd thought he'd learned to cope with it, to disregard it. But it was biting at him again because he couldn't have what he wanted with Bobbie.

The outer-office chatter got a little loud now that the day's work was done, and he got up to close his door. He had to draft a letter to Social Security on behalf of a client residing in Mexico, and the noise wasn't helping his already taut mood. He was just getting back into challenge mode when his extension rang.

He didn't recognize the caller ID and let it go to voice mail while he tried to think.

"Nate? Hi, it's Bobbie. I'm sorry to…" Her voice sounded anxious. He picked up the receiver.

"Bobbie, I'm here. What's the matter?"

"Now, I don't want you to get upset," she said, obviously trying to control her tone.

He was already on his feet. "What?" he demanded.

"Well…Dylan was doing an experiment…."

"Oh, God." Nate imagined fire, ankle-deep water, injury.

"He isn't really hurt," she assured him quickly. "It wasn't that kind of experiment. It seems kids on YouTube are trying to swallow cinnamon by the spoonful and, well…"

That curious craze had even made the news. He recalled images of kids and even some adults vomiting and choking. Somewhere, a teenager had died. "Where are you?"

"In the E.R."

"I'll be right there."

Dylan was pale and pasty-looking. Bobbie sat beside him and dabbed at his mouth with a tissue. The room smelled nasty. Nate imagined the last hour or so had not been pleasant for his nephew. Bobbie smiled at Nate reassuringly.

He spotted a rolling stool and considered sitting on it, but was too agitated. "Are you all right?" he demanded of Dylan. His temper was barely controlled.

The boy's eyes were bloodshot and miserable. He raised them with a resigned expression. "I'm terrible," he replied, his voice raspy, probably from vomiting.

"What were you thinking? We watched that news story together about—"

"I know." Dylan tried to clear his throat. "But…I mean…" He spread his hands helplessly. "It's just swallowing, right? I thought it couldn't be that hard."

"And yet look at where you are! In a hospital!"

"I—"

"People choked in the news story. The mouth can't produce enough saliva to combat the cinnamon, and you end up with a ball of burning mud…"

"I know. I know.

"Somebody died!"

Dylan stiffened defensively. "Everybody dies."

The rigid control Nate had kept on the returning anger snapped. It raged through him like a crazed bear. He had a mental image of Bill the Monster, only the monster in him hadn't been drawn by a cheerful young woman.

Nate caught the stool with his toe and sat down, looking straight at Dylan. "You," he said, jabbing a finger at his chest, "have a long life ahead of you, do you hear me?"

"Nate," Bobbie cautioned quietly.

He ignored her. "And if I have to watch you every minute to make sure you get to live it, I will do that!"

Dylan coughed and sniffed, looking close to tears. But Nate knew pride would never let them fall.

"I'm sorry, okay." Dylan's voice was trembling, defensive.

Nate caught his arm to assure himself of the boy's attention. "You're coming to my office after school from now on," he continued, trying to get control again. On one hand, it felt so good to have an excuse to let his anger fly. On the other, guilt fell over him like a prickly blanket. "You can do your homework in my office," he said more quietly, "and when you're done with that, I'll find odd jobs for you."

Dylan glowered at him. "Cool."

Nate tightened his grip. Bobbie leaned forward. "Nate!" she said more forcefully.

He silenced her with a look, then returned

his attention to Dylan. At least he thought he'd silenced her.

She leaned across the boy to catch Nate's arm in a biting grip. "Bobbie," he warned quietly, "this is my business."

"You're right," she said, maintaining her grip. "Just please handle it carefully." She freed his arm and sat back.

Nate wished himself anywhere but here. He drew a breath for patience, ran a hand over his face and tried another tack. "Do you have any idea what your father would do to me if I let anything happen to you?"

Dylan looked into his eyes, the pain and misery visible behind the rebellious stance. "My father," he said in a raspy whisper, "isn't here. He'll never be here again."

The truth of that reverberated inside Nate like a bullet in a tight space, injuring every time it hit. Again he groped for calm. "There's a lot of him in you, Dylan. I loved him like everything, but he was stubborn and difficult sometimes. So he's with us, believe me."

Dylan didn't seem to know how to respond to that. Which was fine with Nate. For the moment, he was tired of listening.

"And I *am* here. So things are going to change. Grief is one thing, but anger with everyone over things that aren't their fault has to stop."

"Oh, oh." Dylan's eyes widened and he looked around frantically.

Bobbie reached behind her for a basin and placed it strategically. She pointed Nate to a wet facecloth on the small sink in the corner. "Would you get that?"

He took the basin and pushed her hands away. "You get it. I'll do this." Nate worried about the deep spasm in Dylan's thin chest and the tortured sound of his retching. "Where's the doctor, anyway?" He frowned, aware of a sudden incongruity. "Why are you here instead of Stella?"

"Her car's in the shop." Bobbie looked back at him intrepidly, seemingly unaffected by his ill temper. "She called to borrow my truck, and asked if I'd wait for Sheamus to come home from his friend's house. A bunch of his classmates were making cookies to freeze for the food bank event. She said she told you about it."

Nate had a vague memory of that conversation, but at the moment, his brain couldn't quite call it up. Bobbie went on. "Anyway, when she realized my truck's a stick shift, it was easier to let me come with Dylan and for her to wait for Sheamus."

Bobbie took the basin from him and handed him the cloth. "And the doctor is writing a prescription."

Nate wiped the boy's face. Dylan remained impassive under his touch.

She put the basin in the sink and sat down again. "If you have to get back to the office, I'll drive him home and make him comfortable. The doctor said he'll be fine."

Nate was still angry enough to be rude. "Why don't *you* go home, and I'll wait for the prescription."

She stood, presumably to do that, just as the doctor arrived. She was a short young woman with a wide smile and blond hair tied back in a fat knot. She handed Nate a prescription and gave a sheet of paper to Bobbie. "This is a list of instructions for Dylan's care," she said.

"And you…" She caught Dylan's chin in her hand and looked into his eyes with sudden seriousness. "I want you to take better care of yourself. You're a smart boy. Don't do stupid things."

Nate marched out of the E.R. with Dylan hurrying beside him and Bobbie. In the sparsely lit parking lot, he stopped and turned to her.

"Thank you for taking care of Dylan," he said briskly. "I'll take it from here."

She looked back at him with that cool control she'd annoyed him with in the E.R. Mostly because he'd lost *his*. She held out the sheet of paper the doctor had given her. "You might do that more successfully with these instructions."

"Thank you."

"Sure. If Stella has to go home and you need help, call me."

"Aren't you too involved already for someone who's leaving in a couple of months?" It was snide and mean, but at that moment, he felt ruthless. Because she was right; he should be patient with Dylan, but he was finding patience difficult to maintain in the face of the boy's continued hostility. And he hated that his own character was that small.

She turned to Dylan and dropped the frosty demeanor. She wrapped him in her arms. "I hope you feel better. And try to be hopeful, okay? The world's not so bad when you realize everybody has problems and we all just have to deal with them."

Nate aimed the remote at the car and unlocked the doors. "Go ahead," he said to Dylan, "I'll be right there."

As his nephew climbed into the car, Bobbie

started for her truck. "Try to remember that he's just a little boy," she said to Nate over her shoulder. "Good night."

In his growly mood, Nate took instant offense. "I'm well aware of his situation. I live with it around the clock."

She turned back to him and looked right up into his face, her eyes gleaming in the dark. "I know that was scary for you. But shouting at everybody isn't going to help him. Or you."

"And this is all based on your extensive experience with children?" he asked coolly. "I thought you were too busy for that kind of distraction in your life. Children get in the way of art, so how would you know how to handle a little boy determined to hurt himself?" He couldn't believe he'd said that, but the sound of his angry voice rang in his ears.

She was silent for a moment and he thought she wouldn't answer. Then she said in that reasonable tone she'd been using on him all night, and that he'd come to hate, "I don't think he was trying to hurt himself. I think partly he was just a kid doing something stupid, and partly…maybe he just wanted to reassure himself that if something did happen to him, somebody would care enough to be upset."

"Well, I *am* upset!" Nate raised both arms

in exasperation. "So I think even you will have to agree that I've handled this appropriately!"

She turned away from him, climbed into her truck and started the motor.

Determined to finish this argument, he went to her window and twirled his index finger in a "lower the window" gesture.

She did and leaned out. "What?" she demanded. "You're not *my* uncle, so I don't have to sit here and let you yell at me! Don't worry. I'll find another model for the painting, and I promise not to come and mess up your Thanksgiving!"

How could he explain that he was mad enough to throttle Dylan and then her, but still looked forward to Thanksgiving? Nate couldn't. It didn't make sense. So he used guilt.

"You have to come," he said judiciously, ignoring his complete loss of judgment and cool. "You're bringing the pies and rolls. And I have all your art supplies."

"I'll drop off the pies and rolls." She put the truck in gear. "And I'll just buy more supplies if Kiwanis is paying for them."

"You'll come," he roared at her over the sound of the engine, "or I'll tell your father it's all a lie and you *don't have* any friends. Big surprise, why that is!"

She furiously turned the window crank and he had to remove his fingers or let her take them with her. She roared away in a squeal of tires.

Dylan was sobbing when Nate got into the car. Nate was caught off-balance, certain that words of comfort wouldn't be appreciated.

Dylan stopped abruptly, ran a hand over his eyes with the sleeve of his coat and sniffed loudly. Nate started the engine, took the tissues from his pocket and put them in his nephew's lap. He pulled out of the parking space.

"She's not coming for Thanksgiving?" Dylan asked, his voice husky. He yanked a tissue out and put it to his nose.

"She's coming." Nate slowed for the highway entrance and glanced at Dylan. "She's just mad."

"You were yelling at her," he accused.

"Yeah, well, she was yelling at me."

"It wasn't her fault. She was trying to help."

"I know," Nate admitted grudgingly. "But being scared makes me mad, because I don't know what to do and I don't like that feeling. So I took it out on her." He turned onto the highway, which was busy with early evening traffic. At a red light, he stopped and glanced again at Dylan. "You know, just like you do with us when you get mad because you're scared."

Dylan glanced at him with tear-filled eyes. "But you're a grown-up. You're supposed to know what to do."

There it was. The indictment that tortured him constantly. "Sometimes being a grown-up is no different than being a kid. When your emotions are involved, it's hard to think smart."

There was a moment's silence, then Dylan said plaintively, his voice cracking to a squeak, "I want my mom and dad!"

"I know." Nate put a hand out to cover his. "I'm sorry. I want them, too."

With surprising strength, Dylan grabbed the arm he offered, and held on. "Has anybody ever come back from being…dead?"

Nate pulled over, one-handed, to the side of the road. This had been a bad day for Dylan, but the boy's open vulnerability was a first. "Not that I know of," he replied honestly. "Except in the Bible."

It had started to rain and Dylan stared grimly out the windshield. "Has anybody ever gone…there…and come back?"

"I don't think so. I mean, sometimes people

stop breathing or their hearts stop, and that's like being dead, and then a doctor can sometimes bring them back. But people who are really dead don't come back."

"So…that's it? I mean, sometimes when I begin to feel happy about something, I sort of forget that I'm never going to see them again. And it always feels like they're gonna come home. But they don't. And then, when I think about that, I feel so…awful." He had a death grip on Nate's arm, his fingernails digging through his white shirt to the inside of his elbow. "I'm never—ever—going to see them again."

Nate gathered himself to say the words that did not want to be spoken. He took a breath. "That's right."

After a moment, Dylan whispered, "That's why I get mad."

"Yeah. Me, too."

Dylan heaved a deep sigh and freed Nate's arm. "I'm sorry about the cinnamon."

"Good." Realizing what a major breakthrough an apology was, Nate kept commentary to a minimum.

"Do I still have to go to your office?"

"Yes."

"That'll be boring."

Nate turned the key in the ignition. "No,

it won't. You'll have a lot to do." When the traffic thinned, he pulled out onto the road.

"Homework," Dylan said in a disgruntled tone. He dabbed at his eyes and sat back.

"We're moving the supply room around. When your homework's done, you can help Hunter with that."

"Yeah?" There was a little glimmer of hope in Dylan's voice. Nate smiled to himself, feeling as though he'd just been through the car wash without a car.

Stella was beside herself when they got home. She hugged Dylan to her, then held him at arm's length to study him. She frowned over his pallor.

"Do you feel like you can eat anything?" she asked worriedly. "I can make you a soft-boiled egg and some toast."

Dylan shook his head. "Thanks. I think I'll just go to bed." He glanced up at his uncle. "Okay?"

Nate nodded. "Sure. I'll come up in a minute and see if you need anything."

Sheamus followed Dylan, asking him as they climbed the stairs how many times he threw up.

Stella handed Nate a shot of brandy. "Drink that. You look like you've been dragged behind a horse."

He smiled. Similar analogy to a car wash. He took a deep sip and enjoyed the warmth in the pit of his stomach.

"Sorry you had to stay so long," he said, sitting down at the table. "You're looking at a big Christmas bonus."

"Is he okay?" she asked softly. She sat across from him, her purse and coat over her arm.

"Physically, the doctor says he'll be fine. Emotionally, he shared a little of his pain with me on the way home. But there's still a barrier there."

She smiled maternally. "With children, sometimes little breakthroughs are big things. Don't give up. I know how hard you try." She stood and leaned over the table to touch his cheek. "If he has trouble during the night and you need help, call me. And there's a chicken veggie pasta casserole in the fridge if you feel like it. I fed Sheamus."

"Thanks, Stella."

The house was dark and quiet when the door closed behind her. He took another sip of brandy, then headed upstairs to see how Dylan was doing. Nate was surprised to hear quiet, civil conversation coming from his room.

"Did you get a shot?" Sheamus asked.

"No."

"What about those things that shock you?"

"No. That's for when your heart stops."

"Oh." Sheamus sounded disappointed.

Nate rapped twice on the half-closed door. Dylan called a raspy "Come in."

Sheamus sat cross-legged on top of the covers at the foot of the bed and climbed down when Nate appeared. Nate turned on the bedside lamp and switched off the bright overhead light.

"Can I have some ice cream for dessert?" Sheamus asked.

"Sure. Don't forget to put the carton back in the freezer."

"Okay." He ran off.

"How do you feel?" Nate asked Dylan. The boy looked very pale against the pillows.

"Okay. Hungry, but I don't really want to eat anything."

"Yeah. Well, maybe you can have toast and yogurt in the morning."

"That sounds good." He turned onto his side, but toward Nate, not away. "I'm sorry you had to come to the hospital, and I'm sorry Bobbie got mad at you."

Nate pulled the covers up over Dylan's shoulder. "I didn't mind going to the hospital, although I minded that you choked. And

Bobbie being mad at me isn't your fault." He patted his back. "Try to get some sleep. You need anything before I go?"

"Can you close the curtains?" he asked. Then he added, with a surprisingly gentle note in his voice, "Sheamus always thinks something's going to come out of his closet, and I think something might look at me through the window."

Nate crossed the room to close the drapes, and noted the sketch Dylan had been working on the day Bobbie had visited. He'd added a boat on the water. It seemed to be half pirate ship, half fishing trawler. Nate closed the drapes and went back to the bed.

"Unless they have a ladder, or a periscope," he said, turning off the bedside lamp, "nobody's going to be able to look through your window. Good night, Dyl."

"Good night, Uncle Nate."

Nate left the door partially open and the hallway light on, then went down the stairs, trying to decide if he felt like having dinner. Actually, another brandy sounded better.

CHAPTER EIGHT

NATE BECAME CONVINCED there were alien forces at work in his life when even Hunter was quick-tempered and out of sorts. Nate finally called him into his office after a front-desk verbal melee that had everyone slamming things around.

"Please don't yell at Jonni," Nate said, pointing Hunter to the client chair that faced his desk. "She keeps this place together. If she leaves, we'll have to set sail on a tramp steamer for the South Seas."

Hunter collapsed into the chair, his brow furrowed. "I don't see the downside to that."

"Then let me paint you a picture. I'll have two kids with me and a very large dog."

Hunter considered that for a minute, stretching his legs out in front of him. "True. So, no island maidens?"

"I doubt it seriously."

"I don't think they still have tramp steamers, anyway."

Nate sat back in his chair. His personal

problems were so numerous, he didn't know where to start to fix them, so it was better to focus on someone else's. "What's the problem today? You need coffee? Maybe with something in it?"

They kept a bottle of Armagnac in the bathroom file cabinet along with paper towels, toilet tissue and the first aid kit.

Hunter expelled air in a noisy growl. "Sandy invited me to dinner."

"You don't want to go?"

"No."

"Can't you just tell her you have plans?"

"Too late. I accepted."

Nate sat up and frowned across the desk at his friend. "That makes no sense, Hunt."

"Yeah, I got that. But what do I do now?"

"I think courtesy demands that you go."

"What does cowardice demand?"

Really wanting to help, probably because of his own confusion, which he didn't want to confront, Nate went to his office door and pushed it closed. "What are you afraid of?" he asked as he took his chair again. "I mean, besides the fact that being around her is like being tied to the front of a semi."

Hunter was uncharacteristically morose. "I think it's the fact that I kind of...I almost..."

He looked into Nate's face and said with a self-deprecating grimace, "I like her."

"Seriously?"

"Seriously. I ran into her yesterday at the grocery store. She had her girls in the cart and she looked so…I don't know. Alive, I guess. Cheerful, despite all she must have to deal with. And…" He looked suddenly embarrassed and ran a hand over his face.

"I'm the friend," Nate said, "who saw you fall off your motorcycle into a mud pit and didn't laugh. Tell me."

"Okay." Hunter folded and unfolded his arms, then readjusted his long body in the chair. "Remember the morning of the meeting when you said you thought she had a thing for me?"

"Yeah."

"I think she does. There's something in her eyes when she looks at me. I saw it the night of the Monster Bash. I thought then that maybe I was imagining it because we were all being somebody else, you know? But there it was again when she first saw me yesterday at Freddy's. Something softens and gets a little…I'd say 'scared,' but knowing her I can't imagine that's it. Maybe I make her nervous, or something."

Nate smiled. "So, it's nice that you'll get

to spend time with her if you like her. She's pretty and smart, and despite the bulldozer personality, she's a good person. And one dinner isn't a lifetime commitment. If she has any sense at all, an evening spent with you will make her change her mind about being attracted. When's the dinner?"

"It's Thanksgiving at her mom's."

Nate remembered his conversation with Stella. "But your mother thinks you're going camping with the guys."

"I know." Hunter looked distressed. "Mom would freak if she thought I was going to another woman's house for Thanksgiving. My brain's in self-destruct mode. I don't understand why Sandy scares me."

"That's easy," Nate replied. "It's because she has the potential to change your life. And you've got it pretty good right now. No grave responsibilities, no one to consult about everyday decisions."

Hunter stifled a laugh. "Pardon me, but remember my mother? Your housekeeper?"

"Yes, but she doesn't live with you, so you can avoid her if you want to. And she's the best cook in Clatsop County, and I happen to know she's always filling your freezer."

"True. But she has a lot of opinions on everything I do. Even some on what I think."

"Women are just like that. I guess it was a man's world for so long, the need to argue is just built into their DNA from generations of fighting to be heard."

"Bobbie's like that?"

"Bobbie. Sandy. Even Jonni. Name one woman and I'll bet she'll give you an argument on almost anything. Now would you get out of here? I've got a million things to do."

"All right. Don't say anything to Mom about Sandy and Thanksgiving. I'll find a way to explain."

"If she thinks there's even the slightest possibility of getting grandchildren out of this, I'm sure she'll be happy to let you do your thing. So that's the way to approach it. And when I thought you were going camping for Thanksgiving, I invited her to spend it with us."

Hunter saluted him. "You're a pal," he said, and would have closed the office door behind him except that Dylan stood in the doorway. He was neatly groomed, and since coming to the office after school, he'd taken to wearing a pencil behind his ear.

"You're replacing me with him, aren't you?" Hunter teased.

"If you don't watch your step. What's up, Dylan?"

"I put all the green-and-white envelopes for tax season away," he reported cheerfully, "and now Karen wants to send me to Jae's around the corner for cupcakes. She says everyone here needs a little sweetening."

"Excellent idea." Nate beckoned him inside. "Do you know what Hunter and Jonni were fighting about?"

Dylan came closer and whispered, "Jonni was teasing him about Sandy. I think they're boyfriend and girlfriend or something. And he told her to put a sock in it."

"Ah. Okay. So, get the cupcakes and come right back."

"Okay."

Nate watched Dylan walk importantly across the office and out the door, and wondered if he dared even let the thought form that he was making progress with him. Maybe the day would come when the name Raleigh and Raleigh would really define the business again.

NATE DIDN'T SEE Bobbie until the week of Thanksgiving. Now that the weather was definitely cooler, her garage door was always closed. He could usually count on meeting her a couple times a week in their driveways, but hadn't done so once since Dylan's trip to the hospital. Nate wondered if she waited for him to leave before going out to her car, or deliberately stayed away once she was out so that she wouldn't meet him coming home from work.

The painting supplies had been taken from his garage. He called her to make sure they hadn't been stolen. She assured him briskly that she had moved everything to her tiny workroom in the house, then hung up.

Sheamus wandered into the kitchen one evening while Nate looked out the window in the direction of her little house.

"Have you seen Bobbie?" he asked.

Sheamus had his dump truck under his arm, a package of Skittles in it. "Yeah," he replied. "When I was out playing this afternoon. She gave me a cookie."

"When was that?"

"Just before you came home. She went back in the house."

So she *was* avoiding him. Nate wasn't surprised.

"I came inside, too." Sheamus sat in the middle of the kitchen floor and rolled the dump truck back and forth. "It's starting to get cold. When is it winter?"

"Officially, it isn't until December 21,

which is still about four weeks. Pretty soon it'll be time for your big jacket."

His nephew focused on the truck. "Yeah."

Nate knew what was on his mind. "Maybe tomorrow you'll be able to open your closet door."

Sheamus looked hopeful. "You think so?"

"I guess we'll see. And if not tomorrow, then maybe the day after."

Nate tried hard not to apply pressure. He couldn't handle all his own problems. It didn't seem fair to hurry his nephew into solving his.

Dylan appeared beside him, his sketch pad and pens in hand. "When are we going to go Christmas tree shopping?" he asked.

"Yeah!" Sheamus seconded.

"After Thanksgiving," Nate replied. "Kiwanis is going to have a tree lot and Hunter promised to save us a big one."

Dylan's excitement faded just a little. "Mom used to love Christmas."

"We made lots of cookies at Christmas," Sheamus said.

"Yeah."

"We can make cookies," Nate said, hoping to divert a slump into sadness. "I happen to be an excellent cookie maker."

Dylan was openly skeptical. "You are not.

You can't even make pancakes. They come out like CDs—flat and hard."

Nate pretended indignation. Actually, he didn't have to pretend. He'd worked hard on those pancakes.

"Maybe Bobbie would help us, Sheamus suggested."

Dylan shook his head. "Bobbie is hiding from us because she's mad at Uncle Nate 'cause he yelled at her."

"How come you yelled at her?" Sheamus asked in surprise.

"We were having an argument," Nate explained.

"But you're not supposed to yell."

"I forgot."

"You wouldn't let us get away with that," Dylan pointed out with a superior smile. "Maybe if you went over and apologized…"

Outmatched, Nate frowned at both boys. "Don't you guys have homework?"

"Nope. Half day tomorrow, then we're off till next Monday."

Sheamus's wide blue eyes were troubled. "If you don't apologize, we might never have cookies again!"

"Stella can help you with cookies."

"She doesn't like to make cookies," Sheamus said, now seriously distressed. "She says it's…" He turned to Dylan for the word.

"Tedious," Dylan provided. "I think it means it takes a long time and is boring. No more cookies ever, Uncle Nate, unless you apologize."

Nate groaned and promised to think about it. A future without cookies was a sorry fate.

BOBBIE NEEDED a tranquilizer. Her morning art class, moved to Tuesday because of the approaching holiday, had been almost cataclysmic. If it hadn't been for Fernanda and her quick thinking when Eddy painted Miranda Julen's hair chartreuse, she was sure she'd have been fired.

"Bless the waterproof paint," Fernanda said, bustling from the room with Miranda by the hand and her own giant purse over her shoulder. "And the blow-dryer and curling iron in the teachers' bathroom." Left alone with sixty-some steroidal second and third-graders, Bobbie quickly devised a contest. "The best pilgrim," she bargained, tacking up a poster-size caricature of one on the bulletin board, "wins a pen with a pilgrim on it."

She held up the pen she'd found in a gift shop downtown. There were oohs and ahhs. She loved how easy the kids were to please.

She sat Eddy at her desk so she could keep an eye on him, and wandered around the room as the children worked, congratulating herself on handling the hair painting situation so well.

Until she delved into the front pocket of her purse for her truck keys after class and found a chartreuse daisy with a bright pink center painted on it. Next time she sat Eddy at her desk, she'd remember to remove her purse from the knee hole.

The day was alternately stormy and rainy, with scowling clouds hanging over the hills across the river, looking like the brink of doom one minute, then moving on and allowing a bright display of sun the next. She pulled up at a spot on Grand that served as a sort of overlook, and watched a freighter moving up the channel toward Portland. In this moment of sunlight, the superstructure was almost golden, distracting from the worn red-and-black of the hull.

The sun also picked out the red and gold colors in the trees covering Washington's hillsides, and the windshields and chrome on the cars crossing the 4.1-mile Astoria-Megler Bridge. Warmth and a curious sense of belonging filled her being. She enjoyed it for a moment, worried about it for a moment, then sighed and put the truck in gear to go home.

She pulled into her driveway, a little disappointed that the space was empty. She'd thought her father might be here by now. He'd called her from Tillamook that morning and said he was bringing several kinds of cheese, for which the town was famous. He'd taken the van to a mechanic after a sudden loss of power. When the problem didn't occur again, the mechanic suggested it might have been poor fuel purchased the day before in a remote area. So he'd visited the cheese factory, then spent the night in a motel. He should have been on his way right after breakfast.

She was looking forward to seeing him. Much as she'd despaired of having to say goodbye again, she was anxious to spend the holidays with him.

She'd already decided that the day after Thanksgiving she was going shopping for gifts for her father, the Raleigh boys, Sandy and her children, and Fernanda. There had to be a lump of coal somewhere for Nate. In the past, she'd always been too busy, too focused on her art to enjoy the day as most other shoppers did, but this time she was relatively free. She would deliver her commission on Monday. The relief she felt was enormous.

SHE PARKED THE truck, climbed out of it and noticed that the sky was darkening again. She hoped her father was all right. She hesitated a moment and dialed his cell. The call went to voice mail.

Mildly concerned, she shouldered her purse, smiled about the chartreuse daisy, then opened the passenger-side door and hauled out her box of supplies. She was on the back porch steps when a loud crash came from inside the house.

She stopped in surprise and heard the sound of raised voices, then another, louder crash. Monet screeched, followed by a woman's high-pitched scream.

"Did I leave on the television?" she wondered aloud in confusion. The curtain on her back door window prevented her from seeing inside. Then she noticed that the door was slightly ajar.

She struggled to make sense of the situation. Did she have thieves who were fighting with each other? A man and a woman?

Footsteps sounded behind her and Nate leaped onto the porch, carrying an aluminum bat. He pulled her back from the door and pushed her behind him. Shoving the door open, he took a step inside, and stopped with a whispered curse.

Bobbie punched 911 into her cell phone, aimed her thumb over the send button, then stood on tiptoe to look over his shoulder.

She gasped at the sight of what appeared to be some derelict facedown on her kitchen floor. Stella had him pinned to the tiles with a squeegee pressed to the middle of his back. Monet stood on the counter, back arched, screeching loudly.

"Hello, Bobbie." Her father's strangled voice came from the grubby man on the floor. Mud was splashed over his jacket and pants, and his hands, which were flattened against the tiles. His glasses were askew. Unbelievably, he smiled as he craned his neck to look at her. "Flattered as I am by this lady's attentions, would you get her off me, please?" He turned his attention to Nate. "You must be the neighbor with the boys. Hi. I'm Bobbie's father."

"Good God." Nate grabbed Stella by an elbow and yanked the mop away from her. "Stella, what are you doing?"

The older woman's expression went from righteous anger to horror.

"I...ah, he—" As she stammered, Nate handed Bobbie the bat and reached down to help her father to his feet. He adjusted Dennis's glasses and brushed off his muddy beige jacket, though it didn't help much. He shook her dad's hand.

"Hi, Mr. Molloy. Nate Raleigh."

"I saw him climb through Bobbie's window," Stella said, finally pulling her thoughts together. She looked from her employer to her victim in embarrassed confusion. "The back door was open so I went in and he—" she pointed to Dennis "—was rooting through the fridge. I thought he was an intruder." She turned to Bobbie in supplication. "I'm so sorry, but he was dirty and helping himself and…he climbed through the window! God. I'm so sorry."

Nate shook his head at her. "Why didn't you call me?"

"I tried but it just went to voice mail. So I grabbed my cell phone to dial 911 as I ran across the yard and…" She sighed and admitted with obvious reluctance, "I dropped it. I was nervous and clumsy, and I'm sorry." She frowned at him suddenly. "What are you doing home, anyway?"

He held up his cell phone. "Left this in my jeans. I heard screaming and shouting and ran across the yard just as Bobbie was walking in." His stress seemed to deepen. "So, you just walk through an open door that should be locked, and confront and attack a stranger who could be armed?"

Bobbie turned to him impatiently. "Stella's been taking care of herself for a long time." The housekeeper sent her a quick glance of gratitude.

Nate turned on Bobbie. "And you. You'd have walked in on what's obviously some kind of fracas in progress—people shouting, things crashing? That's a good way to get yourself killed."

"Or in this case," Bobbie replied into his scowling face, "talked to death." She reached around him and drew her father toward Stella. "Stella, this is my dad, Dennis Molloy. Daddy, Stella Bristol."

Dennis Molloy was slightly shorter than Nate and very fit for a man in his early sixties. His gray hair was close-cropped and his eyes dark and sparkling with amusement, despite the state of his clothes.

He wrapped his arms around Bobbie, then inclined his head in Stella's direction and said, "I apologize for my scary appearance, but I've spent the large part of this morning standing in the rain on the side of a muddy road trying to get my van to start. I was somewhere between Cannon Beach and Seaside. Cars raced past me, spewing mud and road debris, which accounts for my homeless look." He held his arms out to his side to show off his pants and jacket to full effect.

"Triple A finally had me towed to a shop in Astoria, which promised I'd have the van back after the weekend. Bad alternator. So I took a cab here—after the driver put a tarp down on his backseat—and was hoping to find something to eat in the refrigerator." He smiled in the face of Stella's chagrin. "Bobbie sent me a key on the chance that I arrived when she wasn't home, but it's in my van's glove box, hence the climb through the window."

Stella sighed. "Did I mention how sorry I am?"

Dennis grinned broadly. "Actually, that's the most fun I've had in a very long time. And your take-down technique is pretty impressive."

"Stella's Nate's housekeeper, Dad. And apparently a mean hand with a squeegee."

"Well." He bowed again. "I appreciate your not hurting me. Oh, oh." He put a gentle fingertip to her right cheekbone, where a purple bruise was forming. "That's where I hit you when I flung out my arm." He went to the sink, took the top towel from a folded stack on the counter and ran it under cold water. He wrung it out, folded it and placed it against her cheek. Then put her hand there to hold it. "That shouldn't be too bad. Lucky for you, I'm not that strong."

"I was determined that you weren't going to steal from Nate's neighbor." Stella grinned, then winced. "And I'm not sure what happened, but something distracted you for a moment and I took advantage to hook your ankle and throw you down."

He smiled wryly. "That was the moment I realized I was wrestling with a woman."

Bobbie's father and Nate's housekeeper studied each other a moment longer, neither seeming to notice that they'd exhausted the conversation and that Bobbie and Nate were watching them.

Nate drew Bobbie aside. "I'm sorry Stella went all warrior woman on your father."

Bobbie glanced their way and was pleasantly surprised to see the two were now in the middle of an animated conversation. "He seems to have forgiven her." She folded her arms. "And isn't it a comfort to know that while you're away, the woman in charge of the boys can handle herself?"

He conceded that point. "It is. I just wish she'd have called for help instead. If she was nervous enough to drop the phone, how did she think she was going to handle a man?"

"Hey, she had him pinned when we walked in."

"Yes, she did." Nate ran a hand over his hair and leaned a hip against the counter.

She reached past him to get her teakettle and fill it under the tap. "You're going to have to learn to handle things without yelling at everybody, Nate."

He gave her a dark look. "Everybody does things that require shouting to stop them from getting hurt."

She put the kettle on the burner and turned it on. "Okay," she said, leaning beside him. "I wasn't a paragon of calm that night at the hospital, but your yelling wasn't helping anybody. It had Dylan in tears and made me want to run away from you."

"Oh, you want to run away from me on general principle," he said, folding his arms. "You're afraid to get close enough to me to feel something that might challenge your life plan. It's only been a couple of weeks, but there are feelings here we should deal with."

She turned sideways, leaning one hand on the counter and the other on her hip as she struggled to stop *herself* from shouting. "You don't want me to get close to you. You keep me at a distance, and then blame me for not crossing the gap. Well, I think the truth is you don't like me. You've never liked me because I'm one of those 'variable' women you despise...." She quoted his word with emphasis. "Because they want to do what they want to do without regard for fitting into what you need. You're jealous that you aren't free to do that."

Temper smoldered in his eyes. "Sure, I'm jealous. You can be carefree and I can't. Some of us have too many responsibilities to flit around the globe, following our dreams."

"Yeah," she said flatly. "Waiting for the results of an every-six-months cancer checkup provides such a carefree lifestyle."

He had the grace to look repentant. "I'm sorry. That's not what I—"

"And I told you in the very beginning," she interrupted hotly, "that I couldn't—"

He cut her off. "Yes, you did. It doesn't mean I understand it. Home and family are everything. I used to be like you, living my life my way, but the loss of my brother changed me. I chafe against the confinement, but the boys are my flesh and blood. They're part of *him* and therefore everything to *me*. But you won't let anything mean that much to you."

"You have no idea what's in my head!" Now she was yelling.

"I'm guessing bricks," he said in a controlled tone. Then, without warning, he wrapped an arm around her waist, yanked her to him, closed his mouth over hers and kissed her senseless. She felt his lips, the tip of his tongue, the powerful hand splayed against her back.

She couldn't see, couldn't hear, could only feel and try to think. His words about chafing against confinement occurred to her because that was what she should be doing. But she didn't want to. She'd have happily sunk into the lovely prison of his embrace and let it go on and on.

He loosened his grip suddenly, and she was looking up into his face. Remnants of anger lingered in his eyes, yet he seemed somehow pleased with himself.

"You don't know everything about me, Roberta Molloy." The hand splayed against her back ran up and down her spine, and she trembled in response. He smiled wickedly. "I don't think you know a lot about yourself, either."

Nate pointed to the doorway, where his nephews stood. "Dennis," he said, "I'd like you to meet Dylan and Sheamus, my nephews. Boys, this is Mr. Molloy, Bobbie's father. He's visiting from California."

Dennis went across the room to shake hands with the boys. "Bobbie's told me about you. I'm happy to meet you."

Nate shook hands with Dennis, then turned the boys toward the door and headed out. "Welcome to Astoria," he called over his shoulder.

When Bobbie could breathe again, she noticed her father and Stella staring at her, both looking surprised, yet pleased.

"Stella is staying for coffee," her father said with a smile. "I'll make one for you. You look like you could use it."

NATE PACED ACROSS the living room, every nerve ending vibrating with the sensory memory of Bobbie's mouth under his. Unfortunately, he couldn't focus on it, because clever Dylan had overheard something Nate would have never said aloud. And now he had to deal with it.

The boys sat side by side on the sofa, Sheamus's shorter legs sticking straight out, Dylan's bent but not touching the carpet. He looked indignant.

"Tell me what the word means," Dylan said. Sheamus frowned at his older brother, clearly not sure what the problem was. "You said 'chafe against the confinement' when you were talking about us. I know confinement means being in jail."

Nate closed his eyes and prayed for Ben to help him. His brother had always been so relaxed with the boys. Unlike Nate, who felt ill equipped to deal with them most of the time.

"It doesn't necessarily mean jail," he said, trying not to sound guilty so that they wouldn't think he'd said anything they shouldn't have heard. "It means anything that sort of locks you in to a place or a responsibility."

"And that's us. We lock you up." Dylan wanted to make him suffer. Nate had to appreciate the tactic.

He kicked a footstool to face the sofa, and sat astride it. "Being responsible for the two of you means I have to be here to look out for you," he admitted evenly. "Just like you have to go to school and do your homework. We all have things that lock us in place."

"But what's chafing?" Dylan was determined not to let Nate skate by with an easy explanation.

"When something rubs and makes your skin red. It usually stings."

Dylan thought about that. He looked so

much like Ben in that moment, avid intelligence sorting through data. "So, if you're chafing against confinement, and we're confinement, that means…" He looked Nate in the eye. "It's hurting you that you're stuck with us. It stings that you have to be here."

The kid was good. "I was just explaining to Bobbie," he said, wishing he could erase the last ten minutes, except for the kiss, "why she can fly off to Italy and I can't. That's all that meant. She doesn't have kids, so she can do whatever she wants. The three of us are a family and that's the way I want it."

"But you said you were chafing." Dylan was beginning to bear a close resemblance to an IRS auditor—the one on the Binghams' case.

"I also said," Nate reminded him, "that the two of you are everything to me. Did you hear that part?"

"You probably thought you had to say that."

"No, I didn't. I didn't know you were standing there. Had I known, I wouldn't have said anything about chafing because I wouldn't have wanted you to misunderstand and think what you're thinking now."

Dylan seemed to sink a little. His eyes grew large and dark. "Mom and Dad never said anything about chafing."

Nate leaned forward to put his hand on Dylan's knee. "That's because your dad and mom loved you two so much that they never wanted to go anywhere that didn't include you. And they were so smart. They always understood how you were feeling and what to do for you." He looked from one to the other. "Do you know what a B team is?"

His brow crinkling, Dylan asked, "Like in football?"

"Yes. The kids who don't know as much yet or aren't quite as fast start out in the B team. When they improve, they get to be varsity."

"Yeah?"

"I'm the mom and dad B team. Don't know as much as I'd like and I don't always say or do the right thing." He patted the region of his heart. "But I'm determined to be better, to learn more, to stop doing things wrong."

Tears slipped from Dylan's eyes. That made Sheamus's mouth quiver.

Feeling as though his heart was being sawed with a dull blade, Nate took each boy's hand. "Please believe me when I tell you that there isn't anywhere I'd rather be than right here with you. And pretty soon I'll be better at being like a dad and things won't be so hard for you."

"Don't you want to go with Bobbie?" Dylan asked, sniffling. "You kissed her."

Nate reached for the wad of tissues in his pocket. He peeled off two and handed one to each of the boys. "No, I don't," he said. It came out firmly because it was honest. Then he shrugged. "I'd like it if she stayed here, but she doesn't want to. She has things she has to do."

Dylan dried his eyes and, chin up, said, "Okay. But if you don't want to be here, I can get a job and take care of me and Sheamus."

"Stella could take care of us," Sheamus said brightly.

Dylan gave him a pitying look. "She works for him." He pointed to Nate. "She wouldn't take care of us."

"Listen to me," Nate said a little loudly. Then, remembering Bobbie's advice, he lowered his voice. "You are living with me until one of you becomes president and the other one takes over the Disney Corporation. Is that clear?"

Sheamus raised his hand. "Dibs on Disney!"

Dylan shook his head and smiled feebly at his uncle. "Okay. Can we go out and play?"

"Sure. Jackets. It's getting cold."

Nate poured himself a cup of coffee and

opened the kitchen door as the boys raced past him with an assortment of plastic cars and trucks under their arms.

"That's what you get," he told himself as he headed to his computer and his office duties still undone, "for concentrating on Bobbie when your every thought should be on the boys."

He sat down and powered up. Then he rubbed a sore spot on his chest. For someone who shouldn't matter in his life, Bobbie was taking up a lot of space in it.

CHAPTER NINE

BOBBIE AWOKE TO the sound of voices and the aroma of something wonderful in the kitchen. She recognized her father's soft baritone and had to smile. First full day here and he was cooking for her already. As she drew closer, wrapping her robe around her, she realized Sandy was here.

She sat at the table while Dennis stood at the stove, turning blueberry pancakes. The table was set for two and there were two bowls of berries and yogurt. Bobbie went to hug her friend.

"Where are the girls?" Bobbie asked. On days she wasn't working, Sandy was seldom without them.

"My mom has them," Sandy replied, sipping at a cup of coffee. "She's watching them for us so we can do her shopping."

Bobbie was confused. "Who is 'us'?"

"Hunter and me."

"Hunter Bristol? I didn't know you knew him."

Sandy hunched her shoulders in an artless gesture of nonchalance. "I didn't, until the food bank fund-raiser. I saw him at the Monster Bash and invited him to join us for Thanksgiving."

Bobbie's eyes widened and she reached for Sandy's hands. "You're dating *Hunter Bristol?!*" The question ended in a screech as she threw her arms around Sandy again.

"I am."

"I'm so happy for you!"

There were giggles and squeals, and Dennis turned, spatula in hand. "Ah, this takes me back. Your freshman year in college when you brought Sandy home for Easter. I never heard so much cackling."

"Did you and Nate get supplies for the painting?"

Bobbie blushed violently, and hated herself for it. She liked to think she was cool, usually in control, had faced down death and hadn't flinched—well, not much—but memories of Nate's kiss were crippling her brain and, apparently, elevating her blood pressure.

She opened her mouth to explain that they fought better than they understood each other, but she didn't want to rain on Sandy's parade.

Her friend studied her a moment. "Your

father told me you and Nate shared quite a kiss yesterday."

"Dad," Bobbie complained.

He was unrepentant. "What? It's clear to anyone who looks at the two of you. Sandy'd already figured it out, anyway."

She nodded. "It's true. I knew at our food bank meeting that he thought you were special." She inclined her head. "And you look different today. Ever since…the diagnosis, there's been a part of you holding back, not wanting to step out there for fear…for fear there was nothing under your feet. But you seem more confident today, Bobbie." Sandy assumed a comical Atlas astride the world look, hands on her hips. "You're invincible again. Well." She grabbed the jacket off the chair she'd occupied, put her purse over her shoulder, kissed Dennis on the cheek and gave Bobbie another hug. "Have a wonderful day. And Happy Thanksgiving."

Bobbie walked her to the door, and was about to close it behind her when Sandy turned suddenly with a questioning look. "I almost forgot why I came. So, you've started the painting?"

"Yes. Nate's posing for me as the ship captain."

Sandy frowned at her. "And you're getting things done?"

"Of course."

"Can I see?"

"No. Trust me. I'll call you to come have a look as soon as I've finished."

"The event is December 15. So…dry enough to handle by then?"

"Yes. But if you didn't have such sweet children, I'd hurt you."

Sandy grinned broadly. "And now I have a boyfriend."

"Oh, shut up." Bobbie closed the door on her and walked over to her father, loving the sight of him in jeans and sweatshirt and slippers, cooking at her stove. She wrapped her arms around his middle.

"I like your guy," he said, patting her hand at his waist.

She snagged a blueberry sticking out of one of the pancakes on the griddle. "He's not my guy. He's just a neighbor."

"That wasn't a neighborly kiss," Dennis observed, turning the last pancake and adding it to one of two plates warming in the oven. "And he looks at you like you're his. You want to pour the coffee?"

She took down two cups and said loftily, "No one belongs to anyone, Dad." She put a dash of milk into his cup, then filled it with coffee. "And you're imagining things. He wouldn't want to get involved with me even if I was willing. His mom died of cancer."

"But your prognosis is good. You could be around to be a pain in his side for a long time." She made a face at hime as he went on. "You know what I mean about belonging. Not as in ownership, but as in property of the heart." Using a tea towel as a pot holder, he carried first one plate then the other to the table. "We don't have syrup," he said, "but I thought butter and powdered sugar would be good."

"Sounds perfect."

They focused on breakfast, and Monet came to sit on the extra chair, purring.

"Want to take a walk today?" Dennis asked. "I'd like to find something to take to Nate's tomorrow. A table centerpiece, maybe."

"What if I carved out a pumpkin and we put a small pot of mums in it?"

He grinned at her. "That's my little genius. I don't suppose you want to talk about Nate and the boys?"

"No. It's complicated and will never be what you'd like it to be. Even though I've already explained to you on the phone that what you'd like isn't possible. I'm going to Florence."

"Then," he asked gently, "why are you kissing him as though he has a place in your future?"

"Daddy...*he* kissed *me*."

"Yeah. You fought him off so hard. You think you have an iffy future. But don't you think having a family to live for might lengthen it?"

She dropped her fork with a clatter. "Dad, it's not as though I'm convinced I'm going to expire tomorrow. I'm not! I believe in myself and my ability to stay well as long as possible. But I don't have forever. And I don't know how many ways I can explain this to you...." She drew a breath, a mental picture of Nate suddenly cutting off her air. "I've wanted to do fine art all my life. I have so much to learn. I have to see what happens when I immerse myself in all that inspiration. I have only this chance, Dad."

He looked stricken. He always did when she talked about feeling the limitations of time. She reached across the table to pat his hand.

"Nate understands you're going to leave him?"

She put both hands to her face, then lowered them. "He doesn't have to. He doesn't want to come with me any more than I want to stay with him. There's nothing real between us, Dad."

He shook his head and forked a big bite of pancake. "You're a mystifying generation. Eat up. We have things to do."

While waiting for her father to get ready for their walk, Bobbie sent Laura a quick email, telling her about her dad and Stella's exciting meeting and about Nate's kiss, certain her friend would enjoy the ongoing drama.

She hadn't had a response to her last email, but was sure Laura was busy trying to make a baby.

NATE FOLLOWED STELLA down the grocery store aisle with a cart mounded with the makings of Thanksgiving dinner. Since she'd decided to join them, she'd insisted he cancel the prepared meal he'd ordered. The boys kept adding treats to the cart and Nate had long since lost track of their purchases. His brain was stuttering. He kept remembering Bobbie in his arms.

He was so pathetic. Only a year ago he'd had more women sharing space in his life than was probably prudent, but they'd liked the way he treated them and weren't interested in anything permanent. It had suited his purposes then.

This morning, he was completely distracted by the memory of one kiss he'd given Bobbie no choice to reject, and the feel of her in his arms. Her body was forever imprinted on his, warm and soft and a little delicate. He didn't dare even think *fragile*.

And then, as though the magic of his memories had conjured her, she came around a corner in the produce aisle, a beautifully shaped pumpkin in one arm and a pot of burgundy mums in the other.

Her eyes lit up when she spotted him. Given the way they'd parted, he'd expected hostility. But she was definitely happy to see him. Maybe more than happy. Something inside him melted. He felt all the old anger dissolve into a puddle.

"Hi," she said, the simple word filled with soft emotion. He walked around the cart to greet her, needing to touch her. But the boys' radar told them she was around, and they came running. So he simply took the pumpkin and the plant from her as she greeted them and accepted their hugs.

"Hey, Nate!" Dennis came around the corner with a cart. "Are those Bobbie's? Here, put them down." He pushed the cart up to Nate and held it still so he could place the objects inside. Nate spotted premade piecrusts, cans of pumpkin and mince filling, and a pumpkin cheesecake. Dennis abandoned the cart to greet the boys, then Stella, who'd been half an aisle ahead and was on her way back to say hello, several colorful gourds in her hands.

"Hi!" Dennis took them from her and placed them in their cart. He grinned at Nate. "I make a mean mulled wine. Can I bring some tomorrow?"

"Please. Stella's making eggnog because the boys love it, but I'd prefer the wine."

"Great." Dennis leaned on the cart handle. "You've done such a good job with the boys, according to Bobbie." He indicated the end of the aisle where she and the boys stood, looking up at a honeycomb turkey hanging from a fixture. "Must have been quite a shock to your own life."

Nate was surprised to hear she'd complimented him. "Really. She tells me I shout too much."

"Sometimes you have to shout to be heard."

"That's just what I tried to explain."

Dennis shifted a little uncomfortably. "Would you mind if I asked Stella out to dinner?"

"Ah—no. She very much has her own life.

It would be entirely up to her. Her son is my friend, but he has no say in what she does, either. It's your call. Bear in mind that she's a great lady."

Dennis laughed. "You have to love a woman who takes nothing from nobody."

Nate had his own reason to laugh. "Yes, you do."

Bobbie came up to him. "Do you have a couple of minutes to spare?" she asked. "I need some facial detail for the painting."

"Why don't I just go home with you?" he suggested. He smiled at her dad. "Would you mind going home with Stella and helping her haul in the groceries?"

Dennis didn't even blink. "Is that all right with you?" he asked Stella.

"Um, yes. Okay." Her glance at him had sincere anticipation in it. Nate smiled to himself.

Dylan folded his arms and looked from one to the other. "And what happens to us? Does one of us go with Uncle Nate and one with Mr. Molloy, like the kids in that *Parent Trap* movie? Or are you going to leave us here?"

Nate put his large hand over Dylan's face. "Ha, ha. You're coming with me."

"Oh, goody," Dylan said with a clear lack of enthusiasm, but he grinned at Bobbie.

"Are you going to make us cookies?" Shea-mus asked, catching her hand.

"No, but I did buy some. And some ice cream." She pointed to those objects in her cart.

Dylan tugged on Nate's jacket sleeve. Nate leaned down so he could hear him. "Yeah?"

"I like to go to Bobbie's, but she doesn't have—you know—up-to-date electronics. She's got a TV and that's it. And it's not even a plasma. No Sports Channel, no DVD player."

"Up-to-date electronics?" Nate scoffed playfully at Dylan's criticism. "You won't have time for that. We're going to help Bob-bie make pies and rolls."

"Me?"

"Hey, if I have to do it, you have to do it."

The boy winced. "But then we have to *eat* it tomorrow." He made a face, clearly not trust-ing their skills.

"Right. So we'd better pay attention to what we're doing. And, you know, you might ask Santa for a personal DVD player for such *emergencies*."

Dylan looked both horrified and intrigued. "*Santa?* I'm going to be eleven."

Bobbie and Sheamus led the way down the aisle and Nate pushed the cart to follow, Dylan at his side.

"Everyone believes in Santa at Christmastime," Nate said. "I do, and I'm going to be thirty-six."

His nephew made a face at him. "Come on. *You're* our Santa. So maybe I should ask *you* for a personal DVD player."

"I'll see that your message gets through to him."

"Sometimes," Dylan said with long-suffering tolerance, "you're kind of nutty."

Nate took that with a smile. "That's a criticism I've heard before."

BOBBIE STOOD AT the easel crammed in a corner of her small workroom. Her drafting table had been folded up, and leaned against the closet door, and all her inks and calligraphy materials packed up and put away to make room for her to work on the painting. With her father here, she was sleeping on the sofa.

The kitchen was across the hall and she could hear the boys putting her groceries away. She'd given them free rein to stash things where they thought best, as long as perishables were refrigerated.

"I can't believe the boys don't like my television," she said to Nate as she leaned forward to tilt his chin at a sharper angle. He sat on her windowsill and looked out at the rainy day as though it were the wide Columbia in the painting. She felt stubble under her fingertips and the hard line of his jaw.

"Oh, they like it, they'd just like it better if you had all the ESPN channels."

"My father," she said, her voice diminishing in volume as she focused on perfecting the line of his jaw, "likes your housekeeper."

"I've noticed."

Satisfied that she had the angle correct, she made a few adjusting brushstrokes. Then she looked up and simply admired his profile for a moment. "I think you should ask his intentions. He always asked that of my boyfriends."

"He intends to invite her to dinner. I don't have to know anything else. She's a very capable woman. And Hunter would kill him if he didn't treat her like a lady."

"Dad wouldn't know how to hurt anyone."

"So, if they develop a relationship, you and I might be connected beyond January. I mean, what if they end up together and you come to visit? I'll be here, disturbing your uncomplicated artist's life."

"If they got serious," she speculated, peering around the canvas at him, "she might quit her job. Then you'd have to get married. Maybe call that client in Portland or the model. One of those variable women might have had a change of heart and decided she'd like a family, after all."

"You know, for someone who doesn't want a relationship, you tend to bring it up a lot. Maybe deep down you wish you had one. Or—and this is just occurring to me—maybe you don't know how to have one."

She blew air between her lips in a very unladylike raspberry. "How hard is it to have a relationship? You have things in common and you care about each other. Big deal. Anybody can do it."

She knew she was talking nonsense, but didn't want to get into a serious discussion.

Sheamus appeared suddenly in the doorway, holding up a bag of cookies. "Can we have one of these?"

Bobbie dropped her brush in a jar of water. "Lunch before cookies," she said. "Tomato soup and grilled cheese sandwiches?"

Sheamus cheered, hearing the menu, and went to tell Dylan.

"You can move now," she told Nate as she dried her hands on a rag, pretending she'd forgotten about the subject under discussion.

Nate took the old hat off and placed it carefully on a bookshelf.

"Now you go from artist's model to sous-chef," she said. "First, we have to take this off." She went to help him remove the jacket, and hung it back up in its paper wrapper. He had to think she was as removed as she pretended to be.

He carefully pulled off the shirt and stood there in a white T-shirt molded to a sturdy chest and shoulders.

The urge to touch him was overwhelming. His watchful gaze caught hers. He took her hand and placed it on a warm, solid pectoral muscle. "Nothing to be afraid of," he said softly. "It's just me. Or does that scare you? If you really believe what you just said about relationships, it's clear you haven't had one. Been too devoted to your art, maybe? A little bit afraid of a world that doesn't exist on canvas or pretty paper, but in real flesh and blood?"

HE HAD HER. Her eyes went darker, wider, and in her small, pale face they seemed enormous. Her lips firmed, but her hand under his trembled. "You'd like to think that, wouldn't you?" she asked. "That I'm a poor, repressed innocent and that's why I won't be anything but your neighbor? Did it ever occur to you that I may just not be attracted?"

"Oh, you're attracted," he said with a small

smile. "You can deny it all you want, but your body betrays you. Every time I touch you, you tremble. You're just afraid of the kind of intimacy we could share, because you're not sure you're strong enough to care for me and still walk away."

"I told you once," she said, enunciating carefully, "that I can stand up to anything."

"Yeah," he said. "Big talk."

He got precisely what he wanted when she grabbed a fistful of the front of his T-shirt, pulled him down while she stood on tiptoe, and claimed his mouth. Then he lost awareness of everything but the warm, mobile lips reshaping his, the hand that still clutched his shirt, the other that wandered over his shoulder and into his hair.

He was out of breath when she finally drew back and gulped in air. She looked into his eyes with a shocked and horrified expression. Then she ran from the room and left him standing there.

AFTER LUNCH, BOBBIE wrapped kitchen towels around the boys' spindly bodies, and everyone was given a job. She made quick bread biscuit dough, spread it on the floured countertop and rolled it out. She gave each boy a glass with the rim dipped in flour, and placed them at either end of the flattened dough. She showed the two how to cut a biscuit with the rim of the glass and place it on the parchment-covered tin.

Nate watched her work. The unspoken rule seemed to be to pretend that the moment in her studio had never happened. She was doing it beautifully, but he felt the effort like an anvil on his shoulders.

Apart from that, he'd have liked to employ her method, whatever it was, of getting the boys' rapt attention. She watched them begin their jobs, seemed satisfied with their efforts, and handed Nate the jar of mincemeat.

"I'll pour that into a piecrust," she promised, "if you can get the lid off."

"What? Out of a jar?" He gave the lid a quick turn and handed it back to her. "No large stone pot with bits of lamb and beef and fruit and brandy?"

"Get real, Raleigh. Thank you." She walked across the room to where the piecrust waited, then smiled at him over her shoulder. Brat. Like smiling at him wasn't hard at all. "This is the here and now."

The first batch of biscuits went into the oven and the boys began to work on the second tin. Bobbie handed Nate a bowl with pumpkin puree in it and seasonings on top.

"Would you mix those in, please?" She stuck a wooden spoon in the bowl and placed a prepared piecrust on the table beside him. "Then turn it out into this."

"Gotcha," he said.

As she went back to check on the boys, she gave him another look over her shoulder that he interpreted as "No, you don't," though she didn't say the words. What was he going to do, he wondered, if she could just walk away?

He mixed the spices in and caught the familiar aroma of traditional pumpkin pie. It took him back to his childhood and the loud, cheerful holiday celebrations with grandparents and aunts and uncles who were all gone now. The nostalgia was poignant for a moment. Then he caught sight of the boys and thought of life carrying on despite loss.

The back door opened after a brief two-rap knock and Sandy walked in, carrying a plate of what looked like homemade candy. Hunter followed her, seemingly relieved to see Nate there.

"Hey!" He walked around the women, slapped each boy on the shoulder as he passed and came to greet Nate. "What are you up to? I didn't know you had culinary skills."

Nate pulled a chair out for him. "I don't.

I'm just stirring. Hard to get that wrong. What are you doing?"

Hunter sat as though he really needed to. "Sandy had a bunch of errands to run for her mom, who's cooking tomorrow, so I'm providing chauffeur service."

"Your mother still thinks you're going camping?"

"No. I finally told her the truth. Then I brought Sandy and the girls by to introduce them. You were right. Mom was a little annoyed with me for not being honest with her, but thrilled that I'm seeing someone and that she has children. Sandy's mother invited her to join us, but Mom told them she was cooking for all of you."

"I'm sorry. She could have gone with you. We wouldn't have minded."

"No, she wants to cook for you. And..." He leaned closer to say quietly, "I think she likes spending time with Bobbie's father. Last time I talked to her she seemed happy as a clam. Where does that expression come from, anyway? How do we know clams are happy?" Hunter kept smiling though his eyes were troubled.

"You okay?" Nate asked in a low voice.

"Yeah." He nodded. "I'm just glad to see another guy. I'm on estrogen overload today."

Nate laughed sympathetically. "Come on over Friday. The boys and Bobbie's dad and I are going to watch college football all day, and guy movies. The girls are going shopping."

"Great. I'd love to. I'll bring pizza."

"Good."

"Hunter?" Sandy said his name with a sweet lilt Nate wasn't used to hearing in her voice. Stella always said Hunter's name with pride, and at work, the women either spoke his name with playful abuse or reverence when he found solutions for impossible clients.

He gave Nate a harried look before he pasted on a smile and turned to Sandy. "Coming."

She caught his hand as he went toward her, and they walked out together. Nate had never seen Sandy so taken with a man. And he'd never seen Hunter look so frightened. He followed Bobbie out into the chill air to wave them off.

A crash reverberated from inside and Sheamus shouted as they turned back to the house. Bobbie ran in, Nate right behind her. They found Sheamus standing in the middle of the kitchen, with unbaked rolls all over the floor.

His chin quivered and his blue eyes were wide with guilt.

"I hit the tin with my elbow," he said as Dylan picked up the circles of dough. Nate got down to help him. "I didn't mean to do it, it just—"

Bobbie put a fingertip over his mouth. "It's all right. It's just dough."

"It *was* an accident," Dylan corroborated, getting to his feet, dough in hand. "He was reaching for the glass and accidentally hit the full pan with his elbow, and it tipped off the counter. Shall I throw these away?"

Bobbie glanced at Nate, who looked up from his task in surprise. She must have recognized, just as he had, that it was unusual for Dylan to come to Sheamus's defense.

"Yes. I'd made extra, anyway, so we'll still have plenty." She pinched Sheamus's chin. "You're more important to us than the rolls, Sheamus. Everything's okay."

He sniffed. "I'm really sorry."

She kissed the top of his head. "Nothing to be sorry about. Go ahead and finish. We'll take a break when the last batch goes in the oven, and have milk and cookies."

Sheamus smiled, his eyes bright, and went back to work.

"I'll scrub the floor for you," Nate said,

tossing the rolls he'd picked up into the trash, "as soon as we're all done. Do you have a swab mop," he asked, "to help me get into character?"

"Aren't you cute?"

"So you've told me."

"You'll have to use a Swiffer. In reality, we're stuck with this century."

They looked at each other, all the complications of their nonrelationship and the kisses that kept happening anyway as visible in her eyes as he was sure they were in his. While he might pretend to accept that there was no possibility they could sail off to Europe together as their turn-of-the-century counterparts might have done, he refused to give up hope. In the past or in the present, he just wanted to be near her. He found himself ignoring the cost of caring about a woman who didn't have forever because now seemed to stop time in its tracks.

CHAPTER TEN

NATE HAD TUCKED in the boys, and sat down with a glass of brandy to read the *Daily Astorian*. He found a Black Friday sale insert and put it aside for Stella, who was planning to shop with Bobbie and Sandy. She was out to dinner with Dennis tonight.

The pair had spent the afternoon cleaning and preparing vegetables and making dressing. There was an interesting looking corn concoction in a bowl in the refrigerator and a cranberry-and-orange mixture Nate presumed was a fancier take on cranberry jelly. She'd mashed carrots and rutabagas together—a dish Dennis always made, apparently—and there was a plastic bag of brussels sprouts that were Nate's particular favorite.

So preparations for Thanksgiving were under control, and the boys were excited that Bobbie and Dennis would be here to celebrate with them. Nate had had trouble getting them to go to bed.

It was nearly ten o'clock. He'd brought up

the card table from the basement and washed it as he'd promised Stella.

He was happy to have time to read the paper. He didn't want to sit in the dark and think about the turn-of-the-century captain and the suffragist, who might have had different options than he and Bobbie had. He didn't want to remember the sadness in her eyes when she'd looked at him in the captain's clothes, and he didn't want to recall her sweetness with Sheamus when he'd dropped the rolls.

Nate did, however, like remembering the way she'd grabbed him and kissed him. He let himself dwell on it for a moment, then groaned and forced himself back to reality.

Finding the sports section, he folded the paper back to study the stats. The brandy glass had almost reached his lips when he heard a sharp "Pssst!"

He looked up to see Dylan hanging over the railing. Nate opened his mouth to warn him of the danger of falling when the boy straightened and made an urgent beckoning gesture, then put his fingertip to his lips for silence.

A little concerned, Nate started quickly up the stairs, and Dylan turned to shush him. At least he was smiling.

Nate followed him to the half-open door of

Sheamus's room. Dylan pointed through the opening to his brother, who sat on the floor in front of the closet door, his back to them.

The little boy was looking up at the poster of Bill the Monster, one arm around Arnold, who sat beside him.

Sheamus seemed to be speaking to the door, or, rather, the monster on the other side of it.

"…not afraid of you anymore," he was saying. "I used to feel all alone, and that was scary. But I feel better now. And Bobbie says I'm more important to her than the biscuit dough. Biscuits aren't very important, but not getting mad when somebody's messy is. And I'm more important than that."

Sheamus got up on his knees. Arnold rose to his feet, tail swishing, awaiting his master's next move. "It's starting to get cold," Sheamus told the closet door, "and I want my scarf. And my coat. And my boots. And my basketball. Bobbie said she likes to play basketball, but she doesn't have a ball. I'm gonna let her play with mine."

His voice got a little louder. "I'm gonna open the door, so if you're in there, Bill, you better go. Arnold might hurt you."

When Sheamus stood, Dylan shifted his weight anxiously, as tense as Nate. Placing a palm on his nephew's shoulder, Nate watched as Sheamus reach for the doorknob.

Arnold pranced a little, as though a steak waited on the other side of the door.

Nate held his breath as Sheamus turned the knob. Then with a mighty yank, he pulled the door open and jumped back. Arnold barked and wagged his tail. No steak? No monster?

Sheamus giggled and stepped cautiously forward, his hand on the dog's collar. He looked left, then right, pushed clothes aside and peered under them, got down on the floor and crawled back and forth. Arnold, enjoying the game, licked his face.

Dylan turned to look up at Nate and said with sudden seriousness, "He did it. He finally did it." Then, after a moment, he walked across the hall to his own room and closed the door.

Nate felt as though a part of his life that had gone missing when he'd lost Ben and Sherrie had been restored. He felt lighter, strangely hopeful at the little boy's victory.

Sheamus got to his feet, reached up to the pegs on the inside of the closet door and pulled down the simply knit yellow scarf Sherrie had made him. He twirled it around his neck and wrapped his arms around himself.

Nate walked into the room, trying not to

make a big deal out of what this meant. He had to clear his throat.

"Hey," he said. "You opened the closet. And you found your scarf."

Sheamus beamed up at him, then without warning, shed a very large tear. He held up an end of the scarf and rubbed it against his face. "My mom made this."

Nate squatted down in front of him. "I know. Now you can wear it all winter long to stay warm."

"I'm gonna wear it to bed, okay?"

"Sure." Nate untangled it from around his neck and placed it so that the ends fell loosely. "We won't tie it, so it doesn't choke you if you roll around. Want me to tuck you in again?"

"Okay." He climbed into his bed and lay back against the pillow.

Nate pulled up the blankets, tucked in Sheamus's feet, then leaned over to kiss his forehead.

"I did it, Uncle Nate," he said, wriggling a little in his excitement. "I opened the door."

"I told you you would when you were ready."

"Where do you think Bill went?"

"I think when you stopped being afraid, he left."

Sheamus gave him one of those insightful looks. "Does that mean he wasn't really there?"

Nate laughed. "It means that when you're afraid, it feels like there's a monster in your life, but when you do something brave, you realize how strong you really are, and monsters go away like they were never there."

Sheamus reached his arms up and Nate leaned down for a hug.

"I love you, Uncle Nate," he said.

"I love you, too, buddy." Nate arranged the blankets around his shoulders, ruffled Arnold's ears, then turned off the light and left the room, leaving the door half-open.

God, he needed that brandy.

He passed Dylan's closed door and knocked lightly once. "You okay in there? You need anything before I go downstairs?"

There was a moment's silence, then Dylan replied, "I'm sketching because I can't go to sleep. Okay?"

"Okay. Good night."

"Good night."

THERE WAS MORE FOOD ON Nate's table, Bobbie thought, than she'd eaten in the last year. Even her father refrained from cautioning her against a second helping of dressing or that wonderful corn pudding. He was eating non-stop himself.

She loved to listen to him talk to Stella. Bobbie didn't think a great love affair was in the works there, but they seemed to have a lot of cultural memories to share, and were on the way to developing a strong friendship.

The boys apparently had undergone a change. Nate had told her that Sheamus had had an epiphany and opened his closet door. She was so happy the boy had taken such an important step, and it was clear that Nate was, too.

Sheamus seemed to swagger just a little as he did what he could to help in the kitchen. He took Bobbie's hand and dragged her to the toy box to show her the basketball.

"Is that the one from your closet?" she asked, pretending ignorance.

He nodded, beaming. "Uncle Nate says we can play basketball after dinner."

"Wonderful."

Dylan was also different, though the change was a little harder to figure out. He was polite and helpful, but more restrained than usual. There was no hostility, no biting humor, no harassment of Sheamus.

Stella put a hand to his head when he turned down Bobbie's offer of pumpkin pie.

"Are you okay?" she asked in concern. "You haven't eaten very much, and I've never seen you refuse dessert."

"I'm fine," he insisted. "I had three dinner rolls, and I think I just filled myself up. I'll have some pie later."

Stella would have persisted, but Nate shook his head at her. "He was up late last night working on his sketch. You want to lie down for a while, Dyl?"

"Yeah. May I be excused?"

"Sure."

Dylan smiled briefly at everyone, then walked away from the table.

"What's wrong with him?" Stella asked Nate softly. "I know he didn't have three rolls. He had one, and left half of it." She pointed to his plate, which had most of the food still on it. Then she frowned as something seemed to occur to her. "Oh." She'd started to clear away some plates, then stopped and sat down again, looking at Nate. She handed Sheamus her water glass. "Would you get me some more, please?" she asked.

He took the glass and went for the filtration pitcher in the refrigerator. While he was busy, she asked, just above a whisper, "Do you think he's missing his parents? He's told me several times how much they loved the holidays. This must be hard."

"Thanksgiving was always a big deal for our family," Nate said. "Dylan's been convinced since we began planning it that it would be awful this year. But he was happy that Bobbie and Dennis were coming. I thought it might be all right for him, after all."

Sheamus was back with Stella's water. The conversation stopped, a slight pall falling over the sunny afternoon.

"I'll have pumpkin pie," Sheamus said excitedly. "With ice cream and whipped cream."

"You don't have room for all that," Bobbie teased, squeezing his shoulders as she passed him. "I'll give the ice cream to Stella and half of the pie to Uncle Nate."

He opened his mouth to protest, then, realizing she was playing with him, laughed with everyone else.

After dessert, everyone pitched in to clean up. While working with Stella on making all the leftovers fit into the refrigerator, Bobbie received a text from Laura and Sean, wishing her a Happy Thanksgiving. Know that I'm thankful for you, it read. She held the phone to her chest for a moment.

"Old boyfriend?" Nate asked with a grin.

"My friend Laura." She put her phone on

the table. "We had chemo at the same time. We helped pull each other through."

"Ah. Didn't mean to pry."

"It's all right."

Nate transferred the turkey carcass to a smaller platter while Dennis cleaned off the table. He gave Sheamus the cotton napkins to take to the laundry room.

Dennis held up the salt and pepper. "Do these stay on the table?"

"Leave them out for sandwiches later." When everyone looked horrified at the thought of more food, Nate added, "We're going to play basketball and work off all those calories."

"I could play with the Trailblazers for a whole season," Bobbie said with a laugh, "and not be ready for a sandwich."

Dennis cleared his throat. "I've thought about joining Doctors Without Borders," he said, rolling down the sleeves of his blue flannel shirt. "But I'm afraid to commit to taking off at a moment's notice for an emergency, or agreeing to spend time halfway around the world."

Bobbie kissed his cheek as she reached past him to the table for the place mats. "That's because you don't want to leave me, but I'll be okay. I'll be in Florence, so there's no need for you to stay handy to take care of me. And there's also the fact that I'm just fine."

"I know that. I'd just like you to be able to reach me if you need me." He looked at her directly, daring her to argue.

Stella closed the refrigerator door and dusted off her hands. "I'm probably going to die on the job," she said, "and be carried out of here in an apron with a spoon in my hand."

Nate put an arm around her shoulders. "Good. Not your being carried out of here. I mean, your wanting to stay. I promise you regular raises and combat pay. And vacations."

Tired of the adult chitchat, Sheamus announced, with a smile in Nate's direction, "I'm going upstairs to get my cold weather jacket."

He smiled back. "Okay. You want to check on Dylan while you're up there? If he's awake, ask him if he wants to join us."

Sheamus ran off.

Dennis shrugged into his jacket, handed Bobbie's to Nate and helped Stella into hers. With her back to Nate, pushing her arms into the sleeves, Bobbie watched her father treat Stella with his customary gentle care. "You're never going to retire?"

"No." Stella turned to Dennis, snapping her

jacket closed. She made a wry face. "If you're joining Doctors Without Borders, it sounds as though you aren't, either."

His brow furrowed. "Aren't you tempted to travel, take up a hobby?"

"These guys are my hobby and I love my home."

Dennis pushed the door open and they walked out into the brisk, brilliant autumn afternoon. Bobbie hurried to catch up, not wanting to miss their conversation.

"I knit like a fiend in my spare time." She kicked at the rusty mountain ash leaves all over the driveway. "And I'm taking an online class in design."

Bobbie wondered if her father was thinking about how he could fit into such a life. Or if Stella could fit into his. But there seemed to be no urgency with either of them.

Nate's voice came from behind Bobbie. "Stella, are there things you want to do for yourself that you're not finding time for? Because we can work that out somehow."

She shook her head. "No. I do enjoy having a male coffee and dinner companion, though. That way the conversation doesn't always come down to grandchildren—of which I have *none*."

"Ah, but Hunter's dating now and Sandy has two little girls."

Stella nodded, a smile forming. "That's true. But it's still nice to have a man around."

Nate turned to Bobbie. "Told ya!"

Bobbie laughed and hooked her arm in his. "Get over yourself, Raleigh. You're about to be trounced at basketball by the Free Throw Champion of Whittier High School women's basketball team."

He gave her a light shove on the shoulder. "Oh, yeah? Shall we make a wager on this? Because I was Facts and Figures Club captain at Oregon State."

She blinked at him. "And how does that relate to basketball?"

"It shows my determination and fearless self-esteem in the face of bullying."

She laughed again and instinctively wrapped her arms around his neck, a gesture that seemed fraught with electric significance. He took advantage of the moment to hold her to him, and she relished having the excuse to let him. She felt as though she'd swallowed butterflies.

She finally pushed herself away, looking into his eyes with accusation she didn't really feel.

"Phony baloney," he said under his breath. "Don't blame me for that."

Sheamus came out of the house frowning, the basketball tucked under his arm, his jacket hanging open. "Dylan's crying," he said.

"Okay." Nate's expression changed and he began backing toward the house. "You all go ahead and play...."

Stella started to follow. "Shall I come?"

"No. Stay and play."

"I'll go with Nate." Bobbie fell in step beside him as he turned toward the house. "Okay?" she asked him.

"Please." He opened the door and held it for her, looking worried.

CHAPTER ELEVEN

"I'M NOT CLAIMING to know what to do," she said softly as she ran up the stairs behind him. "I just thought you might like backup."

"I do. I never know what to do."

Serious sobbing was audible even before they reached the top of the stairs. Nate followed the sound, ignored the closed door and went inside, Bobbie right behind him.

There was a medium-size lump under the blue-and-gray quilt in the middle of Dylan's bed. Arnold lay beside it, whining. Nate sat on the other side and touched the top of the blanket.

"Dylan? What is it?"

"Go away!"

"I'm not going away. I have to know what's wrong. Are you sick?"

"No. So you can *go away!*"

"Well…" Nate hesitated. "There're all kinds of sick. Sometimes it's not your head or your stomach, but…your heart. Or maybe your feelings."

Dylan cried harder and said nothing.

Bobbie saw Nate square his shoulders. "Are you missing your mom and dad?" he asked. "Because there's nothing wrong with that. Especially at Thanksgiving. It was always such an important holiday for our family. You can tell me if that's it."

Dylan burst out from under the blanket, his dark hair mussed, his face red and swollen, his eyes tortured. He sat up, holding a rumpled piece of paper. Bobbie recognized it as a page from the Canson sketch pad she'd given him.

"I thought I could do it, but I can't!" he wept. "I wanted to because…" His voice choked.

Bobbie sat behind him and rubbed his back. "It's okay, Dylan. It's going to be okay."

Nate asked quietly, "What is it that you can't do?"

Dylan shoved the paper at him. "I can't think about what happened! Sheamus could do it! He opened his closet. I know what it means. He didn't really think there was a monster there, but he was just scared. Scared of everything. Because our mom and dad are gone and never coming back!" Dylan dissolved into noisy tears and Nate wrapped him in his arms.

Holding the boy closely, he opened the piece of paper and studied it. Bobbie saw the reaction in his eyes, then the look of misery that matched Dylan's as Nate handed it to her.

It was Dylan's sketch; the expressive lines she'd praised, indicating the movement of water, the solidity of rock. But since she'd seen it, he'd added some things. There were a few seagulls in the air, an interesting boat in the distance that was probably more creative than accurate. It was tipping sideways, as though overtaken by a wave.

Then, with a thud of her heart, she noticed people in the water. People drowning. Near the boat, two figures held hands under the water as it claimed them. Dylan's parents, she guessed. Bobbie clapped a palm to her mouth to hold back her own sob.

"Dylan," Nate said, his voice raspy. "Do you know how brave it is that you faced this? Because you did. You put it down on paper. It's an ugly thing to know, but you made yourself look at it. A lot of adults can't do that."

Dylan wrapped his arms around Nate and held on. "I thought I could do it. But I can't."

"But you did. The fact that it hurts and makes you cry doesn't mean you can't do it. You did."

Dylan finally quieted. "I hated that Sheamus always cried," he said, sniffing. "Now *I* can't stop."

"It's all right, Dyl. I cry about them all the time."

Dylan drew back, looking into Nate's tear-filled eyes. Then he fell against him again. "I guess we're a couple of dorks."

"I guess we are. Emotion isn't a bad thing. It doesn't mean you're wimpy if you cry. It just means you have feelings."

"Yeah." Dylan sounded unconvinced. He finally sat up.

Bobbie hugged him. "Want me to make you some cocoa?"

Dylan shook his head. "I feel kind of sick." He made an urgent move to get off the bed. Nate walked him into the bathroom just in time.

Bobbie straightened his sheets, smoothed out the picture he'd drawn and placed it inside his sketch pad. She opened his drapes to the sunny afternoon and could see her father, Stella and Sheamus taking turns shooting baskets. Her dad looked youthful and remarkably agile, and Stella was laughing.

Dennis lifted Sheamus on his shoulders and the boy shot. The ball bounced off the rim

of the basket and hit her father in the head.
Sheamus and Stella laughed hysterically.

Bobbie felt a twinge in the region of her
heart. This was what she'd wanted for her father all along. She wanted him to find someone to hang out with, so that she could go
to Italy without having to worry about him
worrying about *her*. He'd have his own life
to keep in order. At least, that was her theory.

Of course, this situation wasn't without its
problems, because he lived in Southern California and Stella lived here. Bobbie hoped
they would work that out, because she was
leaving.

In all the years of planning her life in Florence, Bobbie had never thought she'd miss
having a husband and family. Now she was
afraid she might. Still, she'd promised herself.
Every human being had to reach out and find
the limits of their capabilities.

Dylan came out of the bathroom, pale but
clear-eyed.

Nate yanked the quilt off the bed. "You
want to come downstairs, curl up on the sofa
and watch football?"

Dylan actually smiled.

Nate pointed him forward. "Go ahead.
Bobbie, can you grab a pillow?"

She did as he asked, and they made a comfortable cocoon for Dylan on the sofa. Nate handed him the remote. "I'll get you a glass of 7 Up. That'll taste good and help your stomach, too."

"Thanks." Dylan snuggled into his quilt and aimed the remote at the TV.

Stella, Dennis and Sheamus came through the back door as Nate poured the soft drink into a glass.

"How is he?" Stella asked quietly. Dennis and Sheamus simply went into the living room to see for themselves.

Nate gave her a brief report of what had happened while Bobbie poured coffee.

Stella's eyes filled. "Poor kid. Can I take him that?"

Nate handed her the glass.

She elbowed Bobbie as she passed her. "Good work with the art supplies. You seem to be two for two with the boys. I'm sure having that image out of his head and onto paper will give him a new perspective on everything."

Bobbie smiled but shrugged off the praise. "He did it himself. I just gave him the sketch pad and pens."

When Nate and she were alone, he caught her hand and drew her to him. "You have done a lot for Dylan," he said, "besides giving him the supplies. You've been kind and caring, you praised his work, gave him some advice, and I'm sure that helped convince him that he could create that picture." Nate pulled her into his arms and simply held her. "It was painful, and I'm sure he'll still have some bad moments, but it's an important step."

Bobbie leaned into Nate and let herself enjoy the moment. She noticed through the kitchen window that long afternoon shadows already fell on the yard. Thanksgiving Day was almost over. In less than a month, it would be Christmas and then New Year's, and before she knew it, time for her to go.

Nate kissed the top of her head and looked down at her. "You've got a death grip on me, woman. Is there something you want to tell me?"

She hesitated, gathering fortitude before pushing way and squaring her shoulders. She had to stop this. Now.

"You have to let me go, Nate."

He held up both hands. "I'm not touching you." He smiled easily as though he understood an important truth. "What's holding you captive is your own ambivalence. It isn't anything I'm doing. You care more than you want to."

She swatted his arm, exasperated. "And you shouldn't care at all. You lost your mom to what I've got, remember?"

He folded his arms. "I remember. And as soon as I was old enough to understand that everybody hurts and everybody has to deal with it, I realized I wouldn't have given up having her as my mother to spare myself the grief. She was great. She loved me. I loved her."

"You've had too many losses!" Her voice rose. She sighed and made a conscious effort to lower it. "You don't need another one. Have you no sense of self-preservation?!"

He opened his arms in a gesture of helplessness and laughed. "Apparently not."

Frustrated by his refusal to understand, she caught her jacket off the back of a kitchen chair and stormed out the back door.

"Watch the chrysanthemums!" he called after her.

NATE COULDN'T HELP punching the air in victory the moment she was out of sight. Bobbie was a complicated woman and there was no telling precisely what was going on in her head, but he saw love for him in her eyes, despite her heated claims to the contrary and her insistence that she was leaving. He felt a little like Dylan's impressive Mentos geyser in the punch bowl at the Monster Bash.

Patience was going to be required here, but he could do that. Dealing with the boys had taught him well.

BOBBIE WAS WRITING OUT her shopping list for the following day when her father came home. She'd told Nate she was going to work on the painting, but she didn't think she could look at the image of his face right now with any equanimity.

So she cut coupons, circled items on a newspaper ad, and made copious notes at the bottom of her list.

Dennis picked up Monet to sit beside her on the sofa. The cat purred and allowed himself to be cuddled in her dad's lap.

"Complicated system," he said, indicating the list with a jut of his chin. "With the circles and the arrows, it looks like a football playbook."

Bobbie glanced up at him, laughing. "A three hundred pound front line would come in handy at these sales. How's Stella?"

"Good." He sat back quietly. Bobbie saw that serene, paternal expression that had always defeated her passionate entreaties to do dangerous things when she'd been a girl.

"What's on your mind, Dad?" She pushed the ad and notes aside and gave him her full attention.

"I really like Nate and the boys," he said, leaning his head back to look at the ceiling. "And it's clear they love you. I'm not meddling, I just wonder if you're so dedicated to an old dream that you're ignoring all the new elements in your life."

At her impatient sigh, he added quickly, "I mean, I love you, and I'll support whatever you want to do. I just wonder if your great determination is the best thing here."

She'd been asking herself the same thing and had no good answer.

"I don't know, Dad. And I'm too tired to think about such heavy stuff tonight."

"Okay. I just don't want you to sacrifice all the love and warmth in your life in pursuit of your talent." Monet climbed out of his lap and onto hers. Her dad pointed to the cat. "Love will give back to you. I have no experience with what producing brilliant artwork will give you."

She fell wearily back against the sofa and stroked the purring cat. "Please don't worry, Dad. I'm thinking hard about it. What about Stella? You seem to really like each other, but you live a thousand miles apart. And are you really joining Doctors Without Borders?"

"I'm seriously considering it. And Stella's going to be a good friend, I think. She says she'll come and visit in the spring. We'll just be happy to connect when we can."

"That sounds very comfortable." Bobbie felt jealous that it could be so simple for them. "If only I could work out that kind of a relationship with Nate."

Her father put an arm around her. "Oh, sweetheart, that's the kind of relationship you have when you're old. When you're young and raising a family, it should be about passion and commitment, and working together for a shared goal."

She sighed and relaxed against him for a moment. "The problem is, we have different goals."

"You seem to have strong feelings for each other."

It was the first time she'd seriously considered the question. "We do. But we also keep sparking off each other, so I'm not sure what it means. There is passion, but I have to go and he has to stay. I don't think there's a way to fix that."

"Mmm." Her dad squeezed her shoulder bracingly. "Well, if you decide you want to, there's a way to fix everything." He smiled philosophically. "In relationships, anyway. In cars and in medicine, not so much."

"SIXTEEN PAIRS OF SOCKS," Stella said, rooting through several bags at her feet. "Sweatshirts for the boys, a Mariners hat and a couple of turtlenecks…" She, Bobbie and Sandy sat at a small table at Starbucks, their tall, whipped cream-topped coffee drinks crowded together, a sea of bags at their feet.

Bobbie laughed. "Well, that's all pretty staid. I bought a magic bra."

"Smart woman," Sandy praised, then turned sideways to show off her ample bosom in a red sweater. "But I don't need a magic bra."

Bobbie swatted her arm. "Brag, brag!"

There was quiet for a few moments while they sipped at their drinks and picked at the coffee cake. Conversation buzzed around them as shoppers came and went.

"What was your mother like?" Stella asked Bobbie. There was interest in her expression. She looked youthful today in a pink sweater, her white hair pulled back into a knot.

"Ah…" Bobbie thought about how to answer that in quick, simple terms, without recounting the million examples of how wonderful she'd been. "Very smart," she said, smiling as she remembered. "A clever, crafty person who made a fortune for her church circle at the bazaar every year, a screaming liberal who argued with my more conservative father all the time, and just a warm, loving wife and mother."

Stella's smile was bright. "Do you think she'd mind my spending time with your father?"

"She'd want him to be happy. And so do I. But isn't the distance thing going to be a problem?"

"Not for me. I have my job with Nate, I have my son. I'll want to be around. But I'd like to visit in the spring and see what his life in California is like." Stella patted Bobbie's hand affectionately. "It's hard to imagine that I met him only four days ago." She put her hand over her eyes and made a small sound of distress. "It's a wonder I didn't kill him when I pinned him to the floor with the mop."

"What?" Sandy asked.

Laughing, Stella told her the story.

Sandy laughed, too, then her expression turned wistful as she picked coffee cake crumbs off her napkin with her index finger.

Stella dabbed at her lips with her napkin, then picked up her purse. "Excuse me, girls, while I run to the ladies'. Don't touch my coffee cake."

"What can I do for you?" Bobbie asked Sandy. "Besides get you a fork?"

She sat back in her chair with a look of dismay. "I don't think you can do anything for me," she said frankly, "but if you don't mind listening to me whine a little…"

"By all means. Whine away."

"I think the only reason Hunter agreed to go out with me was because he didn't know how to say no." Sandy made that simple declaration, then leaned forward again, her eyes dark with distress. "I don't really understand what's wrong, but I'm definitely sensing that I want this relationship more than he does. He seemed to like my mom, and he's surprisingly good with the girls for a man who has no experience with children. But when we're together, he looks like he'd rather be anywhere else than with me."

"You're a hard driver, Sandy, and he's kind of laid-back." Bobbie placed an apologetic hand on her arm. "Maybe you scare him a little. Sometimes you scare me, and I know and love you."

Sandy nodded and fiddled with her spoon. "Yeah. I just like him so much. And the feeling seemed to be mutual, but I think he's pulling away."

Bobbie put an arm around her shoulders. "This is something you can't force to work out through sheer will and determination. He knows how you feel, so let him come the rest of the way. Give him time to get to know all your wonderful qualities."

Stella returned, frowning at the serious expressions on their faces. "Everything okay?" She studied Sandy worriedly. "Sandy?"

"We're fine, Stella." Sandy caught her hand and pulled her gently into her chair. "Bobbie was just giving me advice. Sort of like a life coach. But she plans to leave her own budding romance behind, and live a life of celibacy in Italy?"

"Celibacy?" Bobbie teased. "Who said anything about celibacy? Solitude, maybe."

Sandy laughed and downed the last of her latte. "Yeah. You're such a wild woman. Why don't you just take Nate and the boys with you?"

Bobbie groaned and let her head fall back. "Please! I just went through that with my father. I have to go alone. Sandy, you know why it's so important to me."

Her friend was suddenly quiet. "I think I do, Bobbie. But I wonder if you do."

Oh, no. Not another one.

"What does that mean?" she asked, her tone testy.

Sandy didn't seem to want to say.

Bobbie leaned toward her. "You can tell me. I may slug you after, but you can tell me."

She began intrepidly. "You made this promise to yourself when you weren't sure you'd survive treatment. I think it's come to mean life to you. You think you have to fulfill the promise—move to Florence, make art— or..." She sighed and forced the words out. "Or you'll die."

Bobbie rolled her eyes. "That's ridiculous. My life depends on those contrary mutating genes, not on where I choose to live."

Sandy patted her hand. "Then why are we arguing? Let's get to Ross's before all the good stuff is gone."

"Fine." They stood, gathering up packages. Bobbie punched Sandy on the arm before she picked up her bags. She smiled at Stella's surprise. "I told her I'd slug her."

Sandy punched her back. "And sometimes *I* scare *you?*"

DYLAN WASN'T SURE he understood what was going on here. Uncle Nate, Dennis, Hunter, he and Sheamus were scattered across the

living room, watching football and eating all
kinds of stuff he and Sheamus weren't usually allowed to eat unless there were vegetables with it. They had pizza without the salad;
hot wings without celery and carrot sticks;
jalapeño and cheddar potato chips, corn chips
with guacamole—he thought that was kind of
gross, but everybody else seemed to like it;
and taquitos with hot sauce. He really liked
those.

It was a great day. All the women were
shopping and the men did nothing but sit
around and watch football. He sat on the sofa
between Uncle Nate and Hunter, and Sheamus sat on the love seat with Dennis. They
passed food around and he and Sheamus had
as much pop as they wanted.

By the middle of the afternoon, Uncle Nate
had put the food away but left the chips, and
brought out cookies they'd gone to the bakery
for this morning. Then he handed everyone a
Snickers ice cream bar from the freezer.

They put their feet on the coffee table and
burped out loud. They did have to say, "Excuse me."

When Uncle Nate went to the kitchen to get
Dennis more coffee, Dylan elbowed Hunter.
"How come we get to do this?" he asked.

"Because it's a day without women," Uncle

Nate's friend said. "We still have to be sort of civilized, but we can eat what we want without having to worry about whether or not it's fattening, or good for us, and enjoy the fact that there's no one around telling us to put our feet down, or wanting us to turn off football and watch the Hallmark Channel. It doesn't happen very often, so we try to take advantage of it when it does."

"We don't like having women around?"

"No, it's not that at all. But sometimes we have more fun as guys when they're not here."

Dylan didn't quite get that, but didn't care. He was having a great time. And his uncle seemed to be nicer lately. Or maybe it was just that things didn't seem quite as awful to Dylan as they had for a long time. The last few days, everybody was getting along better in the house, but he'd noticed that Bobbie hadn't come over today before going shopping. She and Uncle Nate usually saw each other every day. He'd even seen them hugging. It would be cool if she moved in, but he'd heard his uncle say she was going to Italy after Christmas. That was across the ocean and you had to fly there, or take a cruise.

Hunter and Uncle Nate had talked about women while making coffee in the kitchen. Hunter was saying he didn't understand them,

and Uncle Nate said he'd like to help him, but
didn't understand them, either. Dennis had
said that you had to love them without understanding them or you'd go crazy.

Hunter had asked him how you could ever
love something you didn't understand. Dennis had smiled and told him that if he loved
a woman, he'd find out.

Hunter leaned toward Dylan now and
asked, "Would you go get us another ice
cream bar?"

"Uncle Nate usually only lets us have one
at a time," he answered, then remembered
that this was Life without Women Day and
that rule might not apply.

"Me, too!" Sheamus pleaded, then turned
to Dennis. "You want another one?"

Bobbie's father nodded. "Yes, please."

Dylan went into the kitchen and relayed
the unanimous request to his uncle, who was
pouring coffee into this tall thing that kept it
warm.

"Sure." He pointed to the freezer at the bottom of the fridge. "Help yourself."

Dylan hadn't thought about it before, but
since he'd drawn the picture and had to think
about what had happened to his parents, it
didn't exactly hurt less, but he felt a little better about the fact that he and Sheamus and

Uncle Nate were still here. And that Uncle Nate was taking care of them.

"Do you know Justin Parker?" he asked as he dug the ice cream bars out of the freezer.

His uncle screwed the top on the coffee thing. "Think so. The blond kid that helped you with the Mentos geyser."

"Yeah. Did you know his mom died?"

Uncle Nate turned to look at him. "No. I know Mr. and Mrs. Berg have a foster home and he lives with them."

"Yeah. When his mom died, his dad left. Justin doesn't know where he is." He was having trouble holding four bars and his uncle reached above his head to get a bowl for him to drop them in.

"That's terrible about Justin."

"Yeah. And people don't like to adopt older kids."

"Who told you that?"

"Justin. Some other foster kid told him. So, Mr. and Mrs. Berg are nice and everything, but he's really lonesome." Dylan drew a deep breath and looked into his uncle's eyes. He was beginning to realize that saying thank-you about big things was hard. He sucked it up. "I'm really glad Sheamus and I didn't have to go live with a foster family," he said quickly. "I'm glad Dad had a brother."

Uncle Nate was quiet for a minute, then he said, his voice a little funny, "Yeah, me, too. It helps me a lot to have you and Sheamus."

Dylan didn't know what to say after that, so he ran off with the ice cream bars. But he felt good. And it had been such a long time since he'd been anything near happy.

NATE WENT TO Rolling Thunder Barbecue for ribs, beans, potato salad and rolls. When he returned home, a bright yellow envelope stuck out of his mailbox. "I KNOW WHAT YOU DID" was written in capital letters on the front. He ripped it open and unfolded a plain white note card. "And that was the sweetest, most generous thing anyone's ever done for us," it read. "Thank you, Nate! Our daughter sent us a check. Here you are. We'll tell everyone we know what a good man you are."

Nate pocketed the note and smiled to himself. He was beginning to understand that there were all kinds of things in life that simply didn't show up on a profit and loss statement.

He went inside to serve dinner and turn on *The Dirty Dozen*. Sheamus was fast asleep, but Dylan was wide-awake and soon totally absorbed in the movie.

While completely upside down about his relationship with Bobbie, Nate was happy and hopeful over his brief conversation with Dylan about his friend in foster care. Nate knew it didn't mean all their problems were resolved, but there was an understanding at the base of their relationship that could be built on as Dylan grew older and communication probably got harder.

They were all in a stupor of overindulgence when the women returned around 8:00 p.m. Nate heard them in the kitchen and was a little surprised to hear laughter, since they'd been up since 5:00 a.m. Maybe being without men was as good for them as being without women had been for him and Hunter and Dennis.

Still, each man's head turned toward the kitchen and the bubbling sound of female conversation. There was crunching plastic, rustling paper and—he couldn't quite believe his ears—giggles.

He got up to investigate. They were all standing around the table, an enormous pile of bags, paper and a lot of things they'd bought strewn across it.

Bobbie had a knitted hat made to resemble a raccoon sitting atop her head. It was too small for her, but he gathered from her remarks that it was one of two she'd bought, for Addie and Zoey.

Sandy ran a hand over a dark blue sweater. "My!" Stella said. "Cashmere. Is that for Hunter?"

Stella had pulled on a plush yellow bathrobe for her daughter and she looked a little like a tall Easter "Peep" when she leaned over to touch the sweater.

"I can't believe," Nate said, walking bravely into the middle of their estrogen-infested area, "that you've been shopping for fifteen hours."

All three women turned to him with smiles. Despite their joviality, they did look tired.

"We shopped for about twelve hours," Bobbie corrected, covering a yawn. She looked soft and sleepy. He felt completely disarmed. "We spent the other three eating and drinking coffee."

The room was suddenly filled with Hunter and Dennis, the boys and Arnold.

Bobbie pulled a squeaky toy shaped like a bone out of a bag and tossed it at the dog, which leaped into the air bit down on it, making any conversation impossible for the next minute. A one-note squeak repeated over and over.

Nate smiled at her flatly. "Thanks a lot, Bobbie."

"Sure." She studied him as though he puzzled her, then he realized she was probably uncertain what to do about her feelings for him. Another point for his side.

She turned with a smile to everyone else. "Hi, Dad. Hi, guys. Hey, Hunter." She delved into another bag and surfaced with two miniature Christmas trees. She worked a switch on the bottom and they lit up, each decorated with tiny ornaments. She held them out to the boys. "For your rooms."

"Cool." Dylan took his from her. "Thank you, Bobbie."

"You're welcome. I bought a couple of other little things to put you in the holiday spirit, but I'm not sure which bag they're in. I'll bring them by tomorrow."

Sheamus held his tree as though it were a puppy. "My own tree!" he said. He smiled up at Nate. "I wish Bobbie lived *here!*"

A sudden silence fell and vague discomfort filled the room.

Bobbie pulled the raccoon hat off her head and ruffled Sheamus's hair. "Well, I'm close enough that you can run over anytime," she said bracingly.

"Yeah." Sheamus sounded halfhearted, but with another look at his tree, he perked up again and took off to put it in his room. Dylan followed, and Arnold raced after them, squeaking his toy as he pranced in their wake.

"Need a ride home?" Hunter asked Sandy.

She seemed surprised by the invitation. "Yes, please," she replied, watching him a little warily as he picked up her things

"Okay, well..." Arms loaded with Sandy's purchases, Hunter started for the door. "Thanks, Nate. Most fun I've had in ages. Take care, Dennis. Bye, guys!" he shouted toward the stairs.

Sandy ran ahead of him to open the door. Nate flipped on the outside lights. He couldn't hear their conversation as they packed the back of Hunter's car, but it sounded increasingly agitated. By the time they were both in the front seat, voices were raised and they were too busy arguing to wave as Hunter backed out of the driveway. Nate watched them go, wondering what had happened.

In the kitchen, Dennis and Stella seemed to be making a date for breakfast. *Good,* he thought.

Bobbie was moving her purchases from bag to bag, trying, he guessed, to make a more manageable burden.

"Want me to help you carry that stuff home?" he asked.

She gave him that wary look again. "I've got it," she said. "Thanks, though."

"Don't forget to get your car washed this weekend at the mini-mart," he told her as Dennis took some bags from her, preparing to leave. "All proceeds for the food bank. And the Urban and the coffee house are donating half their proceeds. Why don't we all meet for dinner Sunday night, my treat?"

"Deal," Dennis said. "But I'll split the bill with you. And isn't there a bake sale somewhere?"

"St. Mary's," Nate replied. "Next weekend. I think the schedule was in Wednesday's paper."

Dennis made a face and tipped his head toward his daughter. "That's too bad. This one used it for strategizing her shopping. Anything of a news nature is illegible or cut out."

Nate laughed. He turned to catch Bobbie's glance, but she was already out the door. "We won't miss anything, trust me. See you Sunday."

"And I'll see you in the morning!" Stella shouted to Dennis over Nate's shoulder.

"Watch out for the chrysanthemums!" Nate warned as they reached the edge of his property. He saw them move more slowly, step carefully over the mums, then finally reach the path lit by Bobbie's back porch light. He closed the door and turned to find Stella right behind him. She was smiling brightly.

"I feel thirty years old tonight," she said. "Well, my feet feel sixty-seven, but the woman inside feels thirty. When I *was* thirty, I had children and a job, and shopping had to be done quickly. Today, we just had fun. It was wonderful."

"I'm glad you had fun. And I'm glad you're enjoying Dennis's company." Nate teased her with a frown. "But if he talks you into moving to California, the boys and I will be very upset."

"That won't happen." She gathered up shopping bags, letting him carry half as he walked her to the door. "What are you going to do about Bobbie?"

"I'm working on that."

"Have you told her that you love her?"

He sighed. "No, she wouldn't want to hear it. At least, that's been the case in the past. Things may be shifting in my favor, but I'm not buying any advertising yet."

Stella opened the front door and took the bags from him. One of them tipped sideways and spilled more than a dozen pairs of socks onto the porch.

Nate looked from them to her. "Is there a centipede on your list?" he asked.

CHAPTER TWELVE

BOBBIE DELIVERED HER commission on Monday to praise and flattering enthusiasm from the law firm's partners. Sandy winked at her as one of the men took down four flower prints hanging across the back of the room and personally replaced them with her quotes from Oliver Wendell Holmes scripted in calligraphy on her handmade paper. Bobbie was proud of the pieces and thought how much in her life had changed since she'd come to Astoria to complete them.

And now she could focus full-time on the painting for the fund-raiser.

The following Friday, she was ready to abandon her workroom for a day with her energetic art class. She had the children hard at work on stars with glitter, bells, candy canes, snowflakes and other symbols of Christmas. Fernanda patrolled the room to prevent anyone from gluing hair or fingers. There was glitter everywhere, but it gave her little students a sort of fairy-tale look Bobbie enjoyed as she walked among them.

Crystal Moreno, a usually quiet and hard-working little girl with long dark hair and enormous eyes, chose to draw on her star rather than apply glitter. The subject appeared to be female, with long brown hair and wide red lips. Crystal had put glitter in her eyes.

"That's a pretty face," Bobbie exclaimed. "Is she someone you know?"

"That's my mom," she said, adding eye-lashes.

"Well, she's very pretty. She'll like that star a lot."

"It's for my dad," the girl said matter-of-factly. "He's in jail and can't come home for Christmas. He didn't do anything bad," she added, as though accustomed to having to ex-plain herself. "We didn't have food one time 'cause he didn't have a job anymore, and he took money from a store."

Horrified that this little child had to deal with such a thing, Bobbie got down on one knee beside her desk, wanting to offer com-fort, but not sure what to say. Fortunately, Crystal was chatty.

"He wants my mom to get a divorce," she said, looking lost. "But she got mad at him when he said that. They had a fight. I'm going to give this to him when we visit."

"I'm sure he'll love it. But what about one with your face, too. And…do you have brothers and sisters?"

"I have a little sister."

"I'll get you two more stars. If you don't finish today, don't worry. I'll help you next week. Maybe we could even put them on a string to remind your dad how you're all waiting for him to come home."

The little girl brightened visibly. "Okay."

Bobbie stood to find Fernanda right behind her. "I'll get the stars," the woman said.

Bobbie continued to circulate among the children, making a mental note to tell Nate about the family and see if one of the holiday gift baskets could be earmarked for them.

The session ended in an enthusiastic but chaotic cleanup and a spirited race for the door when it was time for lunch. Crystal came to wrap her arms around Bobbie's waist, then ran off to follow her friends.

Fernanda helped Bobbie store the unfinished ornaments until the next week's session. "Have you ever thought of getting licensed to hold art therapy classes?" she asked. "You seem to have a gift for helping children with their problems through artwork."

Bobbie dismissed her praise with a shake of her head. "Thank you, but I operate more on gut instinct than knowledge. And, really, I don't know how much it'll help." Just yesterday she'd have said, "Besides, I'm moving to Italy after the holidays," but today, for the first time since she'd made the decision to go, she wasn't sure she would.

"You should think about it, Bobbie. My husband is a psychologist. I know he could point you in the right direction for classes to become certified."

"Thank you, Fernanda." Bobbie gave her a quick hug, then brushed glitter off her shoulder. "I'm going to miss you when this is over. Only one more class."

"I'll miss you. This had been more fun than it usually is. And that's all thanks to you."

"That's sweet of you, Fernanda. See you next week. I'm bringing cookies."

"Great. I'll arrange for milk and hot chocolate."

On her way home, Bobbie pulled up at her favorite viewing spot overlooking the river. It was a beautiful day, with big puffy clouds floating in a row above the subtly purple hills on the Washington side. The water was like glass today, only a red-and-black freighter at anchor disturbing the surface.

It was difficult to admit how much she would hate leaving Astoria. She'd come to love the town and the people so much. Nate in particular. And her feelings for him were now so strong that she wanted to stay with him.

Her painting of him was a testament to her feelings. Though he was shown only in profile, he looked handsome, slightly brooding, a young man of the sea at his prime. He gazed over the river as though dreaming of a woman he'd left behind in some exotic locale. Bobbie wanted to think that in quiet moments, he dreamed of *her*. She was proud of the painting, though it was as much a reflection of how she felt as it was an image of him and the old riverfront.

He was everything a woman could ever want—if she didn't want to go to Florence, too.

Bobbie sat staring at the mountains and the clouds, and wondered why she'd felt so driven to make this trip. Was Sandy right— that the idea gave her hope, and as long as she did what she'd promised herself, she believed she wouldn't die?

Bobbie considered that. Last year she'd have told anyone who asked that if she wasn't able to devote herself completely to her art, her life would be shortened. That was before she'd fallen in love with Nate, Dylan and Sheamus. Research had proved that love could lengthen a life, but, ideally, she'd want to stay with them for what she could give them, not for what they could give her. The question was, could she still be a loving, giving woman if she let her dream go and stayed with them?

The answer, she realized with sudden insight, was that she could if she was determined to. Love wasn't a blast of emotion showered on one by fate. It was a decision made and recommitted to every day.

She felt a stirring of character muscle—a fragile one, she decided, laughing at the word. She could do this.

If Nate still wanted her to.

SANDY MADE A TURN in front of the mirror at Clarissa's in a long-sleeved, loose-fitting, emerald-green gown.

"Too much for Astoria?" She looked doubtfully at her reflection.

Bobbie went to stand beside her in a red taffeta dress that hugged her waist and skimmed her ankles. It had a V-neck and cap sleeves, simplicity lending it drama. Her hair was growing, she noted in some surprise as she studied herself. Her curls had quieted and the little bit of length gave more volume. She was herself again—not quite the girl in her art school graduation photo, but who wanted to go backward, anyway?

"There's no such thing as 'too much' for the holidays. Turn around and let's see the back."

Sandy turned dutifully, looking elegant and graceful.

"It's exquisite," Bobbie said, thrilled by a new sense of comfort with herself. She patted her hair. "You think we should use glitter hair spray?"

Sandy gave her an affectionate shove. "No. You don't need anything artificial to make you sparkle. You're in love with Nate, aren't you?"

Bobbie drew a deep breath and said it aloud. "I'm in love with Nate."

"Does he know?

"I think so. He just doesn't know that I know."

After giving her a hug, Sandy turned her toward the dressing rooms. "I'm so happy. Let's go get some lunch, then not eat again until the dance. One rice cracker and I won't be able to fit into this!"

NATE HOSTED THE last formal meeting of the
food bank committee before the highlight
event on Saturday. Sandy's report on the raffle items collected was very impressive, and
various subcommittee reports on decorations,
menu, entertainment, cleanup and scores of
other details showed they were on track and
on time.

Even Sandy seemed a little stunned. Actually, Nate thought, she seemed sedated. Her
usually lively personality was nowhere in ev-
idence, though her organizational skills certainly were. He wondered if her behavior had
anything to do with Hunter's sudden call from
an important client who needed him across
town immediately—just before the meeting
began.

"I didn't hear your phone ring," Nate had
challenged when his friend said he had to
leave. Hunter had shrugged into his jacket.
"He texted me," he said flatly. "Want me
to bring pizzas for the office when I come
back?"

"Sure. Thanks."

"Your meeting will be over by then, right?"

"Yes."

"Good. See you around twelve-thirty." And
he'd disappeared just as Sandy's car pulled up.

Sandy tried to force a smile now. "Well, troops. I think we've done it. So, we'll all be there Friday night to set up...." She turned to Nate. "The painting is gorgeous. You are very impressive as an Old Astoria ship captain."

She indicated the picture Bobbie had delivered to Nate the day before. He'd taken down a ship's wheel that had hung near the conference table and put up Bobbie's work.

He turned to look at it. The canvas was almost monochromatic, with the soft gray to dark blue tones of a typical Astoria day in winter. The background was a representation of the Butterfly Fleet, the ship that Nate's sea captain would have sailed to Astoria, and the piers and canneries along the riverbank. Splashes of red, yellow and orange suggested figures on the pier and others barely visible on the boats.

What made his heart swell, though, was the figure in the forefront that represented the several hours he'd posed in Bobbie's workroom. He knew he was not that handsome, didn't have that much character in his chin or heroic attitude in the angle of his head. There was a longing in his every waking moment, though, that matched the expression in the captain's eyes as he looked out on the river.

Bobbie Molloy loved him.

He tore his eyes from the painting and bowed. "Thank you, thank you. Anything for the team."

"I'm sure all those hours spent alone with that pretty artist were hard on you," Jerry Gold said with a flat smile. "Poor guy."

Clarissa, seated next to Jerry, swatted him with her notes. "Leave him alone. We've all been in love. Only trouble is that now he'll *never* get to meetings on time."

Mike Wallis laughed. "Ticket sales are brisk," he said. "We've made several thousand dollars already, and I'm sure sales will increase at the dance when guests can actually see the items in the raffle. The *Daily Astorian*'s photographs in last Friday's paper got the buzz going."

Sandy heaved a sigh. "Well, we should be proud of ourselves. I think we're going to pull this off."

"You've done a superb job," Clarissa declared. "I think we already have more money than anybody's ever raised for anything around here. Well done, Sandy." She began to applaud, and everyone joined her.

To their astonishment, Sandy closed her folder, snatched up her purse and ran from the room, her chin trembling. There was an awkward moment of silence while everyone stared after her.

Clarissa cleared her throat and briskly began to pack up. "She's probably exhausted herself." Then she grinned around the table. "And you all make me want to burst into tears, too. See everyone Friday night?"

The group dispersed to go back to their workplaces. Nate walked them to the door and marveled at how generous they were with their time and enthusiasm.

But what was wrong with Sandy?

He asked Hunter when he came back with the pizza.

The girls were eating in the conference room and Nate made a fresh pot of coffee while Hunter scoured the utility drawer for a server.

"She ran out of here like her heart was broken," Nate said. Hunter glowered at him. "Just because you've been immortalized by the woman you love as a heroic seaman from another age, don't expect everything to work out for everyone."

Okay. So Bobbie's feelings for him were apparent to everyone. Nate had a hard time mustering any embarrassment about that.

"What happened?" he asked bravely.

Hunter slashed him with a look. He was

shorter than Nate but beefier, and had Nate been any less sure of his friendship, he'd have withdrawn the question. "Come on." He grinned. "I'd make kindling of you in a heartbeat."

"Raleigh," Hunter said in complete annoyance. He'd found the server and slammed it on the counter. "It's my business, okay? I owe you a lot, but not an explanation of my romantic failures."

"Failures? She looks at you like she's waited for you her whole life. Disagreeing on some issue doesn't make *you* a failure. What happened?"

Hunter picked up the utensil, and Nate was afraid for a moment that he was about to be served up in eight pieces. But Hunter simply turned around to lean a hip on the counter and groan in anguish.

"I have nothing, Nate, to support a family. I have a twelve-year-old car, I live in an apartment and I still owe thirty-two thousand bucks on the credit card I used to buy equipment and outfit my office before I lost it all. She's serious *now*. She wants a husband and a father for her girls *now*. I'm trying to resist getting too serious until I win the lottery or go to Vegas and make a killing."

"You think either of those things is likely?"

"No. But it's more likely than being able to save enough to marry a family of three." He looked down at his shoes, morose, defeated. "She doesn't understand. She makes a fair amount and has health insurance, but it'd take both of us working full-time to cover my bills, too. The girls will soon be in school and they should live in a house with a yard and a swing set." He looked up at Nate, clearly miserable. "Sandy thinks love will conquer all."

Nate was counting on that working for him. He tried to think clearly. "Do you need a raise?"

Hunter threatened him with the server. "You already pay me more than the big firms pay a CPA. No, I have to find a way out from under the debt I carry from the embezzlement. And I just don't see that happening except month by month in a tediously slow process. The girls will be teenagers before I'm clear."

"Hunter, if she loves you and you love her, you'll figure it—"

"No," he said simply. "I'm not going to let her assume part of my debt."

"And she doesn't get that?"

He grinned mirthlessly. "Not at all. She figures that means I don't really love her, and that I don't want to marry her because I don't want to take on two little girls."

"I suppose you've tried to explain how you feel?"

"You've seen her in action. You don't explain to Sandy. You listen or you comply with whatever it is she wants." He shook his head and straightened. "Well, she's not going to win this one. Come on. Let's go get some of that pizza before Jonni and Karen eat it all."

ON WEDNESDAY, THERE was an afternoon Christmas musical program at school. Bobbie, Dennis and Stella went together and Nate arrived just before it began.

Sheamus seemed more interested in the room's architecture than singing, but Dylan was into it, working his bracelet of bells in accompaniment to the tune. End of the year was exhausting for accountants, but Nate felt grateful to have this pure moment of Christmas cheer.

After the concert, he hurried to say hello to Stella, shook hands with Dennis and was pleasantly surprised when Bobbie caught his hand.

"Hi," she said softly. "I don't suppose you have time to talk?"

He glanced at his watch and shook his head

apologetically. He'd have done anything to be able to say yes, but he had a call scheduled with the Binghams' IRS agent, who was beginning to see things their way. "I'm sorry. I've got an important date with the IRS in about fifteen minutes. Can we talk tonight?"

"Sure. You've been coming home late the last few nights. End-of-the-year deadlines, huh?"

He raised an eyebrow. "Roberta Louise, have you been spying on me?"

"Yeah. Just a little."

"Well, I'll be on time tonight."

"All right, I'll see you then. Go, so you're not late for your call."

He wasn't, and it went well. Nate packed up his briefcase just before five, feeling victorious and really, really satisfied. The IRS had accepted the Binghams' offer and the reverse mortgage process had begun.

In a happy mood, he now focused on what it was Bobbie might want to talk about. Still distracted by the thought, he locked the office door behind him and started off in the direction of his car, until the blare of a horn stopped him. He looked up to find a familiar red truck parked in front. The passenger door swung open and Bobbie leaned across the seat, one hand on the steering wheel, the other beckoning to him.

"Hey, sailor," she said with a flirtatious batting of her eyelashes. She wore a white turtleneck with a silver snowflake pendant around her neck. "Can I take you somewhere?"

He stared, wondering if he'd heard her correctly. She really did want to talk. "Ah…"

"Stella and my father are with the boys," she coaxed. "Nothing to worry about. My dad's a doctor."

Nate put a hand to his heart. "I feel like *I* need a doctor. You're sure you have the right sailor?"

"I'm positive," she said with flattering certainty. "Get in before I embarrass us both by hauling you in."

He slipped his briefcase behind the seat and climbed into the front, his heart palpitating just a little. "What's going on?" he asked.

"I told you we need to talk." She checked her side mirror and pulled into traffic. Darkness had fallen and Astoria's rush hour was fully in play. Headlights swerved around them and a horn honked loudly. "I want to take you to one of my favorite places."

He buckled his seat belt. "We're going to Florence?"

She drove with scary abandon. Or maybe

he was dreaming and the world was flying past him.

"No." She laughed lightly. "There's an overlook on Grand where I always stop on my way home from school. I'd like to share it with you."

"You want to share something special with me," he taunted gently, holding on as she drove hell-for-leather. "You who insists that this relationship can never be anything but—"

"Yeah, well, that's all about to change." She smiled at the road. "If you still want it to, that is?"

If he still wanted it to change. He had to lean back and draw a breath. And that had nothing to do with the fact that they nearly rammed a camper moving too slowly for her. She swerved and roared ahead of it.

"So, you're telling me you're…staying?"

"Would you like me to?"

She made a quick right turn and drove up the Sixteenth Street hill to Grand and turned right again. She pulled up in the middle of the block and parked where a deep lawn attached to the Grandview B and B sloped down, clearing a dramatic view of rooftops and the Columbia River. It was breathtaking during the day. Tonight, several cargo ships had dropped anchor in the channel, waiting for space to offload upriver in Portland. They were brilliantly lit under a rare starry winter sky, their glow reflected in the water.

She was out of the truck before he could do the gentlemanly thing and hold her door. She ran around the hood, caught his hand and drew him to the edge of the lawn. "Look at that!" she breathed, awe in her voice. "I'll never get used to how magnificent that is. I've painted it in my mind a dozen times, but I have to really do it when all my work responsibilities are met. I've decided that I can't leave it." She tightened her grip on his hand and turned to look up at him. "Or you."

She added the last two words very softly. He was sure he'd misheard her.

"Did you say," he asked, barely breathing, "that you didn't want to leave me? Nathan Jeremy Raleigh. Me?"

Her face was lit by the spotlights surrounding the B and B. Her eyes were a little anxious, but filled with a wonderful softness as they looked into his.

"I love you, Nathan Jeremy Raleigh," she said, without pausing for breath, "and while I was sure for so long that any deviation from my Italy plan was lax and cowardly, I just realized that I promised *myself,* and that I can cut *myself* some slack. Plans can change when events warrant it, no matter how true to yourself you want to be."

She turned to place her hands at his waist and lean into him. The tender surrender of that action touched him to the center of his being.

He looped his arms around her. She felt so slight in his embrace. He had to hear the words. "So, you're staying?"

Her eyes widened. "Do you still *want* me to stay?"

"More than I want my next breath."

She wrapped her arms around him and held on. "Then I'm staying. But I'd like to reserve the right to go to Florence for a month one summer. Maybe take you and the boys with me."

He'd never been the kind of man who'd been able to get in touch with his feminine side. All he'd ever found there was the desire for more hot wings, more football, a greater need to keep emotional stuff close to his core. The boys might have forced him to dig deep and find a paternal side, but there wasn't much female about that. Still, tears bit the backs of his eyes.

Nate blinked quickly and rested his cheek atop her head. Her hair was silky and smelled of pomegranate. "Bobbie, is that a proposal?"

Puzzlement puckered her forehead. She seemed to be thinking back. "Didn't *you* propose to *me?*"

"When?"

"Um…I don't know. I mean, you're always saying we should be together. Hmm. You never did ask me?"

"Not in so many words, but let me correct that. Bobbie, will you marry me?"

"Yes," she replied in a breathless voice.

"Then, yes," he said. "I'll marry you, too."

"Good. That'll work best."

ARMS STILL ENTWINED, they looked into each other's eyes and, curiously, she giggled and he laughed. It had been such an ordeal to get to this point.

She grew suddenly serious. "What we have to talk about sometime is the boys. I mean, they know I was sick, but they should be gently prepared in case…"

He squeezed her to him to stop her. "You know, anyone can die at any time. I don't know that it's necessary to make them worry about it when your foreseeable future is bright."

She seemed about to disagree, then nodded. "It's your call."

He held her even tighter, feeling humbled

yet fiercely possessive. "You're always saying you don't have forever, but I think the only way to approach our lives is as though we do. And who knows that we don't?"

SHE SO WANTED to believe that. In fact, at that moment, she did. All the cavalier acceptance of a shortened life was gone and she wanted to reach old age with Nate more than she'd ever wanted anything.

"You're right," she said, reaching up to kiss him again. "We'll operate on the belief that we do have forever, and that Florence will always be there."

His loving gaze ensnared her. Love rained over her, wound around her, seeped into her pores and probably changed the construction of her DNA. It might even have killed her cancer, she felt so changed.

He leaned over to kiss her thoroughly. "I don't want to leave you," he said. She loved that light in his eyes. But then she couldn't see his eyes because he was kissing her again.

When he finally came up for air, they both laughed. He hesitated before suggesting, "Since the boys are well cared for, let's get something to eat. I'm starving."

They were heading toward her truck when she stopped suddenly, remembering Crystal and her family. "Oh! I wanted to tell you about a little girl in my art class," she said.

"Yes?"

Bobbie explained about Crystal's father.

"Okay." Nate frowned. "I can get them food and presents for Christmas. I'm not sure I can do anything about her dad's jail time, but there might be someone in Sandy's office who could help. I'll call her."

"That would be wonderful."

His frown deepened. "Did you know she and Hunter are off? At least for the moment. He's broke and worried about how to support them if they got married, and she insists she's working so it shouldn't be a problem. She doesn't want to wait. But he doesn't want her to take on his debt from the embezzlement. They're at an impasse."

So that was it. "I wondered what was going on. She hasn't answered my calls. Darn." Bobbie gave Nate a wan smile. "Isn't there someone in your arsenal of friends who can fix *that?*"

"I wish. Let's celebrate *us* right now. Come on, I'll take you to The Rio. Please drive carefully. We have a lot to live for and you're a bit of a cowgirl behind the wheel."

She laughed and kissed him soundly. "I

love you, Nate. Do you want me to pick you up at work Friday to help decorate the Banker's Suite, or will you have time? I know you have deadlines."

"Hunter volunteered to stay and work. I imagine he'd rather put in overtime than have to deal with Sandy. I'll have to go home and change first, so I'll drive you."

"You're afraid of my driving, aren't you?"

"Yes."

"You keep gasping."

"You keep tailgating and cutting people off. But I adore you."

"It's a good thing I adore you, too, or I'd be offended."

He laughed and climbed into the truck as she ran around to the driver's side.

AFTER DINNER, BOBBIE drove Nate to his car, then headed home. Nate returned just after she did, freeing Stella and Bobbie's father of their babysitting duties. Dennis walked into the kitchen and stopped in the doorway as Bobbie puttered with the teakettle. His blue eyes were wide with anticipation, since she'd shared her plan for the evening with him.

"Well?" he asked.

She threw her arms around him and held

him fiercely. "You're going to get to pay for a wedding, Dad!"

He cheered loudly and lifted her off her feet.

CHAPTER THIRTEEN

BOBBIE WENT TO Sandy's Thursday night with a Christmas movie for the girls, a bottle of white zinfandel and a big bag of Cheetos. Sandy did not seem happy to see her.

"I've got so much to do before tomorrow." She pointed to a kitchen table covered with gold stars and several rolls of fishing line. "I have to—"

"I'm here to help," Bobbie said, trying to push her way in.

Sandy stopped her. "You're here to talk about Hunter and I don't want to."

Bobbie stood her ground. "A year ago when I didn't want to talk about my fear of dying, you made me do it. You said you'd read that it was important to face it, then put it aside. Well, that's what you have to do with Hunter. Let's talk and see if it's something that can be fixed, and if it can't, he's not the only wolf in the forest."

Sandy blinked. "Wolf in the forest?"

"Fish in the sea is so cliché. Especially in Astoria."

Sandy rolled her eyes and let her in. The girls jumped up and down when they saw her because she usually brought presents. They were ecstatic with the movie. Sandy went into the living room to start it for them. When she returned, she handed Bobbie a spool of fishing line and a pair of scissors. "I need ten two-foot lengths, ten eighteen-inch lengths and about twenty twelve-inch lengths. We're going to tie them to the stars and attach them to the Banker's Suite ceiling."

Bobbie put the wine in the refrigerator and the Cheetos bag on the counter. She reached for a yardstick on the far side of the table and sat down to work.

"He doesn't love me," Sandy said, reaching for a box of plain ornaments in red, green, gold and silver. She applied a sticker to each one. It read "An Old Astoria Christmas."

"You know that isn't the problem," Bobbie scolded gently as she reeled out a length of line. "Are those ornaments table favors?"

"Yes. And how do *you* know what the problem is?"

"Nate told me."

She looked indignant. "Hunter told *him?*"

"Well, of course. He's entitled to a confidant. He's as upset as you are. He's just trying to do the noble thing, Sandy."

"I know. But if we wait until he can support us without me helping to pay off his old debts, we'll never be able to be together. What purpose does that serve? He gets to maintain his pride while the girls and I go without a husband and father?"

Bobbie smiled at her patiently. "It isn't simply pride. He knows you've worked hard to take care of the girls on your own, and he doesn't want you to have to take on his problems."

Sandy dropped an ornament back on the table and started to cry. "I thought this was going to work," she wept. "I thought I'd finally found someone who'd be the kind of man I was looking for when I got married the first time."

"Come on. You're mad at him because you can't have your way. That isn't fair. Give him a little time to come up with a solution."

"And what would that be that wouldn't take us into old age?"

"I don't know, but miracles happen all the time. And it's the season. Don't be angry at him for refusing to use you."

Sandy put both hands over her face and continued to sob. "I just want to love him."

"Trust is part of loving. Trust him to find a solution and don't just walk off because you can't have it all your way."

Sandy glared at her. "You're going to Italy and leaving a wonderful man and two of the cutest little boys behind so you can have things *your* way."

Bobbie enjoyed being able to deny that. "Actually, I'm not. I'm staying with Nate and we're getting married."

Sandy sat a moment in stunned silence, then screamed. Her daughters came running in to see what had happened. Still sobbing, she wrapped Bobbie in a bear hug, then drew the worried girls between them. "I'm so happy for you! Oh, that's wonderful! But what made you change your mind?"

"Love, I guess. It's so strong." Bobbie rubbed that spot in her chest where warmth had invaded the day she'd met Nate, knowing for certain now that it wasn't radiation burn. "I still want to be a fine artist, want it passionately, but I'll have to find a way to do that while being a wife and mother."

"Oh, Bobbie. And the best part is you'll be nearby. Do you think your dad will move here?" Sandy narrowed her eyes and asked cautiously, "Is there something going on between him and Stella?"

"Friendship, at this point." Bobbie laughed and hugged her again. "He's talking about joining Doctors Without Borders and she really likes working for Nate, so while they love being together, I don't know that anything immediate is going to happen. She plans to visit him in the spring in California."

Sandy pushed Bobbie gently back to the table. "You get to work again, I'll open the wine and we can plan your engagement party! I'll bet Laura will be excited. Anything new with her on the baby front?"

Bobbie reeled out more fishing line and began cutting. "I got a Happy Thanksgiving text from her, but I haven't heard from her since. She hasn't even answered my cell phone messages. They're probably busy with Christmas stuff."

"Maybe you should call Sean."

"I will."

Bobbie attached a length of line to a large gold foil star and held it up to be sure it was the right length. It bobbed and spun and caught the light in a way that portrayed the warmth of the season—the warmth she felt. She couldn't recall ever being this happy.

"BOBBIE! GUESS WHAT happened?" Crystal came to wrap her arms around her as their last art class began.

Fernanda distributed large envelopes on which Bobbie had placed Christmas stickers. "When you're finished with your ornaments," she told the class, "put them in here to keep them from getting messy."

"What happened?" Bobbie asked in a whisper as Fernanda went on to give them instructions about putting their names on the envelopes.

"Santa came!" The little girl's eyes were enormous, her cheeks pink with excitement. "I didn't get to see him. And I don't know why he came early. But he brought dolls for me and my little sister, jackets for us and my mom, and lots and lots of food. And he did something with the furnace, too, 'cause Mom turned it on so we could get warm!"

Bless Nate and his connections, Bobbie thought with a swell of pride and gratitude. "Wow! That's wonderful."

"Yeah! And my dad gets to come home for Christmas!"

That was beyond anything she'd hoped for. "Really?"

"Yeah. He has to go back afterward. But he might not have to stay as long as we thought."

She hugged Bobbie again. "He's going to love my ornaments."

"Yes, he is!"

The bell rang more than an hour later, announcing the end of school until after the holidays and the final art class. Children ran out of the room yelling their goodbyes and waving at her as they passed. Crystal stopped to give her another hug.

"Bye, guys!" Bobbie shouted back, a little off balance at how disappointed she was that this was the end. But it didn't have to be, she realized with a sudden burst of excitement. She wasn't going anywhere. She could teach this class again next fall. Or possibly offer art classes during the year. "Merry Christmas!" she called.

Fernanda helped clean up cookie crumbs and cocoa cups, and put the room back in order. She retrieved her coat and purse, then wrapped her arms around Bobbie. "I'm going to miss you," she said. She pulled a small gift out of her purse and showed her that the tag with Bobbie's name was the back side of her husband's business card.

"If you are staying after all, call Joel. I think you'd be brilliant at art therapy. Merry Christmas."

Bobbie stood alone for a few minutes in the

empty classroom, rain pouring against the windows, and thought about how much she'd enjoyed this time. Art therapy. That was so not where her dreams lay, but she'd loved the sparkle she'd seen in the children when they'd become involved in their projects, and she couldn't deny it had ignited something in her.

She put a hand to her eyes and drew a deep breath, dizzy with the sudden spin her life had taken. She needed quiet and maybe even solitude to think about Fernanda's suggestion, but the Christmas season wasn't the time to hope for that.

She glanced at her watch. There was time to do a little shopping and wrap presents before Nate picked her up tonight. She'd conscripted her father and Stella to help decorate.

By ten that night the Banker's Suite, a beautiful space to begin with, was a re-creation of Christmas in Old Astoria, as the fund-raiser's theme promised. Floor-to-ceiling photographs from the nineteenth century had been affixed to foam core and stood up against the walls as though the old downtown had been brought inside. Lights had been inserted in every window in the photos, and Bobbie had led a group of artistic volunteers in adding color to the figures visible in windows and on the street.

Old nets had been strung along the sides

with additional photos of the waterfront, and the items to be raffled were placed in front of the shops.

Chunky Christmas garlands stretched from wall to wall, just as they did across Commercial Street, and several old globed streetlamps salvaged from Astoria City Hall's basement provided lighting. The foil stars Bobbie had worked on at Sandy's now dangled from the ceiling and twisted gently in the air, catching the light. The atmosphere was touchingly nostalgic.

Everyone stood in a large knot in the middle of the space and gazed around in awed silence until Clarissa said, "I've never seen anything so beautiful." Applause and whoops of satisfaction followed.

Then the weary group dispersed. Nate caught Bobbie's hand. "We're all going to Mr. Fultano's for pizza. Okay with you?"

"Sure. Who's everybody?"

"Your father, Stella, Jerry Gold and his wife, Clarissa, a lot of the crew. But Sandy has to get home to relieve the babysitter."

"Oh. But she's worked so hard." Bobbie turned to see her friend placing the ornament favors on the tables.

"I know. She told Libby she was too tired to party. You can't fix everything, Bobbie." Nate put an arm around her, caught her neck in the crook of his elbow and pulled her toward him to kiss her temple. "Come on. You're okay with anchovies on the pizza, right?"

"I absolutely am *not*. Or olives. I can pick olives off, but anchovies leave a taste. No anchovies!"

He tightened his grip ever so slightly at her emphatic refusal. "Well," he said with sudden gravity. "I'm glad I found this out before we got married."

"You're telling me anchovies are a dealbreaker?"

"No." He lowered his head to kiss her lips. "But I guess we have to take them off the reception menu."

NATE COULD NOT recall feeling so... He didn't have a word for it. He *had* to cultivate that feminine side. A woman would probably have a word for happiness that seemed to color everything, even the things one was usually *un*happy about.

But it was all right. He didn't have to define it; it was wonderful, a life-revelation to simply feel it. And he did every time he looked at Bobbie in the red dress that hugged her tiny waist and small breasts, with the skirt that floated out around her and whispered when she walked.

Holding her in his arms while they danced in this holiday fairyland was exquisite. Her small body nestled comfortably against his and filled him with a sense of possession he knew he could never express aloud. It wasn't that he wanted to own her, but to protect and indulge her—a thought he knew she'd hate as much as the sense of possession.

"You're very quiet," she observed as they swayed to a bluesy Sinatra medley played by a local band. Couples in elegant dress danced around them, many talking and laughing, but some, like him, overtaken with the mood, the ambience and the partner in their arms.

In the middle of the room, Dennis and Stella chatted happily, arms wrapped around each other, smiles on their faces.

Hunter talked and laughed with Jerry Gold and his wife, who were out for the first time since the baby was born—if you didn't count pizza after decorating the night before—and Sandy danced very decorously with a senior partner in the firm she worked for.

"I'm afraid to speak," Nate admitted.

"Since when?" Bobbie teased.

"Since I've started having possessive thoughts. You'd misunderstand."

She surprised him by smiling. "No, I wouldn't. You don't mean you think of me as chattel, but that your heart wants to own me. Two very different things."

"How very insightful of you!"

She pretended modesty. "It's nothing. My father explained it to me."

That surprised Nate again. "How does he know?"

"Oh, it seems you've been looking at me possessively for a long time. Ah! Time for the raffle. I want the winter wardrobe from Clarissa's! I bought ten tickets!"

They went back to their tables when the music stopped, and Clarissa called Sandy up to draw names from a large basket decorated with a Christmas bow. She held it up so that Sandy couldn't see inside.

Jerry Gold produced a cobalt-blue scarf, which Clarissa explained represented the winter wardrobe from her store. He then wound it around his throat and threw the long, beaded end over his shoulder with great style. Everyone laughed, then fell silent. Sandy reached up into the basket and handed Clarissa the folded square of paper she'd chosen. Clarissa opened it and read, "Cecelia Moreno!"

Bobbie stared in disbelief, then squealed

delightedly. Nate whispered in her ear, "That's not your name, Bobbie!"

She turned to wrap her arms around his neck. "I know! That's Crystal's mom! I bought a few tickets for their family."

She went to accept, explaining to Clarissa that the winner wasn't present. Jerry wrapped the blue scarf around Bobbie's neck and Clarissa handed her a silver-and-black gift certificate.

Item after item was handed out. Bobbie's father won a barbecue, Jonni jumped up and down over a golden Labrador puppy from a local breeder, a very cheerful older woman with a sequined poinsettia in her hair won one of Nate's free tax returns. He groaned.

"What?" Bobbie asked.

He winced. "She looks like the type that has her receipts separated into little plastic bags, has no idea where her property tax statement is, and doesn't remember whether or not she made estimated tax payments. I'm guessing by her gown and the rocks on her fingers that she has considerable income."

Bobbie swatted his arm. "That's pessimistic."

"I'll lay you odds."

The announcement of Nate's name made him stop. Jerry was holding up one of Mike

Wallis's baskets from The Cellar on Tenth. Nate went to claim it. It contained three bottles of wine and a large collection of the gourmet food items stocked at The Cellar.

Bobbie spotted chocolate when he placed his winnings on the table, and reached beneath the elegant cellophane wrapped around the basket.

"Hey!" He caught her hand. "This is mine."

She smiled coyly. "But isn't half of everything that's yours now mine, too? At least the chocolate half?"

He was intoxicated with her playful charm and handed her the chocolate. This did not bode well, he thought, for winning future arguments with her.

Clarissa, Sandy and Jerry continued drawing until almost everything had found a home. The painting was the last item in the raffle. Jerry held it up, and Clarissa made Bobbie stand.

"Oh, no," she groaned under her breath.

Nate and her father pushed her to her feet. There was loud applause and Clarissa asked her to come forward and explain the subject.

She groaned again, but Nate nudged her toward the microphone.

He watched her take the mic and suddenly become relaxed. She talked about having come to Astoria to complete a commission, and becoming involved in the community because of Sandy's bullying. Everyone who knew Sandy laughed, and her friend shook a playful fist at her.

"I had so much fun teaching the art class," Bobbie said, her smile verifying that fact, "and enjoyed working with this committee to put on this beautiful evening...." More applause. "So when Sandy suggested a painting reflecting the Old Astoria theme, I was happy to do it. I was already in love with the place, and seeing the old photographs made me love it even more.

"I had a built-in model for the sea captain because, many of you probably know, Nate Raleigh is my neighbor." There were now hoots and applause. "He owed me big because Arnold... Do you all know Arnold?" Impressed oohs. "He chased my cat through my studio, leaped at a shelf that held a lot of my supplies, tipped them all into my bucket of papermaking material and pretty much destroyed it." This revelation brought on teasing, boos and hisses. "So Nate was forced to pose for the project to try to make it up to me. And that's why the ship's captain might look familiar to you.

"Anyway, thank you for being such a caring, supportive community. I've loved being here so much that I've decided to stay." That news was met with applause and cheers.

Sandy gave her a hug and Bobbie came back to the table, her cheeks pink. She took her chair next to Nate and leaned in as he draped his arm around her. He loved knowing she was his, though he didn't dare say that aloud, either.

The room was silent when Sandy drew for the painting. The band did a drumroll as she handed the entry to Clarissa.

"Mike Wallis!" Clarissa exclaimed. The room erupted in applause again. It was well known that Mike had purchased several hundred dollars worth of tickets

Mike accepted the painting from Jerry and announced that it would hang in a prominent place in The Cellar.

The band played for another hour, guests moving in weary circles on the dance floor as the evening began to wind down. On their way out, everyone stopped to congratulate Sandy and Clarissa on a job well done.

"I have to run to the ladies' room before we leave," Bobbie said to Nate, seeing Sandy head off in that direction. "Do you mind waiting a minute?"

"Not at all. Take your time. I'll carry the basket out to the car and come back for you."

"Perfect."

Bobbie found Sandy staring at her reflection in the mirror. When she spotted Bobbie, she smiled thinly and said, "I can't believe it went so well. It was fun, but I'm so happy it's over. I think we made a bundle. We're turning everything over to Nate and we'll know on Monday how much we made."

"You did a superb job, Sandy. It was a wonderful evening. But how are *you?*"

"I'm fine. Anxious to get home and off my feet."

"Did you try to talk to Hunter?"

"No. I don't know what to say."

"How about 'I'll be happy to wait while we work together to figure this out.'"

Sandy shrugged and turned away from the mirror. "I have a ton of things to do before I go home. I've got to—"

Bobbie's cell phone rang just then, but she caught Sandy's arm before she could disappear. It was Laura's husband's name on her caller ID and Bobbie answered quickly, "Hi, Sean!" She smiled as she spoke, so happy to have finally connected with him.

There was a moment's silence before

he said, "Hi, Bobbie." His voice was dark, clouded.

She knew instantly that something was wrong. Sandy had stopped trying to pull away and now took hold of Bobbie's arm. *"What?"* she mouthed.

"What's wrong?" Bobbie made herself ask.

There was a small gasp on the other end of the line, a swallow, a breath. "Laura's gone, Bobbie."

Cymbals crashed in her head. Everything shook. The moment stretched, then snapped back with a vicious sting. She had no voice, but she somehow whispered, "What?"

"She died. Arrhythmia, they said. Sometimes caused by chemo drugs." He drew a ragged breath. "She was tired and we were lying on the bed, talking baby names, and she…she suddenly couldn't breathe. I helped her sit up, and when that didn't help, I called 911. She died in the ambulance."

Bobbie shut off her own shock and pain. "Oh, Sean," she said, groping for words of comfort and coming up empty. "When did this happen?"

"Ah…ten days ago, I think. I'm not sure. I'm sorry I didn't call you. I sort of forgot everything. I ignored my own phone for days, and it wasn't until I got her stuff from the hospital, and took her phone out of her purse and heard all your messages, that I remembered. Her parents and mine thought it would be best to…to have a memorial service after the holidays. She didn't want a funeral. We had talked about it in the very beginning, when we weren't sure she was going to survive." He was quiet a moment, then said, "She loved you, Bobbie. If we got pregnant and had a girl, she wanted to call her Roberta."

Bobbie's throat closed and she felt as though there was gravel from her tonsils to her chest. She was vaguely aware of crushing Sandy's hand. "I would have loved that," she said around a sob.

Someone in the background called Sean's name.

"My mom's here, staying with me," he said. "I've had trouble eating and she's fixing something…."

"Of course. Sean, I'm so sorry. If I can do anything, please call me."

"I will. Bye, Bobbie."

"Bye." She closed her phone and turned to Sandy, grief shutting off her air. She had to drag in a breath. "Laura died, Sean said. Of arrhythmia caused by the chemo drugs."

"Oh, Bobbie!"

"Ten days ago. She's been gone for…ten days."

Bobbie thought about all the wonderful things that had happened to her in the past ten days. She'd realized she was in love, she and Nate had proposed to each other, they'd had this wonderful evening. And all that time, Laura had been gone.

She felt her own life, at least her enthusiasm for it, drain out of her. Laura had fought so hard. She'd put off having the baby she wanted because of the restraints of student poverty, then when cancer had threatened her, she'd fought to live the life she wanted, to have that baby. Roberta.

And for what? Not only to have the dream die, but the dreamer, too?

"Bobbie, let me get Nate." Sandy tried to push her into a tufted love seat in the lounge outside the restroom.

"No," she said firmly. She felt as though she had that disease where everything in the body became like rock. She had no blood, no breath.

The door pushed open and Stella appeared, a brush in her hand, a smile on her lips—until she saw the two of them.

"Get Nate, please," Sandy ordered urgently.

Stella turned instantly to do as she was told.

"I'm going to be okay," Bobbie insisted, heading for the door.

Sandy stayed with her. "Bobbie, please sit down for a minute. Let me get you a brandy."

Nate flung open the door, worry etched on his face, his eyes narrowing as he saw her pain.

"Her friend Laura died," Sandy explained quickly. "Some complication from the chemo drugs. She just got a call from Laura's husband."

NATE HAD NEVER seen that desperation on Bobbie's face before, a terrible grief in her eyes accompanied by an underlying fear. He didn't know what had happened or what to do for her, so he simply opened his arms. At first she resisted, then she seemed to crumple. He took a step toward her and she fell into his embrace, weeping against him as Sandy explained to their friends and family, women *and* men, gathered in the ladies' room what had happened.

"They went through chemo together," Sandy said, tears streaming down her face. "They championed each other's causes. I think they shared something that's hard for the rest of us to understand."

Nate crushed Bobbie to him. He remembered the text she'd received on Thanksgiving. He knew this wasn't about him, but he didn't want this loss to drive a wedge between him and Bobbie when she now finally, *finally,* wanted to be in his life. He admitted that selfish thought, then focused on what he could do for her.

He turned to Hunter. "I'm parked in the old Safeway lot." He reached into his pants pocket and handed Hunter his keys. "Would you mind bringing my car to the front?"

His friend was off in an instant.

"I'll get her coat." Stella hurried through the swinging doors. Sandy handed her Bobbie's purse.

Dennis shook his head, his eyes sad and concerned. He put a hand to his daughter's back, but didn't seem to know what to say, either.

They were in the car and on their way home in five minutes. Bobbie had stopped crying and sat in eerie stillness, staring through the windshield, her coat pulled around her. Nate glanced at her and saw the tightness in her delicate profile, the set to her mouth that he remembered from the day the boys and Arnold had destroyed her studio.

"I'll make you a cup of mulled wine," he

said, putting a hand out to touch her. "Your father showed me how."

She covered it with her own, then said with a sigh, "I'd like to go home, Nate."

He glanced at her again and saw that she was looking at him. And he knew in that instant that everything was changing. He wasn't sure how or why, but the woman who'd proposed to him was gone, replaced by one who still loved him, but could live without him.

"Bobbie…"

She squeezed his hand to stop what he was about to say.

"Okay." He steered into her driveway rather than his and saw her father already waiting at the open door. Nate helped Bobbie out and walked her up the steps. At the top, she turned to him and wrapped her arms around his neck. He was a step below her so they were eye to eye. He didn't like what he saw in the dark depths of her gaze—that old disconnection that had so frustrated him. But now was not the time.

He hugged her tightly. "Try to sleep," he said gently. "I'm just a shout away."

She seemed grateful for that. For just an instant he caught a glimpse of the woman who'd kidnapped him to show him her favorite place. She put a hand to his cheek and her lips to his, and kissed him with the easy affection that had grown between them. When she raised her head, he swore he saw goodbye in her eyes before that terrible sadness swamped it. "We'll talk tomorrow," she said, her voice raspy and thick.

He watched her disappear into her father's arms, and got back into his car.

Stella waited at the open door when he climbed the steps. She greeted him with a hug. "How awful for her," she said. "Is she okay?"

"I'm not sure," he admitted. "But her dad's helped her deal with life and death before."

"Good." Stella hugged him again. "I paid the babysitter and let her go. You owe me big. I'll see you Monday. Try not to worry about... anything. She loves you."

The woman was reading his mind. "Right."

He paced the living room in the dark, sipping at a cup of coffee. He'd had enough to drink at the party, and whatever else happened in his life, he still had two little boys asleep upstairs. He had to stay functional.

On one of his trips from the front door to the kitchen, he saw the lights go out at Bobbie's. It was just before 1:00 a.m. His cell phone rang. It was Dennis.

"How's she doing?" Nate asked.

"She's in her room, trying to rest. I know you're worried about her, but I'll take good care of her. You should get some rest, too." Dennis cleared his throat, as though not certain he had the right to say what he was about to. "I can imagine how worried you are. But I'm praying she's going to wake up in the morning and realize that what happened to her friend was one of those awful, unpredictable things, and she still has a whole life ahead of her. And that she wants to spend it with you."

Nate fell into his chair. "All right. But if she wakes up thinking anything else, I'm going to lose faith in you as a father-in-law."

Dennis uttered a mirthless laugh. "Good night, Nate."

"Good night, Dennis."

CHAPTER FOURTEEN

RAIN BATTERED THE roof and the windows when Bobbie awoke on Sunday. It was after eleven and she could smell coffee and something mapley. Her father's French toast, she guessed. Monet was wrapped in a tight ball against her side and she had one moment of cozy happiness until her new reality came down on her like a sledgehammer.

Laura was gone, a victim of the drugs intended to save her. One of life's dirty tricks. After all they'd been through together, Bobbie felt as if she'd lost part of herself, as if the progress she'd made back to life had been ripped away.

Nate. She groaned from the ache she felt at the thought of him, so caring and comforting last night, so ready to argue with her always. She closed her eyes to hold back tears, but they fell anyway. She had to go talk to him. Today.

She pulled on jeans and a black turtleneck she'd bought for her Astoria walks, and brushed her hair. It still amazed her how normal she looked now, how much like her old self. Then she accepted with grinding pain in that spot where love had been just yesterday that she would never be her old self again. She would always be a woman who'd had cancer and refused to let it hurt anyone else in her life. And the only way to do that was to bar anyone else from admittance.

She left the house through her studio, to avoid a conversation with her father that might divert her from her plan. She'd decided in the middle of the night that this was how it had to be.

Sheamus answered the back door and smiled brightly at her. "Hi, Bobbie!" He stepped aside to let her in. "We're wrapping presents! And we have something for you!"

The gravel she'd had in her throat last night seemed to have collected into one giant lump. She couldn't swallow past it. "Well…" she said faintly. "I'd better stay in here, then. Is your uncle…?"

"Right here." Nate appeared in the doorway from the living room, looking like the ship's captain after a night at the Astoria waterfront taverns. He was tousled and seemed vulnerable, for all the toughness in his eyes.

She was sure he knew why she was here. But he offered politely, "Cocoa? Tea?"

She didn't want to prolong this, but did want to spend time with him, as difficult as it would be. "Tea would be nice," she replied.

"Water just boiled." He went to the cupboard for two Christmas cups and a box of Christmas spice tea he'd bought when they'd gone to the bake sale at St. Mary's. He poured boiling water over the two tea bags and carried the cups to the table.

He sat opposite her and crossed his forearms on the place mat. "Go ahead," he said. He seemed sort of disengaged despite the flash in his eyes and the hard line of his jaw.

She dragged her tea bag through the water in her cup and met his gaze. "Go ahead?" she asked.

"You're here to tell me you're leaving," he said in an even, unimpassioned voice. "Go ahead."

The direct approach as a tactic to take the wind out of her sails worked very well. She stammered a moment, took a sip of tea, then said with as much dignity as she could muster, "I've thought about it carefully, and I think it's the best thing for all of us."

"In what universe," he asked calmly, "would that be better for all of us?" When she took too long to answer, he did. "I'll tell you. In the universe where only what *you* want matters. You can go your own way and not worry about whether the boys and I are tough enough to deal with whatever happens to you. You can put everything into your art, because it doesn't ask anything of you but your commitment to your talent. If you die, your art only becomes more valuable."

She looked at him in hurt surprise. "I explained—"

"I know," he interrupted. "Art requires your undivided attention, your complete dedication to what's in your gut, yada, yada. And that doesn't fit with family, because love requires that you be there to give it, and get it back, and all those tyrannical little details incomprehensible to the free spirit."

She was too stunned to be angry. He'd argued with her before, but he'd never been cruel. "Nate," she whispered, her eyes brimming.

"Look," he said, his voice rising slightly, the flame in his eyes sparking, "if you don't love me and the boys, that's one thing. But don't give me this tragic tale of the Lone Wolf Lady going off on her own because her life is just too grim to share." He jabbed two fingertips at his chest. "We've dealt with grim, believe me. We can do it."

"Nate," she pleaded quietly, "the boys have already lost both parents, and you carried them through the horror of that and got them to a place where their lives make sense again. What if what happened to Laura happens to me? Or what if the cancer comes back?" He opened his mouth to reply, but she cut him off. "I know. *You're* very heroic. You've proved that on several levels. But Dylan and Sheamus are two little boys who shouldn't be asked to go through that again."

"We don't know that anything will happen to you. Your prognosis at this point is good."

"And that's the way I'd been thinking. I love you and them so much that I forgot what it's like to have that malignancy inside you, and feel it trying to kill you. It makes you balance on the balls of your feet, ready to go either way, to live or to die, because the disease makes the decision, you don't. And Laura's death reminded me of that."

Bobbie reached across the table to cover his hand with hers. He didn't move, but she saw something soften in his eyes. "If it was just you and me, I'd stay. But it isn't. It's them, too. And I won't put them at risk like that."

AND THAT WAS how she got him. He would gladly take the chance himself, but he couldn't force it on the boys. He turned his hand to hold hers, looked into her pleading gaze, and hated himself for everything he'd said. Pain burned in his chest.

"I'm sorry." Tears sprang to his eyes and he fought them down. She came around the table and he pushed back his chair to take her in his lap. They wept together.

"I'm leaving day after tomorrow," she said, straightening up. He closed his eyes against that fact and she kissed his temple and added quickly, "Dad has Stella and you and the boys to spend the holiday with, and the sooner I'm gone the better."

"I could go into a few reasons why that isn't true."

"Please don't. My mind's made up."

"All right then." Nate put her on her feet. "Wait right here. I have something for you." He disappeared into the living room and returned with a large dress box. It was wrapped in signature Tony's Boutique burgundy and silver. He put it on the table.

"Nate," she began to protest.

"Just open it," he said. "I'm on my last reserves of self-control."

She removed the ribbon, tugged off the lid

and dug into the tissue. She pulled out the red wool jacket with the irregular collar and closure that she'd admired the day she'd sketched him on the waterfront. She held it to herself, more tears falling.

"Try it on," he said. "I want to remember you in it."

Hands trembling, she slipped into it and fastened the buttons.

She looked beautiful, he thought. It was just the sort of offbeat, eccentric thing to underscore who she was. He would remember her in this kitchen, helping the boys with their sketches, helping him with Thanksgiving dinner, talking, teasing, being everything he'd ever wanted—but apparently couldn't have.

He reached into the bottom of the box and handed her a five-pound bag of Thundermuck coffee. "That's the stuff you liked so much the night you helped Sheamus build Bill the Monster."

She walked into Nate's arms again, sobbed for several moments, then drew back and looked up at him, misery in her eyes. "I'll love you forever," she said.

"Yeah." He held her close. "Me, too."

He helped her put the coat back in the box, fitted the coffee into a corner, put the lid on and carried it to the door for her. Then he watched her walk across their driveways with it.

From the living room came soft sounds of laughter. Stella and the boys were decorating the Christmas tree she'd bought with them early that morning.

Nate's heartbreak drowned out the sounds.

NATE TOOK THE boys Christmas shopping for Stella and Dennis, to get them out of the house. He explained about Bobbie having to leave, and though he tried to make it sound positive—she was fulfilling a dream, and they might be able to visit her one day—he wasn't fooling anyone. Sheamus cried and Dylan sank into a mood that reminded Nate of the old days. Getting them out into the rampant Christmas cheer seemed like the best solution, even if it was only temporary.

Sheamus wanted to buy Stella a purse set that included wallet, eyeglass holder, cigarette pouch and makeup bag.

Dylan rolled his eyes. "Shea! She doesn't smoke and she doesn't wear glasses. She wouldn't use half that stuff. What about a woolly hat to keep her warm? Or when she stays overnight with us, she has that ratty brown robe. A new one would be something she could really use."

Sheamus folded his arms and struck a stubborn pose. "Okay, but I like the wallet."

"Let's look at robes," Nate suggested. "Good idea, Dylan. Then we can get a wallet, too, that isn't part of a set."

Both boys agreed that would work.

They decided on pink for Stella's robe. Nate decided to ignore the gender stereotyping.

The boys were convinced that Dennis would love a dark blue hooded sweatshirt with ASTORIA embroidered on the left side in gold. "'Cause he isn't from here," Dylan explained.

"Good point." Nate paid for the purchase.

"Can we get a TV for Hunter?" Sheamus stopped to watch a colorful, exceptionally clear cartoon on a dozen screens in the electronics section. "'Cause he likes ours so much."

"That's too expensive," Dylan said. He looked up at Nate questioningly, "Isn't it?"

Nate smiled for the first time since he'd walked into the ladies' room at the Banker's Suite last night. A television for Hunter. He liked the idea. And it fit into the plan he'd been considering while the boys were shopping.

He bought a 46" flat screen television, and the fixtures to mount it on the wall. The boys were excited. He paid extra to have it delivered immediately. "We'll follow the delivery truck to Hunter's," he said to the boys, "then we're all going to go to McDonald's, okay?"

He became the hero of the hour.

"Why don't *we* just deliver it?" Dylan asked.

"Because Hunter's apartment is on the second floor. You think you can help me carry it up?"

Dylan grinned. "Right. He's gonna be so surprised!"

When the truck arrived in front of Hunter's apartment building, Nate parked across the street, and he and the boys followed the deliverymen up the stairs. Hunter came to the door in jeans and a gray sweatshirt, munching on an apple. He looked surprised by the small crowd at his door. His eyes were bloodshot, as though he hadn't slept well.

Nate led the way into the apartment. "Hey, good morning!" he said. "These two elves and I, and these gentlemen from Santa's Workshop, represent the Union for Fairness to members of the Rotten List."

Dylan laughed.

"In the interest of turning you around so that next year you make the Nice list, we're providing you with a gesture of our faith in you. Where would you like it?"

Hunter frowned as he read the box, "Forty-six-inch LED HDTV." He turned to them in astonishment. For a minute, Nate was sure Hunter was going to make a suggestion about where to put it that the boys shouldn't hear, but at the last minute he said instead, "You can't give me—"

"Pick a spot," Nate said, "because in a rented place we want to put the screws in only once. Right here where the current TV is?" There was a lot of bare wall and a very small television.

The men went to work. They disconnected and moved the old set and stand aside, then, with a whir of power tools, put up the new one.

"You'll have to upgrade your cable service," Nate said. "We can do that at the office on Monday. Come on. We're going to lunch."

"What is wrong with you?" Hunter demanded.

Nate ignored him and pointed to the hall closet. "Dylan, get his jacket."

There was a little satisfaction for Nate in seeing his friend confused and speechless. At the office, he was seldom confused about anything, and always had an answer to the knottiest problem. Hunter reminded him a lot of Ben. He'd saved Nate's hide a few times since he'd taken over the office.

Nate and the boys led him forcibly out to the car and into the passenger seat.

"People saw you kidnap me, you know," he told Nate. "You'll never get away with this. Whatever it is."

Nate simply smiled, parked at McDonalds, ordered a Happy Meal for Sheamus, then Big Mac meals for the rest of them.

"We were Christmas shopping," Nate explained to the still perplexed Hunter after they'd eaten, "and the boys thought you should have a television."

"Thanks, guys." Hunter sent a smile the boys' way, clearly still in a stupor. "But you can't give me such a big item just like that."

"Why make life more complicated than it has to be? How about dessert?" The boys were already on their feet. Nate looked at the long line at the counter and saw his chance. "You guys mind going to get it while I talk to Hunter? Four hot fudge sundaes. Hot fudge okay with you?"

Hunter nodded dazedly. The boys ran off to join the line.

Nate pinned his friend with a look. "Okay, here it is. I've only got till the boys come back, so don't interrupt me. I'm giving you the money to pay off the rest of your debts from the embezzlement…hey!"

Hunter glowered and tried to interrupt, but Nate glowered back. "I don't want the boys to hear me talking about Bobbie moving to Italy, so just let me finish."

"I thought you were en—"

"Are you not hearing me?"

Hunter sat back. "Sorry. You can explain that later."

"I'm also going to give you a down payment on a house. So you can call Sandy tonight and tell her you want to talk. You don't have to tell her how you got this money. It's a gift from me to you, because I'm just realizing today how cool it is to have people in your life that you can depend on for anything. I'll transfer funds to your account Monday morning."

There was silence while they stared at each other.

"Can I speak now?" Hunter asked.

"Depends. What are you going to say?"

"That you're an idiot and the best friend any man ever had. And much as I want to accept—"

"If you don't, you're fired."

"Like you could do without me."

"That's the point. I can't. We're coming into year-end and tax season, and I don't want you moping around because the woman you love is out of your life." He sighed painfully, and winced a little as it hurt. "It's just happened to me, and the office won't be able to function if it happens to both of us."

Hunter studied him bleakly, then shook his head. "I'm sorry, Nate. Because her friend died?"

"Yeah. Now she's afraid if something happens to her, the boys will be traumatized for the second time in their lives."

"I don't know what to say."

"Just tell me you'll try to work it out with Sandy. Then there'll be a happy future for one of us."

"I promise."

The boys were back with a carry box of sundaes, and the four of them spent the rest of their lunch talking about meeting at Hunter's for the next football Saturday.

BOBBIE STOOD IN the middle of Nate's garage as Stella helped her collect empty boxes. Her father was at home, packing up her books and favorite curios, and a few items from the kitchen to help her get started in a new place. With Sandy's blessing, she was leaving everything else in the house so that her father could stay and spend the holidays in Astoria.

"I think you're making a mistake, Bobbie," Stella said for the fourth time.

"You've made that clear." She gave her a hug. "And I appreciate how you feel, but think! Imagine what it would be like for the boys if they had to—"

Their conversation was interrupted by the sounds of the garage opening. As the door rose, Nate's car braked to a stop, Bobbie and Stella ensnared in its headlights.

Nate leaned out the window. "What's going on?"

"Bobbie needs a few more boxes," Stella said, holding one up. "I'm trying to help."

He popped the trunk and got out of the car. "Yeah. Dennis called me." He pulled half a dozen boxes of various sizes out of the car and carried them into the garage. He smiled soberly at Bobbie. "Will that do it, or do you need more?"

"That should take care of it. Thank you."

She wanted desperately to touch his hand, his arm, but his expression told her to keep her distance. It wasn't hostile, just pained. They looked into each other's eyes, communicating all kinds of feelings for which there were no words.

"Dennis and I are going to dinner," Stella said, looking from one to the other. "Want to come? The two of you can sit on opposite sides of the booth. Or in different booths."

Nate turned to her. She stopped talking.

"Liberty Cab and Shuttle is picking me up at noon tomorrow," Bobbie said, trying to sound as though it was a good thing. "I talked to the boys this afternoon and they said you explained everything. Whatever you told them, they don't seem to hate me. So, thank you."

Nate nodded. "They have a surprising capacity to deal with what they're given."

She wasn't sure if that was a criticism or not. So she smiled in response. "Stella says you have one wardrobe box in the basement I can have. Is it all right if I come back for it in a while?"

"I'll bring it over later," Nate said. It was impossible to tell what he was thinking. And sad to realize it shouldn't matter to her now.

"Thank you," she said.

STELLA AND DENNIS had gone to dinner, and the boys were upstairs getting ready for bed when Nate sank into his chair with a brandy and tried to pull himself together.

He still hadn't recovered from seeing Bobbie in his garage. In the time she'd spent in Astoria, she'd gone from a pixie in grubby clothes to a fresh-faced, beautiful woman with still-short but lustrous hair that he wanted to touch. She'd put on a few extra pounds and they gave her delicate, gamine body some wonderful curves. She'd been gorgeous Saturday night.

And then the sky had fallen.

He sipped at his brandy and reminded himself that he had no right to self-pity. He'd had several months without anger, thanks to her, and now he suspected that even when she was gone, he'd remain free of it. He'd gotten over his own loss, and realized how lucky he was to have the children his brother had left behind. And to have all the memories he'd made with Bobbie.

He felt confident that his connection with her would remain because of his housekeeper and her father. The logistics were a problem now, but Stella and Dennis were too good together to settle for simple friendship. Still, for Nate and Bobbie, being occasional acquaintances might be more difficult than never seeing each other again—if the way Nate had felt in the garage this afternoon was any indication.

Trying to give it all a cheerful spin, he

imagined a future where Sheamus was CEO of the Disney Corporation, Dylan was President of the United States and Bobbie's work was collected internationally. He could be happy in the knowledge that once their lives had all been intertwined.

God. He'd found his feminine side.

"How come you're still up?" Dylan asked, padding down the stairs in his bare feet. "Don't you feel good?"

Sheamus followed right behind him in slippers that lit up when he walked. "It's 'cause Bobbie's going away," he said.

Dylan stopped at the bottom of the stairs to roll his eyes impatiently at his brother. "I was trying not to say that."

Sheamus walked penitently down the rest of the stairs.

"I'm fine," Nate said, beckoning them to join him in the chair. "I'm sad, but we talked about that, remember? It's okay to be sad."

Dylan settled on the arm. "As long as you don't take it out on other people."

"Very good," Nate praised.

Sheamus was about to climb into his lap when he noticed that the tree wasn't lit. "Can I plug in the lights?"

"Sure." He could take it.

Sheamus's pajama-clad bottom squirmed

under the tree until it came to life in gaudy splendor. Colors reflected on every ornament and on the crystal garland that spiraled around the branches.

Sheamus ran back to climb into Nate's lap and lie against his shoulder. "It looks like the trees we used to have," he said, a little wistfully.

Dylan, too, sounded dreamy. "Yeah. Mom made cookies, like Bobbie does. And she smiled and laughed a lot and sang Christmas carols...."

"Like Bobbie does," Sheamus added.

Dylan hooked a casual arm around Nate's neck and said philosophically, "Pretty soon it won't hurt as much that Bobbie can't stay. You'll find a way to be happy, and...and the love Bobbie has for us and that we have for her will last forever, right? That's what you told us."

With his own arm wrapped around Sheamus, Nate enjoyed the luxury of Dylan's display of affection, and the knowledge that he'd actually listened to what Nate had said. "Did it make you feel better when I told you that?"

"No," Dylan said, true to his candid style. "It still hurts sometimes, but it's not as hard to feel happy anymore, and I like the idea that love lasts forever. We'll always love Mom and Dad, and they'll always love us."

"And we love you," Sheamus said, patting Nate's chest. "You're the best uncle anywhere."

Nate drew a choppy breath.

Dylan sighed in a very adult way. "So Bobbie will still love you even though she has to go away to paint different stuff and you have to stay here."

Sheamus sat up, obviously feeling argumentative. "I don't get that. Aren't people who love each other supposed to be together in the same place? Why doesn't she want to stay with us?"

"It's hard to explain," Nate replied.

"I know why," Dylan went on in that matter-of-fact way. "I heard her tell you yesterday in the kitchen that if she got cancer again, or if she died of that chemo stuff like her friend did, she was afraid Sheamus and me would be all messed up."

Nate stared at him, unaware he'd heard that conversation.

As though afraid Nate would question how he'd heard, Dylan explained with a shrug, "I heard her crying, so I listened."

That was true. "Well…that's a pretty scary

thought, isn't it? I mean, if Bobbie became your stepmom and she got sick again?"

Dylan shrugged. "I think it's scarier that she's going away. I mean, she's okay now, right? Think of all the cool stuff we could do together. We could help her pick flowers and leaves for her paper. We have a lot of fun when we all eat together, and that time we went for groceries was great." His voice waned a little. "Even just watching TV and hanging out is fun." He turned on the arm of Nate's chair so that he could look at him. "What if we promised not to freak out if she did get sick again?" He focused on Sheamus. "You'd rather have her here, right? Sick or not?"

"Yeah!"

Dylan refocused on Nate. "So, maybe you could ask her. If we promise to be okay if something bad happens, would she stay?"

CHAPTER FIFTEEN

BOBBIE STARED AT her bare closet, empty hangers swinging as she ran a hand along them, and considered that a fitting metaphor for her heart. It was full to overflowing for everyone she loved, but felt cavernously empty because she was leaving them behind.

She turned to the pile of clothes she intended to hang in the wardrobe box still in Nate's basement. He'd promised to bring it over for her, but had probably forgotten or been distracted. She'd have to run over there herself. Her father had agreed to ship everything to her, but she didn't want him to have to pack anything. He'd done too much already.

She was glad he'd gone to dinner with Stella tonight and left Bobbie to handle all the odds and ends of uprooting her life by herself. She'd been here such a short time she shouldn't even have roots, but she did. Surprisingly deep ones.

She glanced at the clock: 10:22 p.m. She

imagined Nate would still be up, but was reluctant to knock on the door if he wasn't. She went to her porch and saw that his kitchen was in darkness, but a subtle, colorful glow came from the front of the house. The Christmas tree.

She started across the yard, stepping over the chrysanthemums and going quietly up the back steps. Unwilling to wake the boys, she knocked softly on the door.

She waited a moment, and when there was no response, she knocked again a little louder. Still nothing. She tried the knob and it turned under her hand. Nate was definitely up. She knew he had a nighttime routine of locking doors and turning off lights.

As she walked into the dark kitchen she heard voices coming from the living room. Had her father and Stella come here after their late dinner? She smiled to herself, remembering the first time they'd met, and knowing how delighted they were to have found each other.

She went quietly toward the living room doorway, unwilling to startle anyone until she saw who it was. And then she recognized the voices: Dylan's and Sheamus's. What were they doing up so late? Not that it was any of her business. She'd love to see them before she left, but that would be too upsetting for them and for her.

Well, she thought, turning around, maybe she could get the box from Nate before he left for work in the morning. She stopped suddenly as she heard the sound of her name in their conversation.

"...Bobbie became your stepmom and she got sick again?"

She froze in the darkness of the kitchen, unable to breathe. That had been Nate's voice. She'd missed the beginning of the sentence, so she wasn't sure what point he was making. But the word *stepmom* made her put her hands to her mouth so that she wouldn't betray herself with a sound.

"I thinks it's scarier that she's going away." Dylan's voice. "I mean, she's okay now, right? Think of all the cool stuff we could do together." He talked about picking flowers, leaves, eating together, shopping. Then his voice became choked. "Even watching TV and hanging out is fun."

They didn't mind if she became ill again? Of course, they were children, and children always thought bad things couldn't happen to them.

But that probably wasn't true of these two.

Bad things *had* happened to them. They had firsthand experience that life was cruel.

"What if we promised not to freak out if she got sick again?" Dylan went on. "You'd rather have her here, right? Sick or not?"

"Yeah!" Sheamus replied with spirit.

"So maybe you could ask her. If we promised to be okay if something bad happens, would she stay? We wouldn't freak out."

Another brief silence. "We could help her," Dylan murmured. "We're…experienced now."

The knot in her throat dissolved and a sob broke through with noisy violence. How could she deny such generosity?

Because she didn't have forever to give them, she argued with herself.

But they weren't asking for forever. They just wanted now.

And what was forever, anyway, she thought with sudden insight, but the space of time that started at this moment and lasted for as long as she had?

She was so busy sobbing, and trying to cope with the realization that her approach to her future had been all wrong, that she didn't notice the swiftly moving shadow in the dark until it struck her in the chest and threw her backward into a chair that clattered to the floor. She lay immobile, an enormous weight with a rumbling bark stretched out atop her. Then Arnold recognized her and slurped her face with a rubbery tongue.

The kitchen light went on and she blinked against it, closing her eyes and her mouth as Arnold continued to lavish her with kisses.

"Bobbie! What are you...?" Nate's voice.

"Bobbie!" Sheamus.

"Bobbie's here! Why is she crying?" Dylan.

Strong hands pushed Arnold off her, caught her arms and hauled her to her feet. She opened teary eyes and looked into Nate's concerned face.

"What?" he demanded. "Did something happen to Dennis?"

She shook her head, and as violently as the tears had come, happiness and laughter pushed them aside.

"No," she said. "Something happened to *me*."

Nate apparently considered the quick change from tears to laughter a cause for concern. He guided her to the kitchen table and sat her down.

Sheamus took a napkin from the middle of the table and began to fan her.

"What are you doing?" Dylan asked.

"I saw it in a movie," Sheamus replied. "She needs air."

Nate observed that his dream of Sheamus becoming an executive might have to be readjusted to doctor. Reaching for the bottle of brandy, still on the counter, he poured a small measure in a handy juice glass and, pulling a chair around to sit beside Bobbie, handed it to her. The boys hovered on either side.

"Drink a little. Small sips." She tried to argue, but Nate pushed it toward her lips.

She sipped, coughed and sipped again. "I'm fine," she said finally, her voice a little raspy, her cheeks pink. "Isn't this where I started, almost two months ago? Being taken down by Arnold?"

Tongue lolling, tail wagging, Arnold said as clearly as though he had language, "You're welcome!"

Bobbie laughed again. Nate frowned at her. "Bobbie, what *is* it?"

She wrapped an arm around each boy and pulled them to her. "I love you two so much," she said, then sobered suddenly, her eyes brimming again. "I want to stay with you more than anything. I heard you say that you'd promise not to freak out if I got sick, if it would make me stay."

Sheamus nodded. "Dylan says we're tough now."

Bobbie turned to his brother. "Are you really, Dylan?"

Nate was afraid to speak, afraid to breathe, afraid what he'd heard her say was some figment of his imagination, borne out of the urgent wish that she not leave. He waited while Dylan gave her a hug, then looked at her with that alarmingly adult expression he wore now when talking about his parents or his grief.

"We are. Sheamus scared Bill away, and I said goodbye to my mom and dad. I mean, they're still here." He rubbed fingertips over his heart, and added with a swallow, "But I'm not waiting for them to come home anymore." He rested his elbow on her shoulder. "Now Uncle Nate is our new dad, and we think we shouldn't be without a mom just 'cause we're scared of what *could* happen. We want to be brave."

Bobbie pulled Dylan to her again, then looked into Nate's eyes, and everything inside him that wasn't bone melted into a puddle of helpless servitude to the love he saw there.

"Do you want to be brave?" she asked him.

"I *am* brave," he replied without hesitation. "But I need you to be…whole."

She leaned out of her chair to wrap her arms around him. The boys piled on.

"Then I'm in," she said.

He held her away from him for a moment. The boys straightened worriedly. "What about becoming a fine artist?"

"I'm going to work on that as I can," she said, leaning into him again.

She felt an almost physical letting go of the dream. The pull was painful. Then she looked into the three faces hanging on her every word and remembered her father telling her, "We're born to love and be loved."

"Someone at the school suggested art therapy to me. I may just look into that."

Nate drew her closer and pulled the boys in. "Brilliant. So you packed all your things for nothing."

"No, she didn't," Dylan pointed out. "She has to move it all over here."

EPILOGUE

DYLAN STOOD VERY still, even though his nose itched. Hunter, standing beside him, was quiet and serious, and even Sheamus stood like a soldier and didn't move a muscle. Dylan didn't want to be the one to mess up.

"May we have the rings, please?"

Hunter gave Uncle Nate a small ring trimmed in diamonds. Uncle Nate put it on Bobbie's finger and repeated a lot of promises the priest told him to say.

Bobbie looked wonderful. She wore a white dress with a poufy skirt, and a veil with sparkly stuff that Sandy had pulled back out of her face when they got to the altar. Dennis had walked her up the aisle and Dylan saw a tear on his cheek.

Uncle Nate looked pretty great, too, as Sandy gave Bobbie a ring that she put on his finger, then repeated a lot of words after the priest. His uncle wore a dark suit with a funny striped tie and a collar that was weird, but looked kind of nice. Which was a good thing because Dylan was wearing the same clothes himself.

He felt very strange. It was Christmas Eve and he wasn't even thinking about the toys under the tree, and all the great food in the refrigerator. He was thinking that somehow, life had gotten…nice. Happy again.

Stella wore a pretty green dress like Sandy's, and her hair was piled up with flowers in it. She was beautiful.

Sandy and Hunter didn't talk to each other very much, but they were polite. Uncle Nate said he thought they were going to get together; it was just going to take time. Pride was in the way. Dylan wasn't sure what that meant, but he wasn't going to worry about it, because his own life was really cool.

Bobbie had moved everything to their house this morning and he was going to be part of a whole family again. Stella and Dennis would stay with them while Uncle Nate and Bobbie went to British Columbia on their honeymoon, but not till the day after tomorrow.

Dylan thought about his mom and dad and how much fun they always had at weddings and parties. His dad loved Uncle Nate a lot, and he'd be happy that Uncle Nate was so happy.

Dylan could think about them now without crying. Bobbie told him that he was lucky to have so many people in his life who loved him. He'd had his parents, and now he had Uncle Nate and her. And Stella and Dennis. And Hunter. And—he guessed—Sheamus. He glanced down at his brother, who looked up at him, his expression a little panicky because they'd been standing a long time and he probably had to go to the bathroom.

For a while there, Dylan had lost his ability to be a big brother. He'd been mean instead. But now he knew where he stood again—in the same house, with different parents, but the same little brother. And things were going to be okay.

He winked at Sheamus and stood a little straighter so that Sheamus would get the idea to hang in there.

He did, and smiled back at him.

Then the ceremony was over, there was loud, cheerful organ music and Uncle Nate and Bobbie walked up the aisle with him and Sheamus between them.

The big double doors at the back opened and a friend of Bobbie's from her art classes stood there with Arnold on a leash. He had a big green bow on his collar and was very excited to see them.

The lady lost her grip and Arnold shot into the church. He leaped at them, and because their arms were all looped together they went down in a big pile.

Dylan thought he'd remember their laughter as long as he lived.

* * * * *

REQUEST YOUR FREE BOOKS!
2 FREE WHOLESOME ROMANCE NOVELS
IN LARGER PRINT
PLUS 2
FREE
MYSTERY GIFTS

❄❄❄❄❄❄❄❄❄❄❄❄❄❄❄❄❄❄❄❄❄❄❄❄❄❄

HEARTWARMING™

❄❄❄❄❄❄❄❄❄❄❄❄❄❄❄❄❄❄❄❄❄❄❄❄❄❄

Wholesome, tender romances

YES! Please send me 2 FREE Harlequin® Heartwarming Larger-Print novels and my 2 FREE mystery gifts (gifts worth about $10). After receiving them, if I don't wish to receive any more books, I can return the shipping statement marked "cancel." If I don't cancel, I will receive 4 brand-new larger-print novels every month and be billed just $4.99 per book in the U.S. or $5.74 per book in Canada. That's a savings of at least 23% off the cover price. It's quite a bargain! Shipping and handling is just 50¢ per book in the U.S. and 75¢ per book in Canada.* I understand that accepting the 2 free books and gifts places me under no obligation to buy anything. I can always return a shipment and cancel at any time. Even if I never buy another book, the two free books and gifts are mine to keep forever.

161/361 IDN F47N

Name _____ (PLEASE PRINT) _____

Address _____ Apt. # _____

City _____ State/Prov. _____ Zip/Postal Code _____

Signature (if under 18, a parent or guardian must sign) _____

Mail to the **Harlequin® Reader Service:**
IN U.S.A.: P.O. Box 1867, Buffalo, NY 14240-1867
IN CANADA: P.O. Box 609, Fort Erie, Ontario L2A 5X3

* Terms and prices subject to change without notice. Prices do not include applicable taxes. Sales tax applicable in N.Y. Canadian residents will be charged applicable taxes. Offer not valid in Quebec. This offer is limited to one order per household. Not valid for current subscribers to Harlequin Heartwarming larger-print books. All orders subject to credit approval. Credit or debit balances in a customer's account(s) may be offset by any other outstanding balance owed by or to the customer. Please allow 4 to 6 weeks for delivery. Offer available while quantities last.

Your Privacy—The Harlequin® Reader Service is committed to protecting your privacy. Our Privacy Policy is available online at www.ReaderService.com or upon request from the Harlequin Reader Service.

We make a portion of our mailing list available to reputable third parties that offer products we believe may interest you. If you prefer that we not exchange your name with third parties, or if you wish to clarify or modify your communication preferences, please visit us at www.ReaderService.com/consumerchoice or write to us at Harlequin Reader Service Preference Service, P.O. Box 9062, Buffalo, NY 14269. Include your complete name and address.

HWDIR13R

ReaderService.com

Manage your account online!

- Review your order history
- Manage your payments
- Update your address

**We've designed
the Harlequin® Reader Service
website just for you.**

Enjoy all the features!

- Reader excerpts from any series
- Respond to mailings and
  special monthly offers
- Discover new series available to you
- Browse the Bonus Bucks catalog
- Share your feedback

Visit us at:
ReaderService.com

RS13

LARGER-PRINT BOOKS!

GET 2 FREE LARGER-PRINT NOVELS PLUS 2 FREE MYSTERY GIFTS

Love Inspired®

Larger-print novels are now available...

YES! Please send me 2 FREE LARGER-PRINT Love Inspired® novels and my 2 FREE mystery gifts (gifts are worth about $10). After receiving them, if I don't wish to receive any more books, I can return the shipping statement marked "cancel." If I don't cancel, I will receive 6 brand-new novels every month and be billed just $5.24 per book in the U.S. or $5.74 per book in Canada. That's a savings of at least 23% off the cover price. It's quite a bargain! Shipping and handling is just 50¢ per book in the U.S. and 75¢ per book in Canada.* I understand that accepting the 2 free books and gifts places me under no obligation to buy anything. I can always return a shipment and cancel at any time. Even if I never buy another book, the two free books and gifts are mine to keep forever.

122/322 IDN F49Y

Name _____ (PLEASE PRINT) _____

Address _____ Apt. # _____

City _____ State/Prov. _____ Zip/Postal Code _____

Signature (if under 18, a parent or guardian must sign)

Mail to the Harlequin® Reader Service:
IN U.S.A.: P.O. Box 1867, Buffalo, NY 14240-1867
IN CANADA: P.O. Box 609, Fort Erie, Ontario L2A 5X3

Are you a current subscriber to Love Inspired books and want to receive the larger-print edition?
Call 1-800-873-8635 or visit www.ReaderService.com.

* Terms and prices subject to change without notice. Prices do not include applicable taxes. Sales tax applicable in N.Y. Canadian residents will be charged applicable taxes. Offer not valid in Quebec. This offer is limited to one order per household. Not valid for current subscribers to Love Inspired Larger-Print books. All orders subject to credit approval. Credit or debit balances in a customer's account(s) may be offset by any other outstanding balance owed by or to the customer. Please allow 4 to 6 weeks for delivery. Offer available while quantities last.

Your Privacy—The Harlequin® Reader Service is committed to protecting your privacy. Our Privacy Policy is available online at www.ReaderService.com or upon request from the Harlequin Reader Service.

We make a portion of our mailing list available to reputable third parties that offer products we believe may interest you. If you prefer that we not exchange your name with third parties, or if you wish to clarify or modify your communication preferences, please visit us at www.ReaderService.com/consumerchoice or write to us at Harlequin Reader Service Preference Service, P.O. Box 9062, Buffalo, NY 14269. Include your complete name and address.

LILPDIR13R